SHATTERED ICE

SHATTERED ICE

MELTING HEARTS BOOK 3

JORDYN KROSS

ALSO BY JORDYN KROSS

Melting Hearts Series

Prequel Novella - Jack's Frost

Book 1 - Winter's List

Book 2 - Xmas Angel

Book 3 - Shattered Ice

Dirty Daisy Mystery Series

Book 1 - Dirty Daisy

Anthologies

Falling Hard - 2021 Passionate Ink

Published by Scarlet Parlor Press, LLC

Library of Congress Control Number: 2022904487

Publisher's Cataloging-In-Publication Data

(Prepared by The Donohue Group, Inc.)

Names: Kross, Jordyn, author.

Title: Shattered ice / Jordyn Kross.

Description: [Albuquerque, New Mexico] : Scarlet Parlor Press, LLC, [2022] | Series: Melting hearts ; book 3

Identifiers: ISBN 9781733380874 (print) | ISBN 9781733380867 (ebook)

Subjects: LCSH: Women professional employees--Fiction. | Veterans--Fiction. | Middle-aged women--Sexual behavior--Fiction. | Young men--Sexual behavior--Fiction. | Bed and breakfast accommodations--Colorado--Fiction. | Man-woman relationships--Fiction. | LCGFT: Romance fiction. | Erotic fiction.

Classification: LCC PS3611.R776 S53 2022 (print) | LCC PS3611.R776 (ebook) | DDC 813/.6--dc23

Print ISBN-13: 978-1-7333808-7-4

Ebook ISBN-13: 978-1-7333808-6-7

Editor: Colleen Wagner

Cover: Brandi Doane McCann

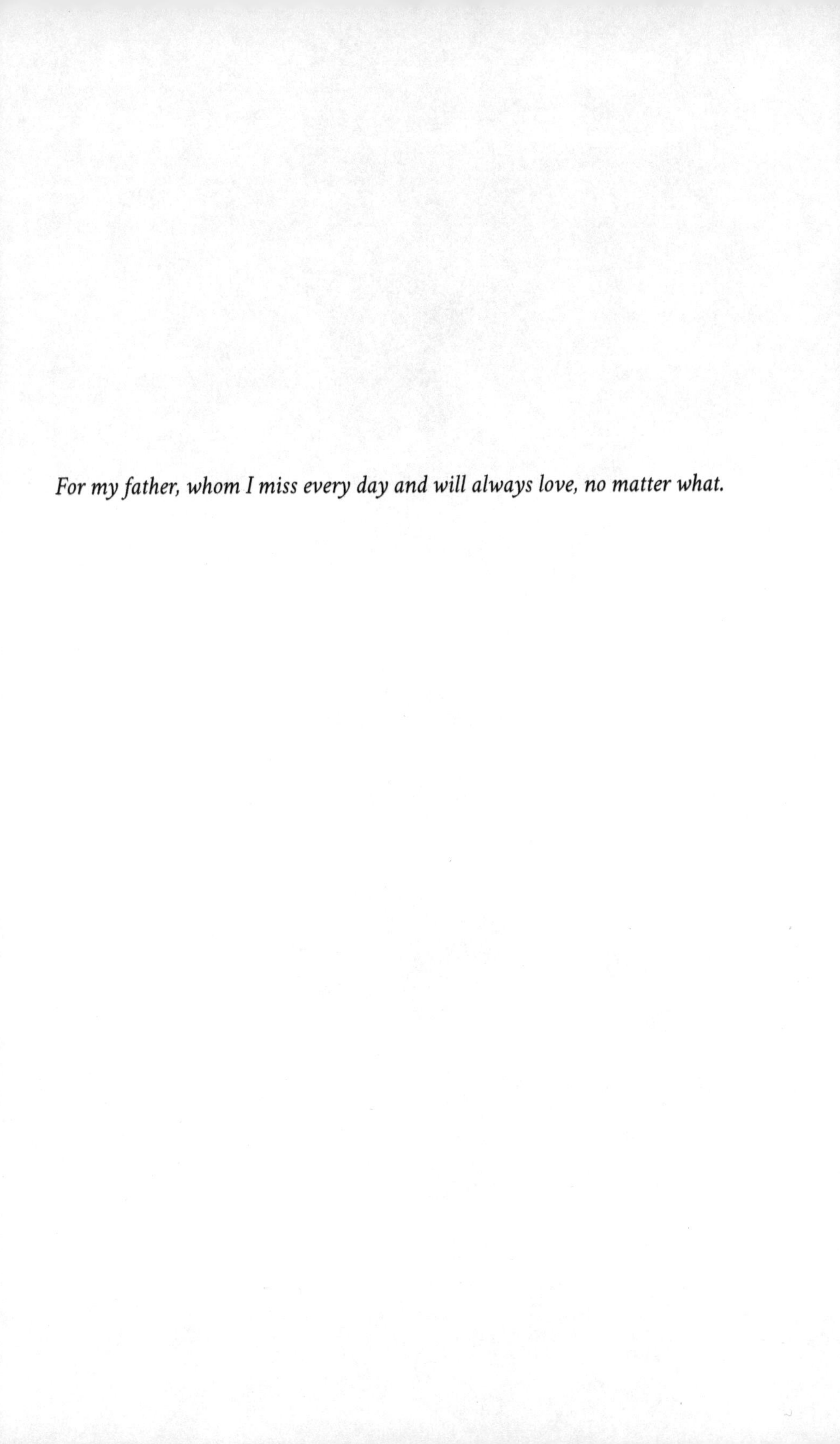

For my father, whom I miss every day and will always love, no matter what.

CHAPTER 1

The frigid air embraced Katherine Wallace as she emerged from the overheated high-rise and paused on the pavement. She'd stood there a thousand times before. Although the city remained unchanged, nothing was the same. Thick clouds filtered the winter sun. The Manhattan streets were nearly empty, everyone at home for New Year's Day, like she should have been. She hesitated in front of her former company car before escaping into Central Park, away from the indifferent concrete and glass.

Late-night revelers had left the salted asphalt paths dirty and slushy, and the icy muck splattered her winter-white stilettos. The same shoes she'd been wearing the previous night when she'd accepted Marcus's ring at midnight. A yellow cab raced by, the noise from the tires on the wet road briefly breaking the silence. Nothing else moved. Even the light snow from earlier in the morning had stopped falling while she'd been inside her office.

Correction.

Her father Richard Wallace's office. Her grandfather James Wallace's law firm. It would never be *hers*, despite the sixteen years she'd devoted to its success.

Past caring about her cashmere coat, she dropped onto a wet

bench. A thin layer of ice had formed over the large pond. Heavy, snow-laden evergreens framed its edges. But the urban oasis, once so inviting and familiar, was bleak and barren and hostile.

"Katie." Richard's tone was harsh. "Come here."

Officially summoned, she rose from the sitting area with practiced poise, tucked away her cell phone, smoothed her skirt, and carefully walked to the chair in front of her father's desk.

"The firm can no longer employ you." His piercing gaze locked to hers. He spoke with complete confidence and authority, as if he were telling the jury his client wasn't guilty.

"Excuse me?" She blinked at him. So that was why he'd called her to come into the office on New Year's Day. A test. Her father enjoyed challenging her loyalty. She sat gracefully before challenging him back. "You're lying."

"I'm not." The flat tone and lack of any of his tells stole her breath.

Her world tilted, and she gripped the arms of the chair.

"You betta watch out. Betta not cry." A sweet little voice shocked her back to the present. A small boy with dark ringlets peeping out from his knit hat appeared. He was too young to be unsupervised, but no one else was nearby. He toddled down the slope toward the water's edge with increasing speed...

Katherine wrenched herself from the bench, stiff from the cold. She tiptoed toward the child, trying not to frighten him. How could someone leave him on his own in such a dangerous place? When she was finally near enough to stop him with a gentle grip on his shoulder, he turned to her. His face lit with a beaming smile on his rosy lips, and she thawed under his warm baby gaze as she folded to his eye level. "Hi. I'm Katherine. What's your name?"

"'Lijah." The lisping drawl was as quiet as the park.

"Elijah." His big brown eyes dug into her long-buried dream, reminding her of what she'd lost before she'd had it. "Do you like the snow?"

"Uh-huh." He nodded at her solemnly—mature beyond his few years. His coat, like the rest of his clothes, was expensive and well-kept. He was a wanted child despite the fact no one was with him.

"Where's your mommy?" asked Katherine.

"Work."

"Who's here with you?"

"Nanny."

A paid stranger had failed to keep that precious gift safe. But she could protect him until whoever it was showed up. "Do you want to make snow angels?"

The little boy nodded, and she guided him away from the pond. In an untouched opening between the trees, they lay in the snow, and she showed him how to move his arms and legs, just like her mother had taught her long ago. Katherine had been a little older than Elijah, and the snow had slipped into the space between her scarf and jacket, making her shiver, but her mom's laughter had kept her warm. Katherine moved her limbs back and forth but found no warmth next to the child who wasn't hers. The sky above remained a blank gray slate.

Elijah's giggle chimed through the air, pulling her back from the emptiness and out of the snow. She clasped his hand, the warmth that radiated from his small grasp foreign to her frigid fingers, and he leaned against her while she showed him what they'd made. His little angel flew next to her larger one.

"Pretty snow," said Elijah.

The yowl of a woman calling his name drowned his words out. Blustering around the corner, a thin twenty-something with an empty stroller in one hand and her phone in the other ran to them.

"There you are." She snatched the child away from Katherine without a word or a second glance and plopped him in the stroller. "We're never coming to the park again if you run off like that."

Elijah still stared at Katherine. He lifted his mittened hand and waved. "Bye."

Katherine tracked the duo as they left the park, and the glow from Elijah's presence faded too quickly. When she could no longer see them, she glanced once more at the angels. Empty impressions, like the footsteps that led away.

Empty.

"I've been working for you and this firm for over ten years. I've done your

marketing, your website, your branding." Katherine had done everything her father had asked, been perfect. For him. He couldn't do that. He wouldn't abandon her, not like that. Without her job, without her father, she'd have nothing. She searched for a reason he could keep her. Something. Anything. "I've done your dirty work. If you wanted information on anyone, I dug until I found what you needed. I'm the best researcher you have."

"Interns are researchers." He stared at his desk.

"You've used me to entertain clients when Mother wouldn't play the game any longer. I've been your right hand. Why would you cut off your arm?" She spoke in a low, measured voice. Aside from her hands clenched in her lap, she posed in a picture of calm serenity. Her long legs were crossed at the ankle and tucked back under the chair.

What are you doing to me? *The silent scream echoed in her head, betrayal battering the protective walls she'd spent years building. How had she not anticipated it? The failed merger. Partners leaving. Clients canceling.*

"I appreciate everything you've done for me and the firm. But we're going through some difficult times."

"It's a minor dip." Katherine balled her hands tighter, resisting the urge to snatch the cut-crystal paperweight and launch it at his forehead. Companies went through cycles. It was normal.

"Every expense is going to be examined."

"I'm not an expense. I'm an employee and your daughter." She clenched her jaw before she started begging. How much would he enjoy seeing her grovel?

"And I can't justify paying our marketer two hundred fifty thousand dollars a year. Especially if she's my daughter." Her father placed his hands on the desk, one in a fist and the other wrapped around it as he leaned toward her and looked her in the eye. "You have to know how hard this is for me. The partners are threatening to— It doesn't matter. My hands are tied."

She forced herself to relax her fingers before the jewel on her engagement ring drew blood. "How long?"

"How long what?"

"How long do I have? What's my last day?" Thirty days at least. He had to give her some time to adjust. To wrap things up, to—

"Today, now."

"You're letting me go without notice?" Bile crept up her throat.

"Your contract doesn't require it."

"Is this a show for the board?" She'd never worked for anyone other than her father. While she'd finished her business degree, she'd begun working in the offices doing whatever needed to be done. The only break she'd taken was during the brief time she'd been married to her ex, Andrew. Over the years, her father had assigned more and more tasks to her. She was integral to the success of the organization. It was all she had. All she was.

"I can give you a good reference. I can put the word out to see what's available, but I can't employ you."

"Can't? Or won't?"

"The semantics are meaningless."

Translation: she *was* meaningless. Her heart turned to stone, a heavy weight in her chest.

Katherine crossed the footbridge over the narrow end of the pond and headed to the opposite side of the park. She'd been engaged for a matter of hours to a man she would never marry. Her father's selection. Maybe that had been his intention all the time, to foist her off so she was no longer *his* problem.

Katherine retrieved her phone, proud that her hand didn't shake. Richard Wallace would never know how much he'd hurt her. "You'll regret this."

"You imagine your importance to be greater than it is. I gave my sad, unemployable daughter a job. Your divorce nearly ruined you. I even found you another husband."

Bastard. She closed her eyes briefly and drew in a breath. He really was the bastard everyone said. She'd seen glimpses of it but made excuses for him because it had been so long since she'd been his target. *"Right, always looking out for me. Always having my best interests at heart while you pimp me out to people you want as clients, business owners who you'd like to represent. Old men you'd let fuck your daughter just for billable hours. Hoping they'd give you details, Daddy? Too bad none of them made it that far."*

"That's out of line."

Katherine dialed her phone. While she waited for an answer, she tugged at the extravagant engagement ring. As much as she hated the idea of being completely alone, she hated the idea of being married to Marcus more. Not to someone so much older than her. Not just because her father thought she should.

"Marcus. It's Katherine. I'm not marrying you. I'm leaving the ring with my father. Perhaps the two of you can make a go of it."

The ring slid down the pen mounted to a marble base with the firm's name etched on a gold plaque. She fished the firm's credit card out of her clutch and dropped it with their cell phone in a pile on his desk.

"Katie girl, don't make more of this than it is." Of course he thought it meant nothing, even used the belittling moniker she hated.

"It's Katherine, and that is the single *point we can agree on. Once again, I made more of this than it was."*

Everything Katherine had done was because she and her father were a team. But, instead of relying on her to deal with the controversy on the board, the failed merger, and potential audit, he'd ripped away everything from her without a thought as to the consequences. At least he'd done it when there'd been no one to see her walk of shame out of her family's firm.

She glanced up at the windows of his office visible over the park's trees. He'd treated her as if *she* were the enemy. She was nearly forty, divorced, and childless. The one thing she'd counted on was belonging to the firm. Katherine turned away and followed the asphalt path with no idea of where she was going except away.

CHAPTER 2

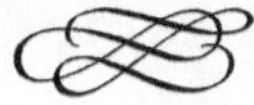

A gold SUV crawling up the gravel driveway of his Colorado lodge caught Gabe Gallegos's eye through the kitchen window. He whipped open the oven and grabbed the tray of muffins with a dish towel. His hand hit the burning edge of the door, and he stumbled, barely catching his balance. *Shit.* He dropped the tin onto the stove and tested the top of one. They seemed done. He'd let them cool while he started the kettle. With quick jabs using his uninjured hand, he tucked his shirt more securely in his waistband, ran his fingers through his starting-to-curl hair, and plastered a confident but welcoming smile on his face.

Two women exited the vehicle. Based on the photo on the Alabaster Bed and Breakfast Association website, the woman wearing the snowflake-themed cardigan and khakis was the president of ABBA, as she'd referred to it. She looked like a grandma or kindergarten teacher, but he wasn't fooled. He'd talked to her on the phone when she'd called to "meet the newest innkeeper in Alabaster." There was a piranha hiding in those support hose and sensible shoes.

The unexpected second woman was a mystery. She was younger and wore dressy jeans and a white button-up shirt underneath an open, dark blue puffy coat. Unsure of what would happen during the meeting, Gabe ran potential scenarios as if he were preparing for a mission.

His objective was clear. His buddy Nick had insisted he secure membership in ABBA so that he could get a web presence for his lodge, support from the other innkeepers, and start connecting with the community. But Nick was back in Tucson with his bride, not facing down the dragon.

He took a deep breath and threw open the door as they neared the front porch. "Welcome to the Ponderosa. You're my first official visitors."

"Hi," the younger woman said, flashing a big grin. "I'm Amy Davis." She thrust out her hand as she entered his home and soon-to-be business.

Gabe shook her hand. It was surprisingly rough and cold and didn't match the happy-go-lucky energy she was projecting. "It's nice to meet you, Amy. Gabriel Gallegos."

"Welcome to Alabaster—" Amy was prevented from saying more as the older woman muscled her way inside.

"Betty Keppel." She held her hand out as well. "We spoke on the phone."

"Yes, of course. Nice to meet you, Betty." He released her hand almost as quickly as he'd taken it, feeling like he'd gripped a venomous snake. The urge to wipe the cold, slimy feeling off on his pants was difficult to resist.

Betty's nose wrinkled as she inspected the tattoos that were visible above his shirt collar, then eyeballed the two-story wood-paneled walls, the chipped Saltillo tile, faded rugs, and the giant cobblestone fireplace that needed to be scrubbed and repointed. Gabe was painfully aware of the repairs and updates his lodge still needed. And she'd likely started her assessment outside as soon as she'd pulled up the driveway and into the parking lot he'd refurbished last fall. But like the windows he'd sealed with Nick's help, those repairs didn't warrant notice like the work still to be done. And clearly his appearance didn't meet with her expectations either.

"Please, take a seat." He pointed toward the oblong wood dining table nestled in a nook of floor-to-ceiling windows that had a perfect view of the snowy pine forest. The table was big enough to seat twelve comfortably but needed some care. His uncle had let the furniture deteriorate when he'd quit maintaining the lodge. The list of things to restore the place to its original glory was longer than Gabe wanted to admit. "Would you like some tea or water? I just made muffins."

"This isn't—" The whistle of the kettle cut Betty off.

"That sounds lovely. I could use a cup of hot tea," Amy replied before Betty could finish whatever she'd been about to say. "Can I help you?"

"No, relax. I'll be right out."

Gabe retreated to the kitchen, happy to have a reason to step away from Betty. He poured the boiling water in a ceramic teapot and covered it with a cozy the way his grandmother had always done, then added another mug and spoon to the tray he'd prepared earlier with three kinds of tea and a bowl of sugar. He retrieved the small carafe of milk and a dish of butter from the refrigerator and placed them next to the sugar before grabbing a plate from the cabinet. The muffins could cool for a few more minutes theoretically, but he was out of time. Using a knife, he freed several of the blue-corn blueberry treats and placed them on the tray. One last check that everything was in order, and then he transported the perfect setup back to the table.

Everything went without a hitch. He poured the water for the tea without spilling a drop, then distributed plates and mugs and passed the butter to Betty. She cut open her muffin, frowning before passing the butter to Amy without a word and without taking any. *What the hell?*

Amy tittered after she cut her muffin open. "High-altitude cooking takes some adjustments."

Gabe pulled one apart. Gooey. The center was undercooked. Heat ran up his neck, and he gritted his teeth. Amy pulled the top free of the undercooked part, added butter, and popped a piece in her mouth.

"You don't have to—"

She moaned. Gabe blinked at her. Betty scowled.

Amy swallowed. "You have to share the recipe. These are delicious. Not too sweet, and the blueberries are the perfect pop of fruitiness. Your guests are going to love them. I'll help you with adjustments."

Betty thumped her mug on the table. "Well, if we're done with the cooking lesson..." Her glare cut off whatever else Amy might have said. "You seem to think you want to run this place as an inn."

Gabe nodded. "My uncle, Juan Casteneda, left it to me in his will, and I'd like to put it back into use. He ran the Ponderosa as a hotel until about six years ago. He passed last year."

"I'm sorry for your loss." The sincerity in Amy's voice was unmistakable.

"Have you ever worked in hospitality or managed a business of any kind?" Betty didn't suffer from the same sympathy as Amy.

"No, but—"

"And you thought...what? You'd just go for it? How hard can it be?" Betty smiled sweetly.

Despite the call to battle, he held his tongue. Gabe focused on Amy. She was staring at the table as if it could reveal the winning lottery numbers. He returned his gaze to Betty. Swallowing his temper, he purposely softened his voice. "I helped my uncle in the summers before he quit renting the place, and I've worked in construction. I know I have—"

"You couldn't have been more than a teenager when you came to help Juan," Betty interrupted.

Gabriel tired of her disrespect and clenched his hands under the table. "As I was saying, I worked construction with my family in California before I joined the military. I spent several summers with my uncle while he ran the lodge when I was in high school. I misspoke when I said I hadn't worked in hospitality—I wasn't paid, but I did work in this very building. I have the experience, the dedication, and the resources to restore it and run it as a professional business. I already have one room just about ready for guests."

"I think your definition of 'ready' and mine differ. Although Alabaster is not Aspen, people have certain expectations. This lodge may have been acceptable in a quaint, rustic way back in the day, but that isn't what our guests desire now. They want upscale accommodations."

After another deep breath, Gabe continued before Betty could start speaking again. "I reached out to the association because I wanted to involve myself in the cares and concerns of my community. This town lives and dies by the tourist dollar. I assumed you'd want to do everything you could to help those who can contribute."

"Your concern and willingness to *contribute* are all very noble, but the B and B association has a standard to maintain. If we let *anyone* use our name and our reputation to promote themselves to guests and the guests are—disappointed..." She paused as she looked around the first floor. "Well, it would reflect badly on all of us. My job as the president of the Alabaster Bed and Breakfast Association is to make sure that *all* the members and properties we promote on our website meet the standards that our guests expect. Especially the returning ones who've experienced our high quality and exceptional hospitality."

Betty placed her hand on Amy's upper arm. "We, the association, don't think that you can meet those standards, Mr. Gallegos. Besides, we have a three-room minimum to join. Keeps out the *amateurs* who like to rent a spare bedroom during high season."

Her condescending smile reappeared as soon as she stopped speaking. She released Amy and pushed back from the table to stand.

"That's it? You pull up here and make a judgment, and that's the end of it?" Gabe was flabbergasted by the audacity of this woman to judge him based on a ten-minute meeting. Hell, more like two minutes. Fuck what his friend had said about making connections. He'd invested everything he had in the lodge, spent nearly every dime on getting the infrastructure up to code. The place was his only chance at a future, and it didn't depend on the dragon, Amy, or ABBA. But it did depend on getting some income from guests—soon.

"You're welcome to attend our meetings...as a non-voting visitor, of course. Perhaps you'll learn something." Betty marched toward the door, and Amy looked back with apology before following like an abused puppy.

Gabe stared at the closed door. Unbelievable. One woman had

walked into his place, judged it and him as unworthy. And that was it? He shook his head and collected the still-full mugs. The B and B association was something that supposedly would have helped him get a jump on the marketing part of the business.

Fuck that.

He could put up a damn website without their help. He'd just add it to the list of things he needed to do, no big deal.

He'd lost a fucking leg, for god's sake. If he could overcome that, everything else was stupid easy.

CHAPTER 3

Katherine kept walking. Her feet had blistered blocks ago, but she savored the pain, letting it mute the building headache. A piercing catcall interrupted the looping memories of everything she'd done for her father. She glanced around. Where the hell *was* she? The neighborhood was completely unfamiliar. It was past time to go back to her condo.

She waved down a taxi. Opening the back door to get in, her heel hooked into a crack in the sidewalk. The snapping sound as she fell into the cab captured her situation perfectly. Having told the driver her address, she closed her eyes and tried to ignore what a terrible start to the new year she'd had so far.

"Ms. Wallace?" The horrified tone in her doorman's voice had her scurrying for the elevator as fast as possible with a broken shoe.

"I'm fine." She waved him off as he came around the desk. "I'll call down if I need anything." The ride to the top of the building never took so long, and with each floor she dreaded the potential ping and pause of another passenger joining her. Luckily, she made it through her door without another person witnessing her catastrophic appearance.

Her shoes went in the trash. The once winter-white coat she

dropped in the dry-cleaning bin. Maybe it was salvageable. Was it too early for a glass of wine? She checked the clock—not even noon. The house phone rang, probably the doorman checking up on her. She answered with an imitation of her confident tone.

"Your friend Natalia is here."

Why? Putting on a show for the idle heiress sounded exhausting. But social niceties required she allow the woman up. Using the few moments before the elevator arrived, Katherine checked her hair, freshened her lipstick, and put on different shoes.

At the sound of the buzz, Katherine opened the door to the currently red head.

"You forgot."

"Forgot what?" Forgot to pretend she wasn't home?

Natalia's lower lip jutted out. "Our date." She dropped onto the pearl-gray sofa in the front room that faced the gas fireplace. "You promised you'd hold my hand while I got my New Year's tattoo. My appointment's in, like, half an hour. Come on, Kiki. You know you want one, too."

Katherine clenched her jaw at the irritating nickname and the fact that she had promised in a moment of weakness the day before Christmas. "Right."

"You can't wear that."

Katherine looked down her cream sheath dress to the navy-blue heels. "What's wrong with what I'm wearing?"

"This isn't a board meeting. It's a tattoo. Relax a little. Don't you have something less harsh? Softer? Maybe a sweater? In that dress, you'd have to strip to get one any place that can't be seen except by your lovers." Natalia gave a flirty smile. "Not that stripping's a bad thing. I just know you won't."

Katherine didn't have lovers, but she wasn't going to admit to that. And she wasn't getting a tattoo. Ever.

"Hey, where's the ring? Thought you said ole Marcus was going to propose."

Drinking with Natalia had been a bad idea. Two glasses of wine and she'd spilled her guts. "He didn't," she lied. "But I'm fine with it. I don't think I'll be seeing him again."

"Good, he's too old for you. You need someone who can get his dick hard without a prescription."

Natalia was mistaken about her needing a hard dick at all. She needed a hot bath and some peace and quiet. But that wouldn't happen until they finished with the ink appointment. Better to get it over with.

After changing into dark jeans and some boots with a cashmere sweater, Katherine still didn't blend with the neighborhood Natalia had dragged her to. A large bearded man in a sleeveless shirt and more ink than skin unlocked the door and flipped the sign to open. "Natalia, babe. Right on time."

"Hey, Axe." Natalia's voice had gone up two octaves. She sashayed up to the man and put a hand on his belt. "You ready to mark me?" As Natalia's fingers slipped lower, Katherine glanced away. Her day kept getting better and better.

Two minutes into the tattooing process, Natalia dropped Katherine's hand and gripped the arms of the chair. Of course she was getting the image on her pelvis near the juncture of her thighs. Clad in a tiny thong and a pullover, Natalia was flirting shamelessly with the artist. He had to be ten years younger, and it was obvious to anyone but Natalia that he was used to toying with customers.

Time ticked by one painful second at a time with nothing to distract Katherine from the disaster her life had become except posters of dragons and butterflies on white-painted cinderblock walls and chipped linoleum floor tiles.

"I need to stretch my legs." Katherine picked up her bag and rose from the backless stool on wheels. "You'll be a while?"

"Another hour or so," Axe answered.

"Don't get lost," Natalia teased.

Katherine walked away before she said something pathetic, like she was already lost beyond finding. She turned right, and a blast of icy wind cut through her clothes. *What am I going to do now?*

Ducking into the alcove of the next storefront, she pushed on the door, which gave way easily. A string of bells dangling from the knob tinkled. Stepping across the threshold, she drew in a breath of spicy, smoky smell she didn't recognize.

"One second." A distracted woman's voice floated through the room. "I'll be right…with you."

Katherine tried to make sense of the space as she moved toward the source of the voice. There were scarves pinned all across the ceiling, vibrant purples and reds and blues, layers and layers concealing any hint of the actual building structure. The shop window was lined with handmade paper, blocking the view from the street.

On the far wall was a mural using the same jewel-toned colors of the scarves. In the middle of the image, a giant gold hand had an eye in the palm. Shelves ran along the side walls, filled with books and boxes and candles and rocks with no sense of order. Scattered throughout were small tables covered with patterned cotton cloths. The tables held miniature statues and bells, copper dishes with lids, more rocks, and crystals.

A glass cabinet halted Katherine's progress. To the right, a small alcove glowed with the light of a computer screen.

"Damn this cockamamie website."

The hiss made Katherine grin. How many times had she uttered something similar? "Need some help?"

The form of a giant woman, almost as tall as Katherine but in flat, plain black shoes, emerged from the shadow. Her shoulders were as broad as the doorway, and her bosom was huge. She had thick gray hair tied into a ponytail. And her eyes, the same silver gray, looked right though Katherine. "You've come for a reading."

"Reading? No. I was next door—"

"I'm Madam Tiana. And you are?"

"Katherine. Having trouble with your website?"

The woman filled the opening and quickly explained her frustration.

"I can fix it for you."

The shopkeeper paused before shrugging. "Sure."

Madam Tiana stepped to the side, allowing Katherine into the nook. Time disappeared as Katherine clicked through several modifications and applied the updates. She pulled up the active site to display the changes. "Better?"

"How did you do that?"

A tiny zing of satisfaction sputtered through Katherine. She wasn't useless. "I'll write down the steps."

"You were sent here." Madam Tiana handed Katherine a pad and pen. "You must let me gift you with a reading, at least."

Katherine shook her head as she wrote. "My friend will be done in a few minutes."

"A three-card. It won't take any time at all."

Katherine set the pad down and checked the clock on the screen. What else was she going to do while she waited? Beat watching ink being stabbed into Natalia. "Sure."

"Come, have a seat." Madam Tiana gestured to one of the chairs behind an engraved wood screen in the opposite corner of the room.

The woman sat in the other chair on the far side and picked up a deck of oversized cards. The little table between them was covered with a shiny purple synthetic cloth. The backs of the cards looked like a night sky. Tiana shuffled them, pulling a chunk of cards away from the pack and then slipping a few back in randomly. The longer she played with the deck, the more difficult it became for Katherine to remain seated. But before she could change her mind and leave, Madam Tiana handed the deck to her.

"As you shuffle, I want you to think of the question you most want the universe to answer. Then hand me the card that resonates for you."

Her world had been stripped from her, and that woman thought some cards were going to guide her? She hesitated before taking the deck and rearranging it. Better to get the reading over with as soon as possible. She drew a random card and handed it to Madam Tiana, who set it faceup on the table and then took the deck from Katherine.

Madam Tiana pulled two more cards from the pile and put them facedown on the table. "The reading today is only a possibility of how your future may unfold. Ultimately, the actions you take can change the final outcome, but this is the path as it appears right now." She pointed at the faceup image. "This card represents your past."

A hairy, horned beast with naked people chained to him. Katherine read the label—*The Devil*—and shivered.

"Don't panic. The Devil card is not the devil represented by Christianity." She tapped the card with her index finger. "Your past has been filled with a feeling of being trapped, perhaps an addiction or an abusive relationship. It can also represent the scapegoat, something you blame your problems on."

The woman paused as if she were waiting for a response. Katherine pursed her lips. It was one thing to let Tiana play her mystic game, but that didn't mean Katherine had to bare her soul.

"You have the power to release yourself from the chains of whatever has held you back." Madam Tiana turned over the card in the middle. "Your present. The Tower."

Katherine should leave, but she couldn't resist looking. People falling out of a burning building while lightning struck. Worse than the Devil.

"You need to be prepared for upheaval in the near future, a tearing down and maybe a release from whatever has held you back in the past."

Katherine had already had a major upheaval. She wasn't ready for more. Her only question was how to get back what she'd lost: her job. Not that she had to work, but she liked having a purpose, something she was good at. She liked being part of her family's legacy even if she wasn't a lawyer. And if the universe was supplying things, she could use a father who wasn't as selfish as her mother. As if they could ever love someone as much as they loved themselves. Katherine stifled her scoff.

And speaking of love: What about love? She could sure use someone who found *her* worthy of love and loyalty. She was tired of fighting, and supposedly the universe was telling her she was going to have to fight harder, have more upheaval. Before Madam Tiana said another word, she should run. Instead, she crossed her arms, leaned back in the chair, and reminded herself that she didn't believe in that crap.

"Do you have any questions so far? Anything you want to clarify or dig into?"

Katherine shook her head.

"Okay, the last card is all about your future and the resources you have to deal with what's coming." Tiana turned the card. "Another major."

Katherine didn't know what that meant, and she wouldn't ask. But the card was different from the first two. An angel was blowing a horn, and people were smiling up at him.

"Judgement is related to an awakening, something dormant within you coming to the forefront. The past is going to be released, and you will find a path of forgiveness for yourself or others. It usually indicates a readiness to live differently, to embrace change, and to find new guides."

What the hell did "find new guides" mean? And could they guide her out of that store?

"That card actually goes really well with the Tower. When you tear down the past, you generally want to resolve the outstanding issues before proceeding. You're making space in your life for a new way of living."

Katherine nodded at the woman as if it all made sense. "I…I have to go. My friend is at the tattoo parlor next door, and she should be done by now. I promised I wouldn't leave her for long. I should check on her, make sure she didn't faint from the needles. Or something." With a deep breath, she willed herself to calm down and stop babbling.

"We were meant to find each other," Madame Tiana said, her tone so sure, so confident. "Normally, I'm closed on New Year's Day. But I was compelled to come in and open up. Now I know why. I'd love to hire you…"

Katherine pulled a twenty from her purse.

A serene smile graced Madam Tiana's lips. "I want you to have this amethyst." She slipped a small purple crystal into a drawstring bag and pressed it into Katherine's hand on top of the money. A polite refusal.

Katherine resisted the unfamiliar urge to hug the woman as she tucked the tiny sack and her cash into an interior pocket of her purse and darted for the door. The day just kept getting weirder.

When Katherine reentered the tattoo shop, it was clear the inking was done, but the appointment wasn't over. Axe's fingers were buried beneath Natalia's panties. Katherine faced the wall, her cheeks heating, unable to unsee that. "I'm going to grab a cab."

"What. About. Brunch," Natalia panted in a squeaky voice.

"Another time."

"*Yes*," Natalia called out.

Katherine didn't stick around to find out what would happen next. She walked past Natalia's car on the curb and waved down her second cab ride of the day. And her last. She missed her driver. Her car. Her life. It'd only been a couple of hours, but her heart ached for the loss of the familiar bubble she'd been wrapped in for so long. In the words of Tiana, she missed her tower. But according to the cards, that safety had been destroyed.

As soon as she was inside the door of her condo, she stripped, letting the clothes fall where they landed. She walked naked into her spa bathroom and started the water in the tub. The day wasn't over, and her entire world had been blown apart.

She stepped into the steaming water and hissed with pain as her blisters reawakened, but she welcomed it.

If the universe was going to upheave her life and force her to rebuild from scratch, then the universe had better be ready. She was Katherine Wallace. And from then on, she was in charge of her life—not Daddy Dearest, not her socialite friends, not her cheating mother, or her oversexed ex-husband. Not one of them had truly valued her. Everybody had put their happiness first, and she had gone along with it. For years.

When was the last time she'd been happy?

Genuinely, bone-deep happy?

Did she know how to be happy?

The questions bounced around unanswered as Katherine searched for a memory. Finally, it came to her. Pine trees, big blues skies, and the best ski slopes in the States. Colorado. She would go to reset, rebuild, and figure out how she'd recover the happiness that had been stolen from her.

CHAPTER 4

Flying commercial was nothing like flying on the corporate jet. Why the hell would anyone do it? The airline staff acted like Katherine's luggage was a huge inconvenience and charged her some fee as a punishment. Like she was going to take a ski vacation and not have clothes? Then she survived practically being strip-searched and fingered at the inspection point. The grouchy woman in blue polyester had insisted Katherine had violated the rules by not taking her shoes off. Seriously, after everyone else had walked across that tile floor in their bare feet or dirty socks, she was expected to wallow in that filth?

No matter how she returned home, it wouldn't be by commercial airline. Not only had she lost her use of the firm's plane, but she'd lost access to their travel agent, too. She'd hire a new agent before she went back to New York, because it had been a mistake thinking she could do it on her own.

Katherine was the last passenger off the plane, taking time to freshen her makeup because she was unsure of where to go. She'd never arrived at an airport without someone to meet her—a car service, her father, someone. An airport bathroom became her immediate sanctuary. Her breath was coming so rapidly she thought she might pass out. A few minutes of washing her hands in startlingly cold water and her rational side took over. First things first —suitcases.

It was a long walk from the concourse where she'd landed to the baggage carousels where an airport employee had assured Katherine she would find her things. The three bags were spinning around and around by themselves. A man in uniform with a luggage rack offered to help her, which was great, but she still needed a driver.

"Where are you headed, miss? Some of the hotels have shuttles."

"I'm staying in Alabaster, near Aspen?"

"Oh, then we need to get you to the rental car counters. You got one you like to use?"

Katherine shook her head. Another thing she'd never dealt with.

"We'll head over there and see what's available."

She followed the older man's dark-blue-coated back. He stayed with her while she rented a small SUV. The car rental clerk had insisted that where Katherine was going, she would need four-wheel drive and looked pointedly at her stack of luggage, insisting that a car trunk wouldn't meet her storage needs.

"Thank you for helping me," she told the porter after he hefted the last bag into the back of the vehicle. She handed the man a hundred-dollar bill and hoped it was enough.

"Be safe now." He was on his way back to the airport building at a brisk pace before she'd even made it into the driver's seat.

How did she get out of the airport? She hadn't driven in years. Probably not since she'd lived in Texas with her ex-husband. She turned on the car and started the heater, but cold air blew out, and she shivered and turned it off. From her purse, she extracted her new phone and opened the map app. The B and B address was on the printout she'd stuffed in her bag at the last minute. The map updated. Four and a half hours? She looked at the time—already well past noon. She'd have to find a place on the road to stop for food. As it was, the sun would be setting when she arrived, and she didn't want to be on snowy mountain roads in the dark if she could avoid it.

She navigated out of the airport. The voice on her phone had her take Peña Boulevard to I-70. That interstate went most of the way to Alabaster. She paused at the first stop sign and yanked off her stiletto. It had been caught in between the gas pedal and the car mat twice already. Driving barefoot only made her feel colder, but she was certain it would be safer. No problem. By the end of the day, she'd be tucked away in a cozy lodge, well on her way to restoring her happiness.

Four hours later, she was starving, frozen, and unsure of where the hell she was. The drive through Denver had been harrowing, and she'd been too nervous to stop for food or even a bathroom break. Trees and snow surrounded her, and the light from the setting sun was nearly gone. The cell reception was spotty, and she wasn't sure the maps were still updating. Heart racing, she pulled over into a picnic-ground parking lot without going all the way into the unplowed section. There were two bars on her phone, but that couldn't be right. It said she still had an hour to go. Panic gripped her chest. She could freeze out there. Or run out of gas. Or be attacked by bears.

She closed her eyes and pulled in a slow breath, straightening her spine. Wallaces did not panic. They took action. She pulled out the sheet from her purse and dialed the Ponderosa Lodge.

The man that answered had a voice that could make millions as a phone-sex operator. It was like hot chocolate spiked with peppermint schnapps. A languid heat slid through her veins, slowing her pulse but leaving her tingling. For a moment, she forgot to speak or breathe. It was a good thing she'd pulled over to call. He growled the name of the lodge into the phone a second time.

"Wow. I mean, help." She shook her head to clear the hormone fog and fatigue. "This is Katherine Wallace, and your hotel is lost." She gritted her teeth. Did she have to sound like a lunatic?

He laughed into the phone, a sound of pleasure and invitation, and the fog was back, twice as thick. "I think you mean you're lost trying to find the lodge. The Ponderosa hasn't moved."

"Well, it's not where it's supposed to be," she snapped, still trying to get control of herself.

"It's right where I left it. Maybe you're not where you're supposed to be. I could help you with that."

"Fine. I'd like to be done traveling for the day. Soon, if at all possible."

"Yep. Snow's coming. Why don't we start with where you are?"

"I'm not exactly sure. I took I-70 to the turnoff for Alabaster. But I don't think I'm on the right road. I should have been there by now."

"I think you missed the fork in the road where you should've gone right, and you went left instead. It's a little tricky. Do you see a mile marker?"

Katherine peered at the nearby road sign and read off the number.

"Not so bad. You're only a mile from where you should've turned. I think the best thing is to put me on speakerphone, turn around, and I'll guide you in."

"I have my map. If you'll just—"

"Don't worry, I won't lose you."

Katherine's insides fluttered at his promise, but she wasn't worried about getting lost again. She was worried she might spontaneously combust if she listened to his voice much longer. "I'm trusting you."

He laughed, and she would have been in flames if she hadn't melted into a puddle already.

Twenty minutes later, she hung up her phone and parked in the empty lot in front of the Ponderosa Lodge. She hadn't caught fire, but perhaps she needed to torch the building? It seemed like it might be better for the owner to start over than to try to fix everything that was wrong with the place. Weathered, yellow-stained wood, cracked concrete steps, paint peeling on the door. And that was just what she could see from the poor outdoor lighting. She couldn't imagine how much worse it would be inside or in the light of day. No wonder there had been so few photos on the website.

There was nothing that could be done. She'd have to stay at least for the night, so she opened the car door and got out. As Katherine came around the car, a man emerged from the entrance, hidden in shadows. He was large and muscular. Young. He lifted his head, revealing the lines of a tattoo on his neck, then crunched his way across the gravel.

Katherine lost her footing and stepped back, bumping into the rental car.

"You must be Katherine." That hot-chocolate voice rolled over her right as the promised snow exploded out of the sky in a downpour of huge flakes.

Katherine wrapped her arms around her middle. She'd been traveling fourteen hours. There were no other vacancies in the area, even if she had another drive in her. But no way could she stay in that rundown lodge with that young man who was sex-in-boots all by herself. "Where is everyone?"

He stared at her like she was still lost. And she *was*—completely lost. What had she done, coming all the way to Colorado without telling a soul where she was going?

"Who?" he asked.

"The other guests, the staff, everyone."

"I'm it. For now. Gabe Gallegos, owner and luggage wrangler for the Ponderosa Lodge. Want to open the back?" He pointed at the key fob in her hand.

She pushed the button once she found the right image, and the hatch popped open with a cheerful tone. Gabe pulled out all three pieces, picked up two. Katherine reached for the third, and he looked at her pointedly. "I've got this. Just head inside."

Katherine lifted her chin and walked toward the rundown lodge that she would have to call home for the night, grateful she wasn't carrying her bag. She'd barely been able to put her shoes on her swollen feet before she'd gotten out of the car. It was all she could do to swallow down the whine that threatened to escape.

A warm fire crackled in the large opening of a rock-clad section of the two-story wood wall. There was a dead animal head of some kind suspended partway up, staring down at her. Katherine avoided the plaid-covered sofa and seated herself on the edge of a leather chair near the hearth, ignoring the book that was propped open on the arm.

"Make yourself comfortable," her host said as he hefted the two bags up the wide wood stairway to what must be the rooms. Her car was visible through the huge multi-paned glass window opposite the fireplace. Her bag leaned against the closed hatch, a layer of snow settling on it. For a moment she considered retrieving it herself, but her feet were screaming, and the gravel and snow would finish off her shoes for good. Besides, Gabe was already heading out the front door, and the fire was finally starting to thaw her bones.

He thumped back inside with her smallest bag. "If you'll follow me? I'll show you your room."

Katherine clenched her jaw and rose, masking a wince. She used the railing to propel herself behind him up thirteen stairs, each one a reminder that her footwear was not appropriate for the mountains. Luckily, her favorite slippers were in the bag he carried.

"Here you are." Gabe held the door open, and Katherine peered inside.

"Oh." Katherine clamped her mouth shut on the single syllable of despair. The room was institutional white, and a lingering fresh-paint smell hung in the air. A drab woven rug covered the wood floors, anchored in place by a queen bed made of knotty pine. The only spot of color was a time-worn quilt and the red numbers illuminating the clock on the knotty-pine nightstand. A single wrought-iron lamp shared the surface.

"My buddy and his wife stayed here and helped me get the room ready. Said the bed is super comfortable."

"I assume you changed the sheets." *Shit.* Katherine wished the words had remained unsaid.

Gabe crossed his arms. "I follow all standard hospitality sanitation protocols, I assure you."

She'd pissed him off but had been far too tired to refrain from blurting the first thing that had come to mind. Fortunately, he wouldn't be mad when she checked out early. She stepped inside, and a matching chest of drawers was revealed behind the door. She turned in a slow circle. The window was covered with a heavy faux-suede drape. At least there wasn't another dead animal glaring down at her. But something was missing. "Where's the bathroom?"

"Down the hall, next door on the right."

Katherine closed her eyes. It had never occurred to her she needed to specify an en suite bath. Rustic indeed. In the morning, she would find a real room in a real resort with real staff and relocate.

"I'll let you get settled. You probably haven't eaten. I have a couple of delivery menus, and, uh, the lodge, it, um, hosts a happy hour. Wine and such, if you'd like."

Katherine paused before answering. She was starving, and he was trying. No point in detailing the extreme shortcomings of his establishment. He either already knew or didn't care. And a glass of wine would be heaven. "Happy hour's fine. I'll be down in a few moments."

Gabe nodded and pulled the door to her room closed sharply. The sound of his footsteps softened and disappeared before she moved to her bags.

One night. Two max.

GABE STOPPED himself from slamming his prosthetic down each stair. Abusing himself or breaking the damn thing, which cost a fortune, wouldn't change the attitude of the ice queen who'd just taken occupancy of his only completed room. The problem with booking rooms over the internet was not knowing who you were renting to. Had he known a character from his niece's favorite movie was going to roar into his life in a four-wheel-drive chariot, he'd have marked the room booked for the foreseeable future instead of spending a day—much less two weeks—with *Jadis* scowling at him in his own home. And the fact that she was gorgeous, smelled like lust, and everything below his brain wanted to spend all kinds of time with her pissed him off even more. Stupid eyeballs, stupid nose, stupid dick.

Talking her through the directions of the lodge, she'd seemed vulnerable and sexy, and he'd wondered what had brought her to Alabaster. There'd been a moment when he'd been guiding her, caring for her, listening to her throaty voice, that he'd imagined they might have a good couple of weeks together. And when she'd stepped out from around the car, all long legs and blond hair, his cock had twitched, speaking to him for the first time in far too long. But as soon as he'd approached, smiling in a way that showed off his dimple, his money smile, she'd recoiled. Hated him on sight. Rejected before he'd had a chance to disappoint her. It had taken everything he had, every rule his uncle had instilled in him about hospitality, to not tell her to get back in her car and keep driving.

It was obvious she didn't have a warm bone in her banging body. And his cock was trying to convince him that ice-cold was fine with him. Last thing he needed was to be sporting a fucking hard-on when she came down for her wine. There would be no hiding that reaction.

As he opened the bottle of merlot and arranged a small charcuterie plate of some cheese, dried fruit, nuts, crackers, and chocolate, he forced himself to recall the painful months of his physical therapy. The five hours a day relearning how to balance, walk, and later run and jump. Focusing on that pain and the loss did what logic couldn't —deflated his damn cock.

He'd have to find a way to deal with his attraction. Maybe remind his body that if she sneered at the lodge, which was basically whole but in need of maintenance, what would she do if he actually got her into bed? Laugh? Run? Worse, look at him with pity? He didn't need any goddamn pity. But he might need to start dating again. Soon. No point in wasting the physical response he was finally having. And redirecting it would be the wiser plan. Gabe huffed out a breath and prepared to make nice. Jadis had traveled from New York, according to the information on her reservation. Between the altitude and the wine and a bit of food, she should crash pretty quickly. But no matter what she said or did, he was going to be the perfect gracious host because he couldn't afford a single bad review.

She came down the stairs as he placed a wineglass next to the plate of food. She looked...perfect.

"That looks perfect." She placed her hand on the back of the chair but didn't sit. "Aren't you joining me? Not quite a happy hour with only one person."

"Of course." Not. He scratched his fingers through his beard. There was no choice. "I was about to grab my glass and the rest of the bottle. Make yourself comfortable."

Gabe took three deep breaths as he took another wineglass from the cabinet. He could be the charming host his uncle had been. He could be so damn charming she would forget the shortcomings of the lodge. Besides, it seemed like she was trying to be nice. Maybe she wasn't a good traveler, and he'd misjudged her.

As soon as he settled in the chair opposite her, he regretted his decision.

"What made you decide to run a B and B?"

A flashback to the ABBA president's visit rolled through him. He popped a piece of cheese in his mouth and considered his answer. "It's a family business."

Katherine's eyebrows shot up. "Really?"

"My uncle left it to me. I used to work for him before I was in the military. I love this place. Some of my happiest memories are from the time I spent with my uncle."

"I can see why you wouldn't let it go even though it needs a complete remodel. Did he keep the rooms so stark, too, or is that something you prefer because you were in the service?"

Gabe focused on the way her lips wrapped around the small pickle as she bit down. If she didn't speak, she was incredibly attractive. Unfortunately, she swallowed, and the seductive silence disappeared.

"I mean, color goes a long way toward making a place feel inviting. And I peeked in the bathroom before I came down. There's a perfect spot to knock a door through. Also, I noticed there isn't a phone? Or a television. Is that normal? I haven't stayed anywhere quite this rustic before."

"People usually come here to ski or hike or do other outdoor activities, not chat on the phone or watch TV. Pretty sure they can Netflix and chill at home." He gulped his wine and softened his tone. "I rushed to get the first room ready. I've been working on the place for months. Sealing cracks, updating the septic, stuff that has to be done. And I need the income to keep making improvements. I've never been much of a decorator, and everything my uncle had was so dated or worn I couldn't use it."

"Stark is better than shabby. Certainly better than shabby chic." Katherine wrinkled her nose. It was almost cute. Almost. "That is so not a thing. There is nothing chic about shabby. I'm not bad with colors. I'd be glad to give you some ideas. I could fix your website, too."

"There's nothing wrong—" Gabe drained his glass. "I'll keep that in mind." He had to change the subject before he lost his shit with her criticism. As he searched for a topic, he refilled their glasses.

"You said this was a family business. Was it just you and your uncle?"

Thank god she'd found a safe topic. "No, I have four brothers and a sister." Angelina, who was spoiled but not abrasive. "They're in California with my mother."

"Do they help you?"

"My brother Michael is a contractor. He came out for a couple of weeks when I first got the place. And Rafe, my second-oldest brother, set up my books. He's a CPA. My youngest brother, Jeremiah, is a concert pianist. He doesn't do anything that could risk his hands." *Yep, let me tell you all about my super-successful family while we discuss my inadequate lodge.*

"What about your sister?"

Gabe shifted in his seat. "She's finishing her pharmacy degree. No time to help me, and she's worse at decorating than I am."

Katherine laughed. And why did he react like she'd stroked her hand up his shaft? *Shit. Keep talking, Gallegos.* "What about you? Any family?"

"I'm an only child. But I was married once." She turned away and drank down her wine.

"Didn't work out?" Gabe refilled her glass, emptying the bottle.

"He liked certain…*things*…that I didn't. But he's happy now. Living with a young woman and another man from my father's law firm."

Ouch.

The wince must have shown on his face, because Katherine waved a hand. "It was a long time ago. I'm completely over it."

Gabe wasn't convinced. She had no siblings. She was traveling alone. Her ex-husband had two lovers. From what he could see, she had no one. "What about your parents?"

The sharp laugh that burst out of her held no humor. "My mother is somewhere in Australia, I expect. And my father fired me from my marketing job in our family's firm on New Year's Day." She took a huge swallow from her glass. "I'm fine on my own. I'm deciding what to do next."

Good for her. But he wouldn't be her next project. "So, skiing? I assume you're here to hit the slopes?"

She blinked at him, her eyes fuzzy from the wine, and she hadn't eaten much. "I am. In fact, I should get some rest." She stood up, backing away as if she'd realized everything she'd just confessed. "I'm going to go tomorrow since there's all this fresh snow falling. I'll see you in the morning."

Gabe nodded and watched her walk away. Two weeks. He could survive that somewhat fragile, somewhat abrasive woman for two weeks. Then she'd be gone, and he could use the money to fix up a second room. As long as he stayed focused on the lodge, he could tolerate anything for fourteen days.

CHAPTER 5

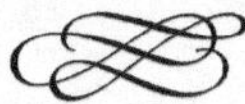

Katherine rolled to a cool spot under the down duvet and white cotton sheets. She'd slept her first long, peaceful slumber in recent memory. The blank walls still cried for color, and the windows could use some liners under the curtains, especially with the way the sunlight reflected off the snow-covered landscape and glowed through the space. But, overall, the room didn't annoy her nearly as much as it had the day before. Maybe it was the anonymity. No one knew where she was. No one had her new cell number. And no one was going to harm her based on the fact Gabe was more of a gentleman than he appeared, military trained, and not at all interested in her. Which was perfect since he was far too young for her, no matter how gorgeous she found him.

Trickles of their conversation the night before flashed back to her. Heat crept up her neck when she recalled sharing some of the dirtier details of her divorce, like her ex-husband living in a ménage. And how her father had fired her. Oh god. Too much wine and not enough food had loosened her tongue. And wait…when had she decided he was gorgeous?

She tossed back the covers. A shower might wash away some of the regret and poor judgment. Once she started moving, her needs became urgent. Toeing her still-packed suitcase open, she snatched her toiletry bag and rushed into the hallway and into the bathroom next door.

Hot water cascaded down Katherine's back, lulling her as she cared for her skin with unthinking routine. She arched her back and ran her hands over her breasts, imagining a faceless lover. Her hand moved lower to press against her clit, stroking a familiar rhythm. Her breath quickened.

Frigid water exploded over her. Icy daggers pelted her skin. The moan she'd been about to release erupted as a screech. She leaned back to avoid the biting assault while twisting the faucet. But nothing worked. She slammed off the water and reached for one of the folded towels, wrapping it— The damn thing didn't go all the way around. She was freezing, frustrated, and furious.

"Katherine?" Gabe pounded on the door. "Are you all right?"

She whipped the door open, ready to share her thoughts on the situation. But the corner of the too-small towel loosened. Before she could grab it, her entire breast made an appearance, nipple at attention with the blast of cold air from the hallway. Gabe's eyes went wide. Heat slammed up her chest to her cheeks as she retrieved the wayward fabric. He turned his head, and the skin on his neck reddened around the fine lines of his tattoo. She swallowed a request for him to finish turning and lift his shirt to better see what exactly he had inked across his broad back. As her eyes trailed down, she noticed the sizable bulge in his pants and snapped back to reality.

"What the hell is wrong with you?" she spat as she fussed with the sorry excuse for a cover. "Cut off the hot water? Too-small towels? All this just for a boob flash?"

"No!" His gaze lashed back to her. "You have a call. A Richard Wallace?"

The breath froze in her lungs.

Her father had found her.

And in less than twenty-four hours. What else could he possibly have to say? Maybe he already missed her and would beg her to come back?

"And for the record, those towels are hotel standard. I don't have to resort to tricks to see a boob." Gabe spun on his heal and headed for the stairs. "Are you going to take the call?"

Katherine swallowed her snarky retort. "Tell him to wait."

Gabe glanced back, opened his mouth, and closed it. Then he descended, leaving her dripping wet in the hallway and mad as hell that she'd booked that place. And why was she the least bit interested in Gabe's tattoo or his huge cock? She didn't need to be interested in a man. *Any* man. Especially a boy-man who was not her type at all.

She threw on some yoga pants and a soft tunic, no bra because she still had fabulous breasts. Not that anybody besides her doctor had seen them in years. She couldn't even remember the last time she'd been around anyone without *makeup*. The last time she'd wanted to wake up with someone, exposing herself as anything less than polished perfection. The last time she'd been vulnerable or wanted to be. But there was no time to get presentable, and, besides, Gabe had already seen her...well, as naked as he was ever going to. No recovering from that.

Twisting her hair into a clip, she went to deal with her father. Gabe reclined in the chair closest to the fireplace with a book. He didn't appear to be reading—more of a pose.

"Where's the phone?" She bit back another complaint about not having a phone in her room. Not as if he could install one before she had to talk to her father.

Gabe lifted from the chair, moved past her to a hallway beyond the stairs she hadn't noticed. "In here."

Katherine walked through the doorway where he'd paused. It was his *bedroom*. A hint of cut lumber lingered in the air. The space was spotless but warm, with thick bedding in russet and olive tones. A chair by the windows held a woven pillow, and there were a few photographs on a tallboy dresser. Snow-covered pines filled the view from the window. All he needed was a candle and some artwork for the perfect nest. A desk sat immediately to her right, and the handset to an old-fashioned princess phone—rotary dial, cord, and all—rested faceup on a stack of DIY magazines. She could just ignore the phone and inspect the pictures.

Bile boiled up in her stomach. If she hung up without speaking, her luggage was still packed—

Ridiculous.

At almost forty years old, she should not respond like a child. She should deal with her father without hesitation. The same way he'd fired her.

Afterward, she'd address the uncomfortable desire she had to flirt with Gabe. To prove she was still attractive. The desire to drop into his bed and pretend she was young enough to have a relationship with a man. Pretend he could be attracted to her despite the fact he had seen through her shattered illusion of perfection. Pretend she could be with someone who got hard because of *her*, not with a pill. Someone who might want her for more than the trinket she would be on his arm. She'd soften her gaze and her heart until he buried himself in her, the way he'd buried himself in the restoration of the inn. They could just fuck without ulterior motives and hidden agendas. She'd wrap herself in the warmth and the peace for a while.

The sound of a throat clearing snapped her out of her fantasy. The second one that day. Something was wrong with her. Gabe leaned on the doorframe, arms crossed. The daydream wasn't real. They wouldn't have sex. But maybe she could use her time here to practice being...softer? That word Natalia rattled at her so often.

She let the corners of her lips lift almost enough to smile, and her gaze met Gabe's.

Her father roared like an old dragon through the speaker. Her mental armor snapped into place. Soft had no purpose in her life.

She reached for the receiver, shooting a glare at Gabe, who took the hint and walked away. After a slow, deep breath, using her most impersonal tone, she said, "Hello, Richard."

G*ABE STALKED BACK* to his chair, leaving Jadis in *his* bedroom. She hadn't been at the Ponderosa for twenty-four hours and already he had a list of things to improve and had given up his bedroom for her personal calls. He sat and closed his eyes, running a hand over his face. An image of her, backlit and surrounded by steam, appeared as if she were still standing in front of him. Ethereal. That was the word he'd been searching for. In that moment, before her towel had slipped and she'd started bitching at him again, she'd been an angel.

And thank you to whoever had made standard hotel bath towels just a bit smaller, a bit narrower, than any other towel for sale. Because *damn.* Her leg had been exposed from the tips of her perfect toes to the point where her toned thigh met her hip. He'd actually had a microsecond to consider if she was natural or waxed bare between her legs. Then her towel had revealed the most perfect breast he could recall having seen in person. He rubbed his palm on the arm of the chair. The itch to cup her perfect flesh and toy with her hard pale pink nipple lingered. Katherine was fucking hot, and she'd nut-punch him if she had any idea what he was sitting there thinking about. Soon he would have to take care of himself as he fantasized about sucking her breasts, licking her naked pussy, and sliding his cock home between her legs.

Gabe groaned and pressed down on the appendage that had earned him the nickname "Thor" in the army. He'd only been half hard, and Katherine had looked at him with horror. She wouldn't be the first one to decline. Size was fantastic for a porn star or a romance novel. But real women expected to be able to walk again after sex. It didn't matter if he knew all kinds of ways to get a lover ready. He could eat pussy like a pro, finger out an orgasm in seconds, and anything else they needed to be able to take him. But most women didn't care to try. And the whole a-baby-can-come-out-of-there argument hadn't worked well the one time he'd tried it. Granted, it was high school, but his soon-to-be ex had stood up and told him, "I don't want to give birth every time I fuck you."

The last time he'd had actual intercourse with anyone had been long before he'd lost his leg. Since then, he hadn't cared to even think about the mechanics of it and what it would mean to fuck with one of his legs missing from the knee down. It didn't matter. Jadis might have lit him up. She might have called out to the protective side he'd buried in the desert years ago. And he might make the effort to provide her with the best accommodations possible, but it wasn't about fucking. It was about taking care of the guests, and it was about the reviews for the hotel. Because if he couldn't even take care of a guest in his uncle's lodge, how was he ever going to take care of a partner?

It was time to pull his head out of his ass and start figuring things out for real. His livelihood was at stake, and he had a jet-setting resort denizen giving him great advice on what to do to fix the place up. Even if it stung like an ice pick being driven into his head every time she pointed out a flaw. He'd just imagine her tits, and it would all be good. Kind of sick, but he would do what he had to in preparation for being the right man for someone someday. But not anytime soon. And not for Katherine, the ice queen.

CHAPTER 6

Katherine held the phone away from her ear as her father bellowed.

"Why the hell are you in Colorado? I need you here."

"How did you find me?"

The bark of laughter stabbed her right in the gut. "I'm on every one of your accounts. I received a warning when a charge came through from out of state."

Of course. As the trustee, he would have been on her accounts. It hadn't occurred to her to remove him or open new ones. He'd always been there behind the scenes, running everything. *Ruining* everything.

"It's none of your business why I'm here. And you made it very clear you no longer require my assistance."

"At the firm."

So he wasn't calling to give her job back. Another wave of loss drained through her.

"Katie. I should have called sooner, but I was giving you time to cool off. I didn't expect you to run away. Why would you do that to me? We're all the other one has."

He was so formulaic: an apology. A magnanimous gesture. An accusation. Victimization. And, finally, alignment.

She clenched her jaw to hold back an ingrained response to appease him. Wow. How did he get away with that type of manipulation? And why hadn't she seen through it sooner?

"I would have thought you'd stay in Aspen if you're running off for a ski vacation."

"It's not a vacation if you have no job." Damn. She closed her eyes. She'd risen to his bait. Such weakness.

"Katie, my hands were tied. I understand your need to hide and lick your wounds for a bit. But why cut Marcus off? He would have paid for everything. Would have come with you, taken care of you. I'm sure he could have found a nicer place to stay. That lodge should be condemned."

An image of her father as a dragon wrapped around the lodge and tearing pieces off flashed through her mind. But according to the psychic, or whatever Madam Tiana was, Katherine was supposed to do the tearing down of the tower. "I don't need Marcus or you to take care of me. I'm a grown woman."

That damn chuckle thudded into her ear. "Come home, Katie."

"Why do you think you're still in charge of what I do?"

"Because I am. I'll give you this brief reprieve. Let you pout. But not for too long."

There was a warning, a threat in his tone. But nothing remained that he could take away. He might have administrative access on her accounts, but the trust had expired years ago. The primary account had originally been set up by her mother's family and added to by her grandfather. Richard Wallace only believed he had power over her. A belief that time would disabuse him of better than any argument she might offer. The man was all mouth, no ears. She sighed. "Bye, Daddy."

The phone settled with a clunk into the cradle, and she closed her eyes. *Stop* flashed in red across the inside of her lids.

Stop reacting.

Stop responding.

Stop relying on a man who had no one's interests but his own at heart.

Her legs went weak, and all the energy left her body. She gripped the desk to hold herself up. Going back to bed held tremendous appeal. Sleep for a week. Bury her head in the covers until it all went away or crashed down on her. Which was more likely.

She drew a slow, deep breath in and steeled her spine. Relying on Richard had been an ongoing mistake. It was time to rip off the leading strings, pick her tits up, and do something. She'd had more balls in her twenties. Where had they gone? Shriveled from lack of use. Or, really, right into her father's pocket. Because she'd let him own her.

How *had* she let herself get so bricked in by the man who was supposed to love her unconditionally? But then, she'd never questioned his motivations.

Whatever action she took would have to be in the form of a plan because it was Saturday and there was no one working in the bank's trust department where her accounts had always been. She'd require professionals to disconnect her life from the hooks of her father. And who could help her with that? No one in the law firm, that was certain. She considered a painfully short list of allies. Ned? No. That bridge was ashes. There had to be more. She wasn't thinking clearly. Rattled by the phone call, it made strategic thinking difficult.

Beyond freeing herself from her father, beyond trying to revive her last moment of real happiness with that getaway, she had to figure out her own brand. What did she have to offer the world as just Katherine? Who was she? What did she want to represent? Everything she'd done before her marriage and since her divorce had been in support of the firm and her father. She hadn't tried to market herself as a woman; her father had provided "suitable" suitors. She'd never even applied for a job.

The one time she'd agreed to do marketing work that didn't involve the firm, her father had made her future ex-husband pay her through the firm. If she'd stood her ground then, her life might have gone in a different direction. But there was nothing to be gained by second-guessing her past decisions.

She would act, but not react. Although she had plenty of dirt on her dad, she didn't want to destroy him, just free herself. The first thing to do was what she did best—research. He said he wouldn't do anything immediately. And, really, what could he do? She scoffed. His self-importance was overblown. If she compared their relative positions, she held the power.

❀

GABE POURED the fresh-brewed coffee into the thermal carafe and placed it on the sideboard near the oval dining table. He'd put out a bowl of mixed fruit, strawberry yogurt, and bakery muffins since he still hadn't been successful with his grandmother's recipe. He could offer eggs if Katherine wanted something hot. Bacon or sausage, too. But his budget couldn't afford to waste food. No point in cooking if she ate like a bird.

She emerged from the doorway, and he opened his mouth to ask if the call had gone well, or something innocuous like that, but he could tell it hadn't. She was smaller, less substantial than the woman he'd led in there. A ghost whose focus was inward.

"Coffee?" he asked softly.

A tiny jolt of her body confirmed she hadn't been aware of his presence. She smiled, but it didn't convince him.

"Yes, thank you."

He ignored the frosty formality of her tone. "There's some food here, or I can make you something hot?"

With a shake of her head, she moved to the buffet. "This is too much. You're only feeding one person. You could have put out a single serving. Or nothing at all."

"Are you okay?" Gabe clenched his jaw. Why had he asked? It was none of his business.

"Fine."

When his sister and his mother used that word, things were not fine. But Katherine was not his problem. He filled a mug and set it next to the sugar and cream. Katherine picked it up, along with a bowl of fruit and yogurt that wouldn't satisfy a small child, and took the chair facing the view. Hands wrapped around her mug and elbows on the table, she looked frozen. Lost.

Damn. He didn't have time to deal with a broken guest. If she ate and disappeared, he would still have time to meet his ski group. Hopefully, she'd forgotten about going skiing. "Any plans for today? The town is cute. Great shopping."

Katherine's gaze moved to him, and she settled her cup on the table without tasting the organic roast. "I'm going to purchase a ski pass and find a good rental place. I came out here to ski, so I might as well get started."

"You can ride along with me." Gabe could have kicked himself. Why had he offered to take her? She had an SUV. She could find her own way. Except that she'd likely get lost. And if he was on the slopes, who would she call? And he was going anyway. And politeness dictated he at least offer. Too bad she hadn't changed her mind.

"*You're* going skiing *today*?"

She probably hadn't meant to sound so condescending. Maybe his guilt about everything that still needed to be done at the lodge was coloring her tone in his ears. "I meet a veterans' group every couple of weeks during the season."

"I'd planned to go solo."

"Just offering a ride." And regretting even that.

"Of course." She waved a hand like she was brushing his comment aside. "A ride would be welcome."

"Great. I'm leaving in forty-five minutes." Gabe went to gather his gear, giving her time to eat what she wanted before he cleared the food and dishes. Either she'd be at the truck when it was time to go or she wouldn't.

Thirty-five minutes later, Gabe had his pile of equipment at the door and was almost done tidying up breakfast. The coffee carafe was empty, so at least she'd liked that. The bakery muffins were untouched. They wouldn't be good later, so he wrapped them up to take. His buddies would make them disappear in a second, and he'd be the hero for the day. He couldn't wait to see them. Men and women who knew his story without being told. He could let down his guard and just be Gabe for a few hours. Not Gabe the vet or the amputee, or Gabe the B and B proprietor. Just Gabe.

Katherine appeared on the stairs as he exited the kitchen. She had on ski pants and surprisingly sturdy boots. Her coat and a small bag were in one hand and her sunglasses in the other. "I'm ready."

Gabe grabbed his bag of essentials, ski bib, gloves, and a single ski boot. His ski was already in the truck's bed. After tucking his outriggers under one arm, he opened the lodge door so Katherine could precede him.

"What are those?" she asked, eyeing the outriggers.

Gabe stepped out behind her and locked up, *so* not ready for that conversation. "My ski poles."

He dropped his bag and lowered the tailgate on the truck. After stowing his equipment securely, he turned. Katherine was a few feet behind him, a curious tilt to her head. *Fuck it.* He lifted his pant leg enough to reveal the aftermarket part that allowed him to walk.

"Oh." She nodded. There wasn't a trace of pity on her face.

Huh. That was different. But they still had a long car ride to get through.

She moved to the passenger side. Opening the door for her would be too much like a date.

He flicked the button on his key fob, letting the chirp signal the cab was unlocked. His hand hovered over the driver's door handle. If she was weird about his leg, personal questions or staring, he'd dump her on the side of the road. *No, you will not,* his mother's voice echoed. Gritting his teeth, he got in and closed the door sharply.

They drove for about ten minutes in total silence. The roads were clear, having been plowed and salted. Katherine faced the passenger window. It was a pretty view, with the snow clumped on the evergreens. Probably didn't see much of that in New York City.

She turned, and Gabe quickly shifted his focus back to the road.

"Is there a rental place you recommend?" she asked.

He'd expected the questions to start at some point, but not about ski equipment. Gabe cleared his throat. "There's a place right at the base. Probably the easiest since you can leave everything but your boots with them overnight if you're planning on renting multiple days."

"Excellent. Drop me there."

Yes, mistress. That imperial tone pissed him off every time, but he wouldn't be rude. "I can wait for you."

"I don't know how long I'll be, and you have people to meet."

The tension in his jaw released. Jadis was being considerate.

"How late will you ski?" she asked. "I assume the local shuttle doesn't go to Alabaster?"

"We're usually done and at the tavern by four thirty or five. I'll meet you there."

Twenty-five comfortably silent minutes later, Gabe pulled over behind a clump of late-model SUVs. Rainbow-hued groups of skiers clomped around the lodge area and waited in lines for the lifts. Katherine got out of his truck with a quick thank-you and a wave.

He kept his eyes on her until she was inside. She hadn't said a word about his prosthetic or how he could ski or any of the other dumb things he'd heard. In the early days, when his gait had been more awkward and his balance less stable, he hadn't been able to hide his injury, and people were damn nosy. Beautiful women would talk to him but with zero attraction on their side, just indulging their curiosity about "the freak." The sting of the memories lingered, and he'd been careful to hide the evidence of his scars from strangers.

But maybe not everyone would see him as a sideshow.

Maybe there was someone out there for him.

Maybe it was time to lower his guard.

CHAPTER 7

*K*atherine winced as the chairlift scooped her up for her second run. It had been far too long since she'd used those particular muscles. But what was she going to do if she wasn't skiing? As nice as the staff was, lingering at the base camp restaurants didn't hold much appeal. Everyone else was in groups, chatting, laughing, including the three twenty-somethings on the lift with her, who looked ready for a photo shoot instead of hitting the slopes. Exactly how she'd remembered that place. But everything had changed. Not just the facility upgrades, but her.

Another run or two and she'd stop for the day, short even for her half-day plan. Not giving up but being gentle with herself. She'd use the time before she had to meet Gabe to flirt with a bartender or start a conversation with somebody. Anybody. She could practice opening up and maybe find some people to ski with while she was in Colorado. If it didn't work, she'd leave and return to the city early, then figure out what to do next.

Anything that didn't involve her father.

The warm laughter from a group on a run below the lift rattled against her chilly isolation. Dressed in bright colors, they moved as a group down the slope, like all the other skiers. But some were in sleds or at least chairs on skis. More than one person had the ski poles with mini skis attached.

And then one man skied out of the group—more graceful on a single ski than she could ever hope to be on two. He traversed back and forth like there was a soundtrack coordinating his moves. Arcs of snow highlighted his sinuous motion. Broad shoulders and tight hips, every muscle in total control. His crew called his name, and heat crawled up her neck.

Gabe.

She'd nearly jumped off the lift to meet the man she was already staying with. Face turned to the mountain to stop staring at him, she willed her growing desire to fade.

Katherine hopped off at a midway point for the easy runs before the lift continued on its way to the more difficult trails. After allowing skiers more eager and agile to pass, she traversed the snow in a zigzag path nowhere near as elegantly as Gabe. There were a lot of people on the run. To be expected with the weekend and the fresh powder the storm had dumped on the mountain. Families moved down the slopes in small clots, calling out to each other in cheerful bursts. The sun glinted off the snow. And the trees, gilded with powder, completed the picture worthy of a postcard.

Up ahead, a young skier, maybe ten or eleven years old with long hair peeking out of their helmet, paused at the edge of the trail. Trouble with a boot or a binding based on the wiggling. Katherine slowly skied closer to offer a hand when a blur to her left snatched her attention.

Another skier. Darting off a black run, headed directly toward the kid adjusting their boot. There was no way that guy would be able to cut away in time to avoid the unaware victim—he was moving too fast. She had to stop him from smashing into the little one. Blood racing, Katherine bent her knees and dug in with her poles, determined to move the child out of the way.

But her trajectory was completely off.

She collided with the out-of-control skier, careening away like a pinball off a flipper. His skis swooped out in an arc, but somehow he managed to recover, navigated the turn, and resumed full speed through the easy run. Did he even realize he'd hit her? She skidded hard, and her left ski twisted at an awkward angle as she went down. The binding failed to release. Oh *damn*. That couldn't be right. She tried to get up. Pain erupted from her ankle past her eyeballs. A scream caught in her throat. It was the worst sprain she'd ever experienced. How was she going to get down the mountain?

"I saw what happened. What were you thinking?"

Katherine blinked through tears to find Gabe glaring down at her. Why him, of all people? The man skied like a god with one leg, and there she was, hobbled on only her second run. "How are you here?"

"Did you hit your head?" He slid the ski forward and lowered to the snow next to her. "The helmet should have protected you."

"No." She sucked in a shuddering breath and swallowed down the rising bile as another wave of pain from her ankle blasted her. At least the agony killed some of her embarrassment. "Where'd you come from? I just saw you. On this run."

"We grabbed the express. But what the hell *was* that? Didn't you see that other guy?"

"I..." The child was gone. Oh, *like hell* was she going to explain herself. "No. Didn't see him."

Gabe looked at her like she was a teenager busted for being out past curfew. She returned it in full measure.

"Don't move. Help is on the way," he said.

She tried to reposition herself again. *Ow. Oh damn.* She closed her eyes and breathed through her nose until the urge to vomit passed. "I don't need medical attention. It's a sprain."

"Too late. My buddy already called it in." He pressed a hand to her shoulder. "You're *not* moving until they get here. And you're going to do what they say."

"I don't recall you being in charge of me. If anything, *I'm* paying *you*. Which makes me the one in charge. So, go ski."

Gabe laughed loudly. "Wrong, Jadis."

Jadis? What the hell was a Jadis? She refused to ask and add to his misguided sense of superiority. The internet would explain without the attitude. She freed her uninjured leg from her ski and positioned her poles. Gabe squeezed her shoulder and leaned in close. The smell of fresh-cut wood and man softened her resolve.

"I brought you out here. And I'm not leaving you. Besides, after our discussion last night, I'm more than your innkeeper."

Before she could figure out what he might mean by being "more than her *innkeeper*," help arrived in the form of ski patrol with a rescue sled. She closed her eyes. Outnumbered, she'd be bullied into allowing them to put her on that thing. And she'd have to spend the rest of her time in Alabaster skiing on a different mountain after such an embarrassing display. But there were four peaks, so she still had three more on which to make a fool of herself.

GABE'S HEART had gone AWOL to live in his throat when he'd seen Katherine and that guy collide. The fact she'd fallen but missed the nearby tree allowed him to take a breath as he rushed to her. Then he'd called her Jadis and professed to be more than a host. The words hadn't been filtered through his brain—gut directly to mouth. Why did his viscera claim he was more important to her?

Protectiveness was going to wreck him one day for real, not just blow him up. A warning his brain would have to heed at some point. But still he followed the ski patrol down the mountain. His crew had offered to stay, but no reason for them to lose the last hours of slope time. *They* hadn't sworn loyalty to the ice queen. Gabe rolled his eyes and hurried to catch up so he could wait while they assessed her.

After stowing his gear and changing back into street clothes, Gabe paced the tiny lobby of the clinic. His only concern should be the loss of income if she had to leave early. If she had more than a sprain—

"You can come back. She's asking for you."

Gabe turned at the medic's voice. "She's good to go?"

The woman waved for him to follow. Tucked into the back corner of the med clinic, surrounded by curtains on a track, Katherine was on a gurney with a white blanket pulled up to her neck and her eyes wide. She'd shrunk since she'd been lying on the slope giving him sass.

"They're transferring me to the hospital. It's likely a fracture, not a sprain. But they gave me something for the pain. So you can leave."

"Is there someone you want me to call?" Her father?

"No." Her voice was empty, and it cut a space into the center of him.

If it were the other way around, he'd be asking her to call his mother and his oldest brother, and it would be a race to see which of his five siblings would accompany his mother to come to him. Hell, they'd tried to fly to Germany after his "Event." And they'd gone to DC for his initial recovery before taking him home to LA, where they had flapped around him until he'd nearly gone nuts. They'd insisted he couldn't visit his uncle unless one of them escorted him. He'd been glad he'd compromised, letting his brother Uriel join him, when news came a few months later that his uncle had died. But even losing Juan had left him with more family than he knew what to do with. How could Katherine be so all alone? How could she stand it?

"I don't need your pity," she said. "I'll be fine."

The *p* word snapped him out of his musings. Exactly what he'd found intolerable in his own family.

"I'm not pitying you," he said. "You've got a broken leg. They'll fix it. No biggie. I was planning on feeding and housing you anyway. Not like you're gonna run off now."

She gaped at him.

He grinned, letting his dimples show. "I need someone to taste-test my muffins."

A blush covered her cheeks. "I don't know what that means."

He bent toward her ear. "You have a dirty mind."

"I...I—" she sputtered.

Gabe laughed. "Jadis. I got you. We'll go to the hospital, then I'll take you back to the inn. We can roast marshmallows or watch movies or whatever until you decide what you want to do next."

"I need my phone. It's in the lockers. The key is on my bibs." She pointed to a folded pile of clothes, and Gabe slapped away the image of what she might be wearing under the blanket.

"You think of someone to call?"

"No, I want to look up this word you keep calling me."

"Should've just asked. And it's the first movie we'll be watching —*The Chronicles of Narnia*. Your cultural education is sorely lacking."

"*My* cultural education? You do know where I'm from? A mecca for the arts."

"Then how'd you miss my niece's favorite movie? And I can tell you, it's just as good the eighty-fifth time you watch it."

"Oh, I don't think so. Get my phone."

Gabe held up his hands like she had him at gunpoint and tried not to laugh. "What?"

She raised an eyebrow, chin lifting in a haughty tilt. "I'll call someone."

"Ghostbusters?" He couldn't resist. And her spark was returning.

"You are *so* not funny."

"I'm hilarious."

"Who told you this? Your six-year-old niece?"

"She's nine. And yes."

"The ambulance is here." The medic's voice interrupted whatever Katherine had been about to respond with.

Her gaze snapped to his. "I'm sorry. I shouldn't have made fun of your niece or her favorite movie. I'm sure it's fantastic. But you're not taking this seriously. I've never ridden in an ambulance, and I'm going to be incapacitated for weeks. I can't expect you to— I should look into getting a nurse or flying home early. Maybe they have rehab at the hospital. You know what I'm facing. I—"

"Jadis." He reached for her hand, and she gripped his tight. "I'll be right behind you. Promise."

CHAPTER 8

Katherine pressed the button to raise the back of the hospital bed as a nurse entered her room. She cheerfully announced Katherine was going home and removed the IV line. Rather than respond with several choice phrases about "home," Katherine kept her mouth tightly shut and her face blank. She couldn't blame the nurse for being happy about the prospect of getting rid of her worst patient. Katherine didn't mean to be difficult, not really. But how many terrible things had to happen in a row before she was allowed to express her displeasure with life? And getting discharged meant more problems to solve. Where would she go, and who would take care of her?

Gabe had valiantly remained by her side in the ER, but after the doctor's decision to keep her overnight "just in case," Katherine insisted he leave. She could call him to take her back to the lodge, but the logistics of getting up and down the stairs—or bathing, or going anywhere—made Katherine's head hurt. Yet there was no one else.

Her friends were in New York but not caretaker material. Her mother was likely already in Australia or on her way for the winter tennis tournaments. And her father was out of the question. In fact, she still needed to call her financial advisor to check on the status of her accounts and get the paperwork started to clear up the ownership. Katherine closed her eyes, exhausted from thinking about all the hurdles. Maybe she could pay the hospital to keep her for the six weeks of recovery.

"Hey, Jadis."

Katherine opened her eyes to find Gabe, freshly showered and smiling, standing in the doorway in a long-sleeved navy-blue shirt, faded jeans, and soft hiking boots. Her stupid heart pounded a little faster.

"Heard they're letting you out of here."

"Pushing me out, you mean."

"That's a good thing," he said, coming into the room. "Hospitals are not healthy places to be. Trust me, I spent years living in them. If they open the door, run."

"Easy for you to say." Katherine pointed at her cast. "Not going to be running anywhere for a while."

He tilted his head in acknowledgement. "At least they let you keep the broken parts."

Katherine winced. She'd been unintentionally insensitive.

"Relax. I was teasing you." Gabe was close enough to bump her shoulder with his hand. "Now, are you walking out of here in that johnny? Because if so, I'm bringing up the rear." Gabe laughed.

"That's not funny." Katherine blinked away the visual of Gabe watching her naked ass. "I have nothing to wear. They cut my ski pants off. Which, if I bill them for the replacement, ought to cover a small part of the hospital expense."

Gabe snorted. "Don't worry. I got you covered." He held up a drawstring bag. "Literally."

"What's that?"

"The clothes you were wearing before we went skiing. They were still on the bed when I went in to tidy. Figured you'd need 'em."

Katherine had the urge to kiss Gabe in relief. Her yoga pants were probably stretchy enough to fit over the cast.

"I'll call the nurse to help you. Unless you'd rather I stayed." As Gabe went for the door, Katherine rolled her eyes. He was sweet and funny when he wanted to be, and she was getting used to his teasing. But even if she stayed with him while she got better, it would be as a paying guest. Nothing more. Friends and lovers always let you down. People you paid did their best or there was always someone else willing to fill in for a price.

After allowing the nurse to help her struggle into her clothes, Katherine assumed the indignities were over. An orderly walked in with a wheelchair, Gabe's handsome face visible over the young man's shoulder.

"I'm *not* sitting in that." Katherine crossed her arms. She hadn't been in one since her hysterectomy.

The orderly piped up. "The hospital requires—"

"I don't care what the hospital requires." Katherine's voice rose with every word, and the air around her thinned. "I'm not sitting in a wheelchair. I assume there are crutches somewhere in this building. Get them." She crossed her arms and tried to hide the way her heart pounded in her chest.

"Ah, lighten up, Jadis." Gabe held up a set of crutches. "I got them right here, but you can't use them in the hospital, and you can't use them until I show you how. I promised the doctor I was an expert."

"Fine. Show me now." She wiped the sweat from her hands on the sheets and tried not to lose her composure completely in front of him.

"Nope, you've gotta ride in the chair. Rules are rules." Gabe leaned back against the wall and crossed one denim-clad leg over the other, clearly ready to wait her out.

She closed her eyes and rolled her lips over her teeth. It was one damn ride. And she wasn't going into surgery to leave a piece of herself behind. Instead, they would wheel her to the nearest exit. If she could only sit in that chair without vomiting or having a full-blown panic attack. With a shaky breath, she blinked back the building tears and attempted to regain control of herself.

Gabe was so close his breath teased her neck. "Look at me."

She focused on him, and his warm brown gaze filled her field of view. He put his hand on hers, stopping the shaking she hadn't been aware of before he'd touched her.

"Count with me." His deep voice wrapped around her like a blanket.

She followed his lead, and they counted softly, eyes locked.

At thirty-seven, her breath completely even, he leaned back. "Good. Ready?"

With a quick nod, she braced herself for a rush of remorse and memories. She wasn't prepared for his strong arm to slide underneath hers and around her back. As he lifted her from the bed, she wrapped her arm around his shoulders and held on. They spun in a graceful move that was all Gabe, and he lowered her into the chair. The frame caged her. Her throat tightened painfully.

"Breathe." His voice broke through her panic.

She drew in a choppy lungful of air.

"As we leave, count all the yellow items you see." Gabe knelt, adjusting the footrests. A soft stroke of her healthy leg as he rose sent shivers into her core.

The chair moved, and she gripped the armrests with a squawk.

Gabe bounded up, taking the handles from the orderly. "I got this."

Katherine exhaled as Gabe turned the chair gently for the door, and the orderly followed, carrying her equipment. Katherine counted a vase, a poster, a warning label, a shirt, and a flower. The more she counted, the easier the air flowed in and out of her lungs and the less her heart tried to pound its way out of her chest.

While she waited in the lobby for Gabe to get his truck, she pulled her phone from the bag he'd brought. She logged into his website and booked her room for the next six weeks, paying in full. Even if she didn't stay with him the entire time, he deserved the money. By paying before she went back, there was no way he could argue with her. He'd already lost hours of skiing, managing his B and B, and who knows what else due to her accident. There weren't a lot of ways to show how much his actions meant to her, but money never disappointed.

GABE PULLED the truck in front of the hospital. He'd seen so many wounded guys freak out over different medical procedures or equipment, but a wheelchair was a first. With her gasping breaths, shaking hands, and wide-eyed gaze, Katherine had all the signs of a panic attack. Best to get her out of that chair as soon as possible. They could talk about it later if she needed. First, he had to get her back to the lodge. A small part of him questioned the urgency he felt, but he squashed it down with an insistence that she was a guest and he was only doing the right thing. He hadn't felt *anything* when he'd moved her from the bed and placed her in that god-awful wheeled contraption. Okay, maybe a minor zing, but it was just compassion, not attraction.

He raced around the truck as fast as he could and entered the hospital lobby. "Your chariot awaits, Jadis."

Katherine tucked away her phone and frowned. "Can I have my crutches now?"

Gabe shook his head. "I'm not gonna let you walk back to the lodge."

"Who says I would go there?"

"Exactly. You're not running away now. You'd want a refund or something." He set the brake on her chair and opened the passenger-side door. Then he adjusted her position to the perfect spot and leaned over her. "Ready?"

"For wha—" He lifted her from the chair, and she locked her arms around his neck. "You can't pick me up."

"Pretty sure we already proved that wrong."

"What about—"

"I know what I'm doing. Trained professional." He set her on the passenger seat and made sure her legs were clear before shutting the door on her rambling speech about how he shouldn't be carrying her. Like he didn't lift all kinds of construction materials and hadn't been trained by physical and occupational therapists for weeks and months. But, of course, she still doubted him.

He grabbed the crutches from the orderly and dropped them in the truck's bed as he made his way back to the driver's side. At least she was quiet when he got in. After starting the truck and making sure the vents were blowing heat in her direction, he carefully made his way home.

At the lodge, they repeated a version of the scene at the hospital, but Katherine didn't protest as much. The pain of being moved and the extra weight of the cast were probably getting to her. "Couch or bed?"

"What do you mean?" She stiffened in his arms.

"You need to rest. Here in the living room, or do you want to go to bed?"

"I'm not ready for...bed." She glanced around the room. "Just put me down here."

He placed her on the couch so that she could see out the window if she wanted. "I moved some things upstairs. You'll be staying in my room."

"No. I can't—"

He held up a hand. "Already done. And before you ask, yes, I changed the sheets."

"I...I wasn't going to."

"Hungry?" Gabe propped her leg up on a cushion and draped the lap blanket from the sofa over her. He knew how to take care of someone. He'd spent years helping his mother with his two younger siblings. Why couldn't Jadis just trust him?

"Maybe. What do you have?"

"Creamy green-chile chicken stew. My uncle's famous after-skiing recipe." Gabe had planned to serve it the night before, even though the lodge didn't technically serve meals other than breakfast. But it was tradition.

"It's got to be better than the horrible breakfast I had hours ago."

"It's my first attempt at using his recipe, but people loved it." He moved toward the kitchen.

"Any coffee?"

The desperate quality in her tone made him pause, then turn to face her. She had craned her neck around to face him. A flashback of his first real noninstitutional cup of coffee after months in rehab rushed through him. "Of course. I'll make a fresh pot."

Gabe placed a tray with two bowls of soup on the ottoman next to the couch. He handed one bowl to Katherine and held his breath as she dipped her spoon in and took her first taste.

A grimace flashed across her face, and she reached for her coffee. "What's the matter?"

She shook her head and set the cup down. "It's a little salty. But good."

How could he have screwed up soup? He slurped a large spoonful and nearly spit it out. "A *little* salty?"

"It's fine." She ate another bite and smiled.

"I could make you something else."

"There's no need."

Gabe got them glasses of water and bread to help choke it down. He wracked his brain for where he could have gone wrong with the recipe as they worked their way through the failure one spoon at a time.

She sighed as she set her empty dish on the tray.

"There's more if you want." He couldn't believe she'd eaten it all.

"No. That was too much. Thank you." Carefully sipping the coffee he'd refilled a few moments ago, she peered over the edge of the mug at him.

"What?"

"How is this going to work? I should probably hire a nurse or something. Or maybe—" Katherine glanced at the front door.

"Already told you, not a problem. Why don't you rest here for a while? I need to take care of a few chores. After that, we'll get your crutches adjusted so you can get around. My bathroom has grab bars and everything you could need for a safe shower."

"Don't *you* need all that stuff? The bathroom upstairs is standard."

"Yeah, you'll have to share with me. But you must be all right with it since I got an email notification from my website that you booked your room for four more weeks."

"I hadn't thought I was kicking you out of your space."

"I offered."

She shifted her weight on the couch. "What if I need more...*personal* help?"

"Uh?" Gabe scrambled for an answer. The only woman he had a connection with was Amy, the other lodge owner, who was trying to help him. Helping Katherine kind of fell under helping him. Maybe? "We can call Amy. She's cool. Owns another B and B. In fact, she's coming by tomorrow to help me with a muffin recipe." At least she would be once Gabe returned her call and accepted her offer.

Katherine's forehead scrunched, and she shook her head.

"Wait until you meet her. Besides, if she can't help, she'll know someone who can." Wouldn't she?

"Fine. But I still need to *do* something. I'm used to working. I'll go crazy sitting around."

"I've got books and lots of movies. We're on for Narnia tonight."

"I mean something extra besides paying for the room." She smoothed her hands over the blanket. "You're going above and beyond, and I'm taking away from your remodeling time. It has to be fair or I'll find another place to stay. I don't take advantage of people."

No, she rubbed them raw and questioned their motives, but she didn't take advantage. With any luck, Jadis would be on her best behavior, and she and Amy would get along. "I'll think of something. Let's call it good for now."

No matter what, he'd make sure she was happy to stay. He'd about had a heart attack when he'd seen the dollars deposited to his account. With that lump of cash, he could make some changes, get a couple of rooms upgraded. Even add another bathroom. But an itch of discomfort pricked the back of his neck. It was too much money. What if she left early? He would wait until she left to do anything major. Besides, it wasn't a hardship to help her out. She was even growing on him. And it would be nice to have someone to watch a movie with. Talk over the improvements he could finally make. Eat lunch with. Temporarily.

CHAPTER 9

a light knock at the door roused Katherine from the half doze, half daydream she'd been listing in for the past hour. She shifted to a sitting position and picked up a book off the nightstand, opening it to a random position. "Yes."

Gabe's face filled the small gap he'd created in the open doorway. "You decent?" He smiled and swung the door wider. "Good book?"

Katherine glanced at the cover. Dog tags and camo and an author name with lots of degrees. She lifted her chin. "Delightful."

"Glad you're enjoying it," Gabe said with a grin. "I need to grab a shower. Amy'll be here in a few."

"Oh. I'll, uh…"

"Relax. I've got coffee brewing. As soon as I'm out, we can eat. Cutting in the new doorway was a messy job." He held out his arms. White dust, wood chips, and sweat covered his long-sleeved t-shirt. "I'll be out in a flash."

Before Katherine could respond, he was enclosed in his en suite bathroom. And it *was* his. Fully functional and retro fit with a built-in bench and multiple grab bars. Taking a shower the night before had been simple and restorative. She'd used the handheld showerhead to divest herself of the institutional haze that had settled into her pores during the short hospital stay. With her cast wrapped in a white garbage bag, she'd been able to relax and wash her hair.

Three days ago, she would have panicked at the idea of meeting a new person without her hair and makeup flawless, dressed perfectly. But that was before she'd been run over on the slopes and had to be put back together. Besides, she'd be going home in a few weeks, never to see the woman—Amy—again. Or Gabe. A subtle sting arced through her chest.

The smell of coffee floated into the room. Katherine placed the book back on the nightstand. The title intrigued her, and she might actually read it. Psychology was always interesting, usually from a marketing perspective. But reading about how people thought and why they did the things they did fascinated her. After combing her fingers through her hair, she retrieved her clip and tied it up in a messy bun. She wrestled the yoga pants she'd had on the previous night over her cast, making a note to order more. Or buy some in town if there was a decent store. Her bra and shirt were folded up on the chair by the windows. She'd have to get up on her crutches to get there.

The bathroom door cracked open a tiny bit. "Just letting out the steam."

Perfect. Katherine would wait and have Gabe bring them to her. She could finish changing after he left. Movement drew her eye back to the bathroom. The door gaped, and the quickly clearing mirror reflected Gabe.

Naked.

He had a towel over his head, rigorously drying his dark hair. He lifted a sculpted tattooed arm, ran the white cloth along the underside and over his ribs. Droplets of water clung to his sparse chest hair but were scrubbed away. And he did all that balanced on one leg. Inked images covered his tanned skin. Deep furrows ran up his damaged leg. But Katherine's mouth dropped open at the sight of his cock resting long and thick against his other leg. A phantom stretch rolled through her pussy. Dear god, would he be even larger when he got hard? Or was it all on display? The stretch transitioned into a clenching ache.

The view shifted as Gabe sat. Katherine picked up the book again, pretending she hadn't been a voyeur. Hadn't been fantasizing about Gabe fucking her with everything he had, making her insides pulse with forgotten need. It had been so long since she'd dreamed of sex in a real way. Rubbing out the odd urge was too familiar, but the idea of a man inside her—a real flesh-and-blood man, not some fantasy—not since she'd been married. And even then, the desire had been intellectual, emotional. Not physical, like she was starving.

Gabe stepped out, fully dressed. "Hungry?"

Katherine nodded, not trusting herself to truly answer that question.

"Need any help?"

"Yes." Katherine cleared her throat. "Could you hand me the clothes on that chair?"

Gabe moved to the chair, and, despite not an inch of his skin showing besides his hands and head, all she saw was gorgeous inked-up golden skin wrapped around hard muscles. He bent, and her eyes would not move from his ass. As he turned, she dropped her chin, forcing her gaze to the page and the blur of words.

"Here you go." Gabe set the pile on her lap. "You want me to come back and help you get to the table?"

"No." Her voice was harsher than she'd intended. "I'm fine. Be out in a moment."

Gabe saluted and left.

She took a few more minutes with her appearance, twisting her hair up a little tighter, applying a touch of makeup. Not up to her usual standards, but the routine settled her to the point she could meet someone new without her nerves putting her on the defense. She adjusted her crutches and carefully made her way out of the room.

Gabe moved around the kitchen, collecting ingredients on the counter. Amy was already seated with a mug in her hand. At least, Katherine assumed the medium-height, medium-build brunette was the person they'd been expecting. The woman was a mannequin of nondescript. Even her hair was medium length. Katherine misjudged her next step and bumped into the table. Amy looked up with brown eyes, and a huge smile broke out over her face like the sun coming out from behind the clouds.

"You must be Katherine." Amy jumped up and pulled back the chair nearest Katherine. "Gabe was just telling me what an ordeal you've been through. First day of skiing, too. What a bummer."

Katherine dropped into the chair and leaned the cursed crutches to the side.

"Coffee?" Amy held up a mug.

Katherine nodded.

"At least you're in a great space. And this muffin recipe Gabe has. Wait 'til you taste them. Out of this world. We're just going to make some adjustments for high altitude." Amy placed the mug, a spoon, a pitcher of cream, and sugar bowl within Katherine's reach as she talked.

"Thank you."

The woman would be perfect to balance out the gruffness of Gabe, but Katherine noted a wedding ring and asked, "You've known Gabe long?"

Amy laughed; it was friendly and real. No bells or chimes, just happiness. "Probably a week or so more than you. I'm just here to steal his recipe." She nudged Gabe. "Kidding."

"Your husband doesn't mind you hanging out with a handsome single man?"

The laugh that time had an edge to it.

"My husband travels a lot." She twisted the ring on her hand. "We should get started." The smile was aimed at Gabe that time.

Katherine nibbled yogurt from the tip of a spoon while Amy guided Gabe in the finer points of high-altitude baking. Adding flour. Adjusting temperatures and times. Chattering the entire time. The woman was delightful, and Katherine tried to find a way back into the conversation. Her comment hadn't been meant to put Amy on edge. But reviewing the exchange, Katherine had been marking her territory. Territory that wasn't hers to mark.

"Ready to test the first batch, Jadis?" Gabe asked as he pulled the hot pan from the oven.

"Let them cool, first," Amy said. "And who's Jadis?"

"Mr. Gallegos thinks he's funny referring to me as the ice queen from Narnia."

"Never heard of her." Amy tilted her head.

"Oh, you're going to regret admitting that." Katherine shook her head. "He's on a mission for everyone to see his niece's favorite movie."

"It's a great movie." Gabe crossed his arms, oven mitts still on his hands, leaning against the counter. Katherine couldn't take her eyes off him.

"Movie night," Amy exclaimed, bouncing a bit. "I'll bring my homemade moose munch."

"Moose munch?" Katherine couldn't hold back a laugh. Amy was infectious.

"Butter-toffee caramel popcorn with chocolate and nuts. Can't watch a movie without it."

"Sounds delicious." Like the treats that had been delivered to the law offices in a festive tin last Christmas. Katherine hadn't eaten any, but the paralegals had fought over the last crumbs.

"You have to make the munch over here so I can learn. Since you're stealing my abuela's blue-corn muffin recipe." Gabe pulled one muffin from the tray and cut it in half. Steam wafted up, and the corners of Gabe's mouth lifted.

"Done," Amy agreed. "Wednesday? I don't have anyone booked that night."

"Where is your inn?"

"Right in town. The Sunflower B and B."

Katherine would check out the website as soon as Amy left. "Sounds cute."

"It is. Not stuffy like this place." Amy winked at Katherine.

"Hey, now." Gabe grumbled as he brought out a plate of perfectly cooked blue muffins with blueberries dotted through them. "The Ponderosa is a classic."

"It needs a lift." Amy took a muffin and slathered butter on it before passing the plates to Katherine.

"That is the most understated way I think to capture what this place needs." Katherine followed Amy's example with the butter, anxious to taste Gabe's creation.

"Color," the women said together.

"I'm being ganged up on here." Gabe's focus shifted from Katherine to Amy and back. The weight of it settled low in Katherine's core. "I just cut a hole in the wall this morning to make a damn *en suite* bathroom, I'll have you know."

"Mmm. Construction and cooking." Amy picked up the other half of the muffin, the first half already gone. "You're going to be quite a catch for someone."

Gabe rolled his eyes. Katherine swallowed down the urge to shout "me." Ridiculous.

"Are you trying to get three rooms in rentable condition?" Amy asked.

"Three?" Katherine wasn't sure there was space for three rooms with bathrooms. What was the significance?

"Yeah, for the Alabaster B and B Association membership, you have to have three rooms," Amy said. "My place has four. Some inns around here are a lot bigger. But I'm by myself." She shrugged.

"Your husband doesn't help?" Katherine asked.

"It's not his thing."

"I don't give a shit about the association." Gabe popped half a muffin in his mouth and chewed it like it owed him money.

"What is it?" Katherine directed her question to Amy, ignoring Gabe's obvious rancor.

"A group of us meet on the third Tuesday of every month to keep up to date on the latest health codes, industry trends, and things. We also share website-hosting expenses and such. It's supposed to be educational and supportive, but they don't let anyone in who's more of a hobbyist. Therefore, the three-room minimum."

Katherine glanced at Gabe, who was glaring at the plate of muffins. The lodge was dated, but it wasn't a "hobby."

"So, shopping?" Amy asked.

"Yes," Katherine agreed automatically. It wasn't New York, but she loved wandering in and out of stores when she had time. Getting inspiration from the colors, the designs. Because what sold in stores, sold online. The themes, the color schemes. An idea formed of how she could repay Gabe for his caretaking hospitality that exceeded the bounds of a hotel proprietor.

"Excellent. Maybe later this week." Amy wiped her hands and stood. "I need to get going, but I think the recipe is perfect. The notes are on the index card." She leaned down and wrapped her arms around Katherine in a hug. "See you Wednesday for movie night." With a quick hug for Gabe, Amy blew out of the lodge like a bubble on a breeze.

"You want any more?" Gabe asked, holding up the plate. Amy was right: he was a total catch. Katherine admired how hard he was working to improve his menu and the lodge. Not everyone would've taken action on her suggestions so quickly.

"Not right now, thanks. They're delicious."

"Cool. I'm going to tidy up and get back to the bathroom remodel. Might be a little loud. What can I do for you?"

"Would you bring me my laptop bag? I have earbuds." And a plan.

A few minutes later, Gabe was upstairs pounding away while Katherine sipped her coffee and logged in to her computer. First, she pulled up the Sunflower B and B. The website was slow to load but delightfully inviting. The theme of azure, honey yellow, and sunset orange created a warm, welcoming vibe. The pictures captured a shabby-chic decor that showed surprising restraint, something uncommon to that decorating style. And it somehow worked. The only thing missing was a picture of Amy with that million-dollar smile that welcomed one and all. Katherine would mention it on movie night.

Tired of the touchpad, Katherine retrieved her wireless mouse from the bag, bringing a small, forgotten pouch with it. She slid open the drawstrings and drew out the oblong purple crystal.

An odd gift. And, more unexplainable, why she'd carried it with her. On a whim, she pulled up Madam Tiana's website. Still working great. She clicked on the "Contact Us" page and copied the email address. Tiana had Katherine's old number, and she'd promised the woman could call if she needed anything. Katherine fired off a quick email updating the psychic with her number and extended travel plans and another thank-you for the stone. That done, Katherine stared at the screen. She could email her friend Natalia. But why?

Instead, she pulled up the Ponderosa Lodge site and started making notes. She'd need the admin credentials to do any edits, but for the time being she could make a list of tasks, like adding Gabe's bio and picture, and research what other resorts in the area were doing on their sites. That was how she would pay Gabe back. Creating a site that was better than anything the association would host for him.

Gabe clomped down the stairs, and Katherine quickly closed the browser with the multiple tabs she'd had open. She'd buried herself in reading travel sites and looking at reviews, gauging where Gabe needed to focus to get the best return on his investment.

"Lost track of time. You hungry?"

Katherine experienced a bone weariness that was unusual for her. "I'm tired."

Gabe nodded. "To be expected."

Katherine closed her laptop and tucked away her notes.

"You can leave your stuff there."

With a sigh, she maneuvered her crutches under her arms as she rose, but the legs of the chair somehow tangled with her feet, and she started to tip. Strong arms wrapped around her middle before she inevitably face-planted. The scent of the muffins softened the stronger cut lumber and soap that clung to his skin. She breathed him in, trying not to be obvious but unable to resist.

"I got you." Gabe nudged the chair back with one of her crutches and dropped it on the seat. "I'll be your other crutch."

She could've suggested so many other ways he could assist her. *Bad Katherine. Put away the cougar claws.*

He guided her to his bedroom and onto the bed. Katherine

stopped herself from pulling him down with her. Or patting the mattress beside her. When had she become so needy? So starved for affection? So desperate for human contact? Must be fatigue.

"I'll check on you in a few," Gabe said as he left.

Katherine's gaze went to the mirror through the bathroom door. The morning's show replayed in slow motion, having the same effect on her body. She didn't have a forever-man in her future, and Gabe certainly wasn't it. But he'd make a damn good "for now."

CHAPTER 10

Gabe ran Katherine's laptop cord to an outlet. "You all set?"

She shifted in the chair before flashing him a warm smile. "I'm good. Should be done with the major parts of the redesign today."

After just three days, they'd fallen into a routine. Breakfast, cleanup, and then work on their separate projects. Gabe still couldn't believe she was willing to redo his website. Getting the shitty one he had to work had been a total nightmare and wasted far too many hours for the end result. Then she'd shown him some of the other sites she'd done—he'd be an idiot to decline. And one thing he'd learned over his recovery: *If you need help, ask. And if someone offers what you need before you ask, say yes.*

He filled her coffee mug. "We should talk about the other rooms at lunch. I'll be done with this bathroom today."

"Excellent. I need more photos."

"Are you still planning on doing *staging*?" He pretended to shiver.

"It's not a dirty word." She rolled her eyes. "And yes, I'm going to take some time to make the rooms look their best. Amy said she'd help. Better get your painting clothes ready."

"Yes, Jadis."

She slapped at him with a laugh, but he stepped out of range and retreated up the stairs with a smile on his face that went all the way to his heart. Like lost dogs, hope and purpose had returned, but with an unfamiliar lightness. Even when he'd joined the service—and that had been everything he'd ever dreamed of—it had been with a serious mindset. He froze in the doorway, slammed with clarity.

He was having fun.

A few hours later, when Gabe checked the swing of the bathroom door, it glided closed with a satisfying click. It was almost impossible to tell where the door had previously opened out to the hallway. Even his construction-guru brother, Michael, would approve of the work. His stomach growled as he tidied up his tools and wiped down the molding and the floor, removing the last traces of construction dust.

Downstairs, Katherine sat in the living room, reading his veterans' psych book. Freshly showered and dressed, with her golden hair tied up, she was getting around better, and a twinge of regret bounced through him that she didn't have to rely on him more. Damn, he had to shake that shit off. They weren't married, for fuck's sake.

"Ready for lunch?" he asked.

"Sure. I called Amy. She can meet us in town in about an hour. Her guests are on the slopes this afternoon." Katherine rose and positioned her crutches like a pro. "She pointed me to some great sites. I have a list of things we…I mean, *you* should consider getting. Amy can help pick accessories that will hold up to the demands of innkeeping. We're fortunate to have her professional advice."

"It's too bad *she's* not the president of ABBA."

"Maybe she will be."

Gabe snorted and went to the kitchen. Katherine took her seat at the table and nudged her laptop to the side. He put together a salad for her and fixed himself a sandwich. They ate and discussed possible reconfigurations for the last two rooms upstairs.

When they'd mostly finished, Katherine pulled up his website. "Look, it's completely simplified. All you have to do to make a room go live is click here and…" Her long fingers, wrapped around the mouse, barely twitched. "See? The system manages itself after that.

And you can update the pictures just by doing this…" She clicked over to another screen and showed him how to upload media. "Easy."

"You're going to write down instructions for me, right?"

"I configured all the notices to go to your text and email." She patted his leg, and everything she'd shown him vanished in a haze of lust. "You won't miss a message."

He scrambled for something to say that wasn't a sexual invitation. "I can't believe you did all this in three days."

Her cheeks turned pink. "It was nothing. Just my way of saying thank you."

"Still…" Gabe stuffed the last bite of sandwich in his mouth to keep from kissing her. And not just a peck on the cheek. His arms ached to hold her while he owned her mouth, pressed her body against his.

Stand down.

It's just a fucking website.

~

AFTER PARKING behind the Sunflower B and B, a brightly painted Victorian gingerbread, Gabe hustled around the truck to help Katherine. He guided her to grip the open door. "Hold on."

"I can do this with my crutches."

"No doubt, but we're going to be walking on salted brick sidewalks and in various stores. This is easier." He grabbed his knee scooter from the truck bed and snapped it open. "With this, if you hit an icy patch, you won't fall and break something else."

"Afraid you won't be able to get rid of me?"

"Ha." More like afraid she'd leave. Afraid he was already too attached. Afraid she didn't feel the same way.

Amy appeared on the back porch. "Right on time. Ready to do some small-town power shopping?"

"Sure. As long as we can stay within budget." Gabe had seen what his mom and sister could do in a store, and his bank card quivered in his wallet.

"I'd be happy to—"

"You're going to be amazed," Amy said, interrupting Katherine. "I'm a deal-finding magnet."

"Katherine has our list. I mean, the list of things for the lodge. Are you two sure we have to add color?"

"Yes," they said in one voice.

Gabe sighed. Hopefully, it wasn't pink, purple, or gold. His sister's childhood bedroom still repulsed him, and she'd repainted years ago.

"We're starting at the hardware store for paint. They can mix up the cans while we hunt and gather." Amy led them down the sidewalk with small piles of snow patchworked on either side. Katherine held the handlebars of the scooter and pushed with her good leg. Gabe brought up the rear and, distracted by her spectacular ass, stumbled over a raised brick.

"Sure *you* don't need this thing?" Katherine glanced back at him with a teasing grin.

Somehow, she'd known what he'd been doing. He couldn't feel bad. An ass like that deserved admiration.

Amy turned into a whirlwind as soon as they arrived at the hardware store that seemed to have been transported from another era. Gabe's brother Michael had mentioned it was a time-warp experience when he'd made a couple of emergency purchases to finish the septic upgrade that summer. But Gabe hadn't expected the small storefront to be overflowing with everything a guy could ever need.

The paint counter was at the back, but on the way there they passed camping accessories, car care, light fixtures, and a cabinet of drawers filled with pulls and knobs all packed together. It was like they'd invaded his grandpa's shed. Definitely not the big-box home-improvement chain he was used to.

They stopped in front of a small lit-up display of paint swatches. Amy began pulling cards and conferring with Katherine. Yep, just like shopping with his mom and sister. Would they notice if he went to check out the woodworking area?

Before he could slide away, Katherine held out three cards to him. "What do you think of these?"

He stepped closer to her, the air of domesticity reeling him in. She pressed her shoulder to his chest as she held up the samples. Nuzzling her neck would be the wrong thing to do, so he stared intently at the three swatches of off-white. "They're identical."

Katherine laughed. "Any preference?"

Yes, for her to laugh like that a hundred times a day. Gabe pointed at the one in the middle.

They repeated the process with olive green and tan. Hell, they should have said they needed camouflage. *That* he understood. But he didn't say anything; instead, he pretended to consider each choice carefully, all the while enjoying Katherine pressed up against him. The last one was a reddish rusty-looking color, and then she pulled away. The cool air punctuated the loss.

Amy called out to an older man in an apron. "Hey, Pete."

"Hey, Miss Amy. Doin' some more decorating?"

"Kind of. Do you know Gabe Gallegos?" Gabe stepped forward at her cue. "He owns the Ponderosa. Needs some updating."

"Mr. Gallegos. Welcome."

"It's just Gabe. And thanks."

"I guess we'll be seeing a lot of you if Miss Amy's got plans."

"Well, her and my friend Katherine." He placed his hand on Katherine's back. It was possessive and unwarranted, but some part of him had worried the clerk might connect him romantically with Amy. And why did he care?

"Nice to meet you, ma'am." Pete nodded. "Now, how many gallons of what?"

After sorting out the order, getting the additional painting supplies, and paying for everything with a promise to return for the cans, they made their way back outside into the wintery air. A small figure stood huddled in the recessed doorway of the hardware store.

"Sebastian?" Amy asked. "What are you doing here? Are you okay?"

A teenager in a surplus jacket that wasn't thick enough for January in Colorado uncurled from the corner. His blond hair was a little long, peeking out from the polar-fleece beanie.

"Looking for a little work." His voice was deeper than Gabe had expected. "Need me to carry anything? Could run some errands for you."

"Oh, honey. Where's your mom?"

Bony shoulders rose and dropped.

Gabe had been scrawny at his age, too, but from Amy's questions there was more to the kid's story.

"I could use your help." Gabe lifted his bag of paint supplies. "Can you run these back to my truck? It's back at the Sunflower. The tail-gate's unlocked. Then Pete's going to have about six cans of paint ready. Need those loaded, too."

The boy took the bag. Gabe opened his wallet and handed Sebastian a ten-dollar bill. "After you get the paint loaded, I'll have more for you. Meet us as the Stone Bear for some food. We can talk about some other work I have that you might be interested in." Gabe glanced at his watch. "In an hour?"

"Okay." Sebastian rushed down the sidewalk, carrying the paint supplies.

As soon as the boy turned the corner, Katherine spoke up. "Who is that? Where are his parents? What's going on?"

Amy looped her arm through Katherine's. "I'll tell you while we shop. I only have a short time before I have to get back to the inn."

In the first store, Amy led them to the back to where artwork and other accessories were stacked randomly. Katherine joined Amy in rifling through the piles. Gabe opened his mouth, but Katherine cut him off. "How long have you known Sebastian?"

The exact topic he'd been planning to bring up.

Amy held up a piece of multicolored metal, and Katherine nodded. Amy handed it to Gabe. "I met Seb this summer. He was looking for work, and I had him help me with my gardening, a few other odd jobs. Quiet and so sweet. He's a hard worker, too."

"What about his mom?" Katherine stacked two pillows on top of the metal in Gabe's arms after getting Amy's nod of approval.

"He doesn't say a lot, but I get the impression she works jobs in other parts of the area, doesn't always come home. Sometimes his supplies run short, but he doesn't really admit it. He just shows up."

"Have you called the authorities?" Gabe couldn't imagine his mother doing that. She'd worked and left them alone, but together and never overnight.

"I have, but they haven't been able to see the situation for themselves. So no results." Amy wrapped her arms around a small blanket and led them back to the cashier.

Gabe paid for the purchases. And she hadn't been lying. Everything had been on sale or clearance. They walked to one more store, Gabe carrying the bags.

"I'm glad we're meeting at a restaurant after this. I always try to feed him when I see him," Amy said.

"In thirty minutes," Gabe reminded them.

"Don't worry. We're almost done." Amy held open the door to another small boutique.

Katherine wheeled her scooter through the doorway. Gabe stayed close to make sure she cleared the transition, then dropped into a chair at the front of the store.

"What about his dad?" Katherine asked as they roamed, her voice rising over the shelves.

"I don't think he's ever been in the picture."

"That's awful." Katherine's voice carried a note of pain. The same pain that punched his own heart at the idea of the kid's parents being so uninvolved.

Gabe paid for the last of the decorative linens and knickknacks. The sting of each seemingly useless purchase pained his wallet much more than lumber or tools. Thank god he'd limited them to an hour. He glanced at his watch. "Let's get to the pub."

Sebastian was in front of the restaurant, bouncing on his toes with a smile for them. "Got the paint. It's all loaded in your truck."

"Good man." Gabe clapped him lightly on the shoulder and ushered him into the small restaurant with exposed brick walls and wooden picnic tables. The heat from the open kitchen was welcoming after walking in the brisk winter afternoon. "Let's get some food. I'm starving."

"Do you want me to take these bags, too?" Sebastian asked.

Before Gabe could reply, Katherine spoke up. "After we eat. In fact, we could use some help unloading at the lodge if you have time?"

Sebastian nodded. He sat next to Katherine, helping her with her crutches.

"And we were planning on pizza and a movie tonight." She met Gabe's eye with an unspoken request for approval, and he gave a slight smile. "Amy's coming."

"Actually, I can't." Amy grimaced. "My guests decided to extend their stay. But you should go, Sebastian."

"Have you ever seen the *Chronicles of Narnia*?" Katherine asked.

"I don't know." Sebastian's gaze darted between them.

"Well, it's Gabe's—" she pointed across the table "—favorite movie. You have to see it. I mean, if you don't have plans."

"It is," Gabe agreed. Would Katherine's lure work?

"Sure." Hooked.

"Oh, and since you delivered all the paint and you're going to be helping us some more, here." Katherine pressed a bill into Sebastian's hand.

Gabe's heart stretched, aching with approval. They hadn't talked about dinner. The woman ate like a bird. They were already on the third meal of their day, and she was planning pizza for later? The more he got to see past her frosty barriers, the more he realized Katherine was as pretty inside as she was on the outside. Maybe more. He was going to miss the hell out of her when she returned to her East Coast life.

Could he find a way to entice her to stay?

CHAPTER 11

Katherine debated washing her coffee mug. Gabe was still taking his morning shower, a sight she could picture far too clearly. If she ran the hot water, she'd freeze him. Somehow appropriate for the ice-queen nickname he'd given her. She looked nothing like the character in the movie they'd watched the night before, despite the fact she'd blown into his life during a snowstorm. But she was far from royalty, and she didn't want him to think she expected him to clean up after her. He would argue it was his job. But it was becoming increasingly uncomfortable to be treated as a guest when they had moved so far beyond that.

"Knock, knock." Amy's voice carried into the kitchen from the entry. "We're here, ready to work."

"In here," Katherine called back. The shower turned off, freeing her to finish the dishes.

A few moments later, Amy and Sebastian appeared around the corner, cheeks pink from the cold. Amy's hair was tied up in a ponytail, her face free of makeup. Katherine had never met a woman so relaxed about her appearance. Maybe because she was married? Or maybe because she was just naturally pretty.

"Any coffee left?" Amy asked.

"I can make a fresh pot." Katherine glanced around Amy to the table where Sebastian sat slumped in a chair, all elbows and legs like most teens his age. "Have you eaten?"

He nodded with a shy smile. "Thanks."

The slight crack in his voice was adorable.

"We ate before we came over," Amy said. "But I need more caffeine."

"I'll make it." Gabe, hair still wet, came into the kitchen, shrinking the space in half and heating it up. "Hey, Sebastian, ever done any painting?"

Sebastian straightened. "Nope."

"Not a problem. I'll show you everything my brother's painting contractor showed me." Gabe wrapped himself around Katherine's back and shifted the water to cold before filling the carafe.

Katherine held herself tight to the counter despite the fact if she tilted her hips back a fraction of an inch, she could press into him. Rub her ass against his long length as it hardened. She shivered with the strain to behave.

"Cold?" Gabe asked, his breath warm at her ear.

"I'm good."

Gabe stepped back. And finished prepping the coffee maker.

Katherine let the heat in her cheeks cool before she turned to Amy, who lifted a single brow. "We...uh...the decor. Let's start in the..."

"Main room?" Amy asked with a laughing lilt to her voice.

Katherine nodded.

"Come on," Gabe said to Sebastian. "We got painting to do, starting with the upstairs bedroom. I've already got the furniture and floors covered. What colors am I supposed to use again? Green and red?"

"No," Amy and Katherine howled in unison.

"Aztec Fire on the back wall with the new bathroom door. And Antique Linen on the other three," Katherine said.

"Red and white." Gabe stomped up the stairs with a small shadow behind him. "Got it."

"Wait."

Gabe paused midway up.

"Sebastian. You can't paint in those clothes." Katherine wasn't sure how much he had to wear. "What if it splatters?"

"Wait for me upstairs," Gabe told Sebastian. "I'll grab an old shirt for you." Then he returned to the ground floor, and as he passed Katherine, he rubbed his knuckles from her elbow to her shoulder and back. "Good call."

His touch was gone before she could catch her breath to respond. The chime on the coffee maker cleared the hormone fog she'd been caught in.

Amy poured a cup of coffee and blew across the rim. Katherine expected the third degree about what was going on between her and Gabe, and she had no idea how to answer.

"Where should we start?" Amy asked.

The tension in Katherine's jaw released. "Deep clean. Then hang the drapes and metal sculpture and place the throw pillows."

"Works for me. I'll take the ladder and the cleaning of Mr. Horny there." She pointed at the antlered head.

"I'll take the windows."

Katherine had freed all the existing curtains and dumped them in a pile for cleaning, all while maintaining her balance on her crutches. She carefully began detailing each pane of glass, wondering how they'd gotten so dirty. And if she was doing it right. She'd never cleaned a window in her life, but she wasn't about to admit that out loud.

"How did movie night go last night?" Amy asked while swinging a feather duster across an antler.

"Sebastian ate his weight in pizza. But he wouldn't stay. Gabe drove him home."

"Yeah, he has a thing about trying to be there for his mom."

"Did you know he doesn't have a reliable heater? And his pantry was practically empty?" Katherine couldn't imagine living without basic services. "Gabe made sure there was plenty of firewood, and I guess they made a stop at a store for canned goods and bottled water. What does his mother do for a living?"

Amy shrugged. "I've never got the complete story."

"I can't believe social services hasn't stepped in." He was a teenager, but, still, someone should care.

"Sebastian is as good at disappearing as his mother if he doesn't want to be found. But he was at my place bright and early. Asked for a ride out here since he knew I was coming over. Of course, I fed him."

"I wish there was more I could do." But her time at the Ponderosa was limited, even though she wasn't sure what she'd do next. Outside the window she was working on, movement in the parking lot drew her attention. "Someone's here."

"Oh shit." Amy came down the ladder. "Let me deal with this."

"That sounds ominous."

"Betty's the president of the B and B association." Amy scooped up the pile of drapes and practically ran to the washer.

The association that had refused Gabe's membership. Seconds later, a middle-aged woman in khaki slacks, a snowman-themed sweater, and hideous pastel blue snow boots with thick black tread tromped her way to the door.

Amy reappeared and swung open the door before the woman even knocked. "Betty, how nice of you to stop by."

Katherine flinched at the saccharine tone in Amy's voice. It was the same one Katherine would use when dealing with one of her father's creepy clients. Something wasn't right. Katherine stiffened her spine and prepared to engage.

"Heard you'd been to the hardware store with Mr. Gallegos. Came to see if he finally cleaned up the place, but based on the outside, I guess not. I didn't expect to find *you* here." Betty stomped into the living room and blazed a critical glance across the entire open space. Her eyebrow lifted when she got to Katherine. "Who's—"

"This is a guest of Mr. Gallegos's. He's upstairs doing some painting. Let me show you the colors. I think you'll be impressed." Amy grabbed on to Betty's arm and drew her to the staircase.

Katherine followed to the base of the stairs, eyes locked on their progress up while Amy continued to kowtow. Betty's voice carried down. "He has his guests cleaning?"

"Friend. She's staying. Temporarily. Helping him out. With his, ah…as a friend. Like me."

"She must be *something*." Betty's innuendo was crystal clear. "I've never put a guest to work, no matter *how* well I know them."

The hair on the back of Katherine's neck lifted. There was a predator inside, and Amy thought she'd pacify her? Not a chance. Katherine carefully placed her crutches on the tread and lifted herself up the first stair.

"And don't you have your own business to run, Amy?" Betty continued. "Or are you short on guests this season?"

"Nope, doing great. They went skiing."

Why did Amy have to justify being at the lodge instead of her place to that woman? Katherine continued her slow ascent, the second floor coming into view.

"Gabe," Amy called out. "Look who stopped by."

Gabe stepped out of the bedroom with an Aztec Fire–dipped paintbrush and a wrinkled brow.

"Mr. Gallegos. I see you're taking my advice and improving this property. At least the inside." Betty glanced past his shoulder. "Looks like you closed off a doorway?"

"Yeah. The paint will hide the change. Won't even be able to see where it was." Gabe's voice was gruff but confused.

"Mmmhmm." Betty arched her neck. "And who's this?"

Gabe glanced behind him. "Sebastian."

"Well, never too young to start, I guess. Always good to keep training the next generation. Keep it in the family."

What was that woman getting at? Katherine kept moving, not about to fall before she got to speak to that *Betty* face-to-face.

"He's not related." Gabe's jaw was locked, but the words escaped between his lips.

"I assumed he *must* be. He's not nearly old enough to work *legally*. You're not exploiting a child for labor, right?"

Amy laughed, and it sounded slightly hysterical. "Oh, he's not really *working*. He's a friend. Of mine. Well, my friend's son. And I'm, ah…keeping an eye on him. And he asked to help."

"I'm sixteen. Old enough to have a job," Sebastian said.

"Is that right?" Betty asked.

Nobody moved. Katherine finally reached the hallway and put herself in Betty's line of sight. "We weren't properly introduced." Katherine looked down her nose at the woman. "I'm Katherine Wallace. And you are?"

"Betty Keppel. President of the Alabaster Bed and Breakfast Association."

"My. What an accomplishment." Katherine tilted her head to the side slightly. "I imagine you must have so many properties to keep up with. And yet you still found time to stop by here?" Uninvited. "Don't *you* own a B and B?"

"Of course," Betty snapped.

"Impressive." Katherine infused the word with the bitter cold of a New York winter, inhaled, and let her inner diva loose. "Running a business, running an association, and running around investigating all the happenings in town. I'm shocked you have time. I mean with that kind of schedule—but maybe *you're* short on guests? And while it's so *thoughtful* of you to visit, I would have assumed only members of the association received this kind of special attention. I hope none of them get jealous of the time you're spending with a *hobbyist*. Speaking of hobbyists, the website you host for your members? I assume you're aware of how desperately dated it is. I imagine for the general public, it would be difficult to discern the difference between Gabe's lodge and your professional innkeepers based on the amateur approach to marketing it embodies."

Amy was shaking her head, but Katherine had more to say.

"You know, after I finish helping Gabe with updating what his uncle left him, I'd be delighted to offer my services to ABBA. A shabby site can be so off-putting to people unfamiliar with the area. Back in the day, websites used to be an afterthought, but now technology is *so* important. The web really is the face of a place. Don't you think?" Katherine showed all of her teeth when she smiled.

Betty's eyes were wide, and her mouth gaped like a fish's.

"I could give you a discounted rate since you're so *supportive* of Gabe and Amy."

"I have to go." Betty whipped around and practically ran down the stairs. Quite a feat for the evil little troll.

Amy dropped her head in her hands. "Oh no."

A ping of regret flashed through Katherine's heart until she turned to Gabe. His smile was huge, and he released a chuckle. She hadn't disappointed him.

Before she could ask him what he really thought, she was cut off by the ping of his phone. He pulled it from his jeans and stared at the screen. Using his thumb, he tapped on the screen twice. "We have a reservation."

"Congrats." Amy's bubbly happiness was back.

"For two. Starting in two days." Gabe's voice was completely flat. "For a week."

"Oh god." Katherine waited until he met her gaze. "When I showed you how to enable the reservation system, I forgot to turn it off."

CHAPTER 12

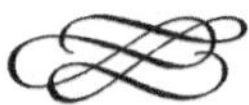

Gabe laughed at the look of horror on Katherine's face. The perfectionist probably rarely made a mistake. "No worries. I can take the couch."

Amy's gaze snapped to him. "I thought you had three rooms."

"I do. But the other two don't have beds. When my buddy was here, we got rid of the old mattresses. Not sure when my uncle replaced them last, but it wasn't this century."

"No." Katherine crossed her arms. "This is my screwup. I'll fix it. Amy, do you have a room I can rent?"

"I'm so sorry. I'm booked up. I think everyone in town is, but I can check."

The hesitation in her voice told Gabe there was zero chance they'd find another room. "I'll be fine."

"You can't sleep in the living room when you have guests," Katherine said. "That's too—"

"Unprofessional," Amy supplied.

"Well, what do you suggest, Jadis?"

"We'll have to share your room." Her eyes widened, and she wasn't so much crossing her arms as gripping herself.

"Works for me." Gabe swallowed a completely inappropriate chuckle. "But don't be getting any ideas."

Katherine's jaw dropped with a gasp. "I. You—"

"Better get to work." Amy turned for the stairs. "We have a lot to finish in two days, and I have to get back to my own business."

Katherine followed, cheeks pinker than usual.

"Come on, man." Gabe clapped Sebastian on the back. "We got some painting to wrap up." Better to get his mind back to Aztec Fire instead of the ice queen he'd be sharing a bed with. And, damn, when he'd warned about getting ideas, he'd been chastising himself, caught in the middle of a thankful prayer that God had put that woman in his bed. And for their first chat in a long time, it probably wasn't what the Almighty had in mind.

He'd have to offer to take the floor. It wasn't right for him to leverage the situation to take things further with Katherine, no matter how attracted he was. His urgency should've been quenched with the jack-off session in the shower earlier. But when he'd come out of his bedroom and found Katherine at the sink, all domesticated and at home, not guest-like at all, his cock had guided him to her. She'd allowed him to crowd her back to fill the coffeepot. For one second, he'd been sure she would press back into him. Maybe if they'd been alone…

Their attraction was mutual and off the charts in the damn kitchen. No way they could share a bed and not succumb. But Gabe would have to keep himself in check and let Jadis come to him. Let her take the lead and be in charge. And didn't that image of her dominating him in bed just about make him come in his jeans.

Fuck.

"I finished all the cut-ins." Sebastian's voice jolted Gabe back to the present—to the room that had to be painted for the guests that were coming to his lodge. Ones that would leave a review and didn't care about how precarious his love life had become. And since Katherine would leave, too, he'd better keep his focus on the mission. Build out the lodge and get it working so he'd have some kind of job.

Gabe scanned the walls of the room and the work Sebastian had done. "Good job, buddy. Let's get the rollers."

A few hours later, Gabe led Sebastian through the process of cleaning up. The red wall would likely need another coat before he could call the painting done. But they'd knocked out the rest of the bedroom and the bathroom, which just left covering up the wall patch in the hallway. No biggie.

As soon as he hit the stairs, the strains of laughter and gossipy chatter hit him. It was like being at home when his sister had friends over. Slowly, the great room came into focus. It was clear Katherine and Amy had been equally successful. The great room shone, but in an inviting, cozy way. "Wow."

Katherine spun toward him, one crutch under her arm and her phone held out like a camera. Gabe swore he heard a click and smiled. Yeah, the second click confirmed it. She'd taken his picture. Lowering her cell, she held out a hand like a game-show beauty. "Well? How do you like it?"

So many very wrong answers came to mind. Her on top or him with his face between her legs. But he bit his tongue and inspected the room more carefully. "You covered the couch."

"Really?" Her eyebrow went up, and irritation in her voice snapped against him like a whip.

"No. I mean yes. The whole room looks great. Perfect place for guests to hang out. I just can't believe a couch cover, some pillows, and…what did you call that metal thing on the wall?"

"Art."

"Uh, yeah, *art* could make this big a difference. I never did like that couch." He mock shivered.

She laughed. "Let me show you the photos I got for the website."

Gabe closed the distance and held still when she leaned against him and swiped through a ton of pictures. She could've been showing him the winning lottery numbers for all he cared. Her closeness, her scent, her tendrils of hair, escaped from their confines, captured his focus.

"What do you think?"

"Perfect."

"I'm glad you're happy with it. Is the bedroom ready?"

Yep, his bedroom was ready for them to share. He lifted his gaze to hers, issuing the silent invitation.

"The painting…" She nudged him.

"Oh. The painting. No. I'll finish tomorrow. That red is a beast. Even with the one-coat brand, it needs a third application."

"Great things take time."

Gabe's heart stuttered. "Some things," he whispered, "are worth the effort."

"Hey, guys," Amy called from the kitchen sink. "I need to run. Get ready for my guests. Sebastian, you want a ride?"

Gabe's awareness expanded beyond the woman at his side. Shit. They had an audience. "Hey, what about dinner?"

"I've got it covered," Amy answered. "Sebastian promised to dine with me."

Gabe appreciated how Amy'd made it sound like Seb was doing her the favor. "Great work today, man." Gabe fished out his wallet and the twenties he'd set aside for that purpose. "You have any time tomorrow? I could use the help."

"Sure," Sebastian said quietly as he stuffed the money in his front pocket.

"Maybe you could stay afterwards and catch another movie with us?" Katherine added.

Not even planned. Exactly what Gabe would have offered.

"'Kay," Sebastian said. But the small smile reached Gabe's heart.

"We've gotta go." Amy waved from the front door, and Sebastian scurried out behind her.

The silence in the room became weighted. They had the lodge to themselves for the night, and with the upstairs bedroom unfinished… should he offer to stay on the couch again? Or let the night play out naturally? For the first time since high school, he wasn't sure what the next move with his woman should be.

His. Damn. Not yet. But maybe.

~

THE CLICK of the front door stirred Katherine to action. Lingering around Gabe was dangerous. The slight hint of sweat, the lines in the muscles of his forearms, the smear of cream paint across the thigh of his tight jeans distracted her. Made her crave more. And due to *her* error, they were going to be sharing a bedroom. He'd made it clear she shouldn't get ideas. But plenty of sexy ideas had formed days ago when she'd seen him in the shower, and plenty more had grown with every passing touch. The closeness in the kitchen earlier, the press of his body to hers while they'd reviewed the pictures—everything he did called to her. But his seduction was accidental, only her interpretation of events, not something Gabe designed to tempt her closer. That had been her ex-husband's style. Every move and smile had been planned for maximum effect. Gabe's mere existence, his day-to-day way of moving through his life, his natural masculinity drew her to him. She had no way to resist except avoidance, and her own mistake had screwed up that plan.

"I should edit the pics and update your website. Turn off future bookings until we, I mean you, get the remaining rooms figured out."

"Wait." Gabe wrapped his hand around her arm.

She gazed at him over her shoulder, trying to ignore the way his touch traveled through her chest.

"We've worked hard today. Do the pictures later. I'll make dinner."

Katherine swallowed down the urge to argue. "Okay. But I'm turning off the bookings now."

"Yeah. Good plan. Find a movie for us?" He released his grip and went toward the kitchen. "We can try out the new couch cover."

An image of them making out on the couch fluttered through her mind and lower. *Get a grip. It's dinner and a movie, not a euphemism for fucking.*

Her libido had become a wayward teenager. It was time to quit reading into every word he said. If he wanted sex, he'd ask. Maybe. Or maybe he was waiting for her to take the lead? Had she interpreted his words correctly, his touches, and the ways he'd looked at her? If she picked the sexiest film she could find, made the first move, she'd know for sure. But what if he'd been serious earlier? What if he really didn't want her that way? The uncertainty tortured her.

Turning off the reservation app took a minute. Finding a sexy movie that didn't involve kidnapping, porn-star characters, or subtitles was infuriatingly difficult. Finally, a sexy rom-com came up on her search. Yeah, it was old, but exactly what she needed to set the mood and make her move. If it failed, she'd order an air mattress for next-day delivery and sleep on the floor until the guests left. Or she might have to fly home if it was horribly awkward.

She bit her lip.

At least she'd have the answer to whether all that heat was him or her imagination.

As soon as dinner was over and they'd cleaned up, Katherine sat on the couch next to Gabe, in the friend zone but close to the line. Would he take her silent invitation and cross it?

She clicked on the remote and started the film.

"Have you seen this one? It's older, like ten years ago, but it looked good, and I must have missed it when it came out."

"Think I might have been in boot camp. It doesn't look familiar."

Boot camp. He'd have been eighteen or so. She'd almost forgotten how much younger he was and fallen into the strange domestic bubble they'd created the past few days. And they could flirt, maybe more, but it could only be temporary. She would go back to New York, and he would find someone closer to his age, someone he could have a family with. He was so good with Sebastian that it was obvious he was meant to be a father.

Was she okay with a fling?

She'd never considered one before, but the man next to her had her considering all kinds of things she'd been avoiding for too long. And it felt damn good. After all, the entire reason she'd come to Colorado was to find her happiness again.

He stretched his arm across the back of the couch as the cutest meet-cute played out on the screen. She tilted toward him and waited. And waited. Nothing. Not even a twitch.

The characters' lips met. Their first kiss.

Katherine glanced at Gabe. His eyes were closed, his breathing regular. He'd fallen asleep. Long eyelashes nearly met his cheeks. His beard, recently trimmed, covered a strong jawline, and his soft lips hid the most open and friendly smile ever to grace a man. At least in her experience. It was honest. *He* was honest. And if she were honest with herself, it would take more than a fling to get over him.

His arm wrapped around her shoulders, tugging her to his chest. "Watch the movie."

Apparently, he hadn't been quite asleep. She let her head rest on his firm pec, the weight and heat of his embrace like a blanket, and stared at the TV. But the only drama playing out was what to do about her potent attraction to the much-younger man who lived two thousand miles from where her life waited for her return.

CHAPTER 13

The flash of previews of various movies and shows on the television roused Gabe. He slowly turned his wrist and glanced at his watch. Past midnight. Blond hair covered the left side of his chest. The woman wrapped in his arm fit perfectly, and he'd stay there all night, but that wasn't good for his leg. He had to move despite his resistance to breaking up that perfect moment.

He rubbed her shoulder and down her arm. "Hey, Jadis. Movie's over," he said in a low voice. She snuggled closer. His cock woke up just fine. Great. "We should go to bed. Got a lot to do later today. Need some real rest."

She shifted, and her half-lidded gaze met his.

Sex. She looked like sex—either ready for it or just had it. He leaned forward, and she arched into him, her soft lips brushing against his. Electricity and peace. She tasted like safety and danger. Her tongue teased into him. The room disappeared, and he wrapped her tighter in his embrace, kissing her like she was the last oasis in the desert. Her hands trailed over his chest and lower. Could she feel the pounding of his heart? She grazed his cock and broke their connection to stare at his crotch.

Shit. Gabe groaned. "It's late. I'll head upstairs."

"Wait." She sat up and brushed her hair back from her face. "That bed's covered with plastic and the paint fumes. We're going to be sharing anyway..."

Jadis had issued an invitation. Not due to necessity. He could move the plastic. The paint was low emissions and probably didn't even have a smell at that point. But there was no way in hell he was turning down sharing a bed with her. No one else was in the lodge. Not that anything had to happen or would happen. They'd just sleep. Next to each other, as close as she preferred. Or as far. Whatever. "Okay."

He helped her up from the couch, got her steadied on her crutches, and then shadowed her to his bedroom.

"I'm going to brush my teeth and change. Then you can have the bath." She tugged open the drawer she'd taken ownership of and closed the door to the bathroom behind her.

Gabe folded back the comforter, dropped onto the bed, and told his cock the rules for the night. *No poking. No coming. No behavior of any kind that will get you banned from your own bedroom. Behave.* His cock ignored him with a twitch. He glanced up to the bathroom door. It hadn't latched. He really should have fixed the balance on the damn thing. But when he saw Katherine's bare back arching down to a perfect round ass, the line drawing his eye to the apex of her thighs, he couldn't feel bad about procrastinating. She was the reason men learned to carve marble to preserve that perfection of undulating softness that only a woman could possess. His hand went to his cock, and he pressed it down in a sad attempt to control his desire. She raised her slim arms, and lavender fabric slid over her skin the same way he wanted to slide his hands down each luscious inch.

She turned, and her gaze met his.

Gabe swallowed. Opened his mouth to apologize.

Jadis smiled.

Oh fuck.

She was seducing him. Most of him was completely ready, but a small part, a tiny voice, asked, *What if...*

"It's all yours." She stood at the end of the bed.

Bathroom. She meant the bathroom, not her body. Not her kisses.

Not the warm heat between her legs. Gabe took a steadying breath as he moved past her. He wasn't fifteen with his first look at a naked woman. He could control himself. Maybe. He closed the door between them and leaned on it. Yes, she'd kissed him. But she'd backed off as soon as she'd felt his cock. So she was attracted, but the "hammer" that had earned him the Thor nickname was a dealbreaker. No problem. He brushed his teeth. He'd give her only what she wanted. No demands.

He removed his t-shirt but left his sweatpants on. After he took off his prosthetic, she wouldn't be in the mood for anything anyway. Gabe checked his beard for any stray flecks of toothpaste and went to face reality.

She leaned against a pillow propped on the headboard, comforter at her waist. Beautiful tits barely covered by silky fabric, nipples beaded and begging. "Come here."

"I…uh…I need to get out of this prosthetic. My leg needs a break."

"Right." She tugged the covers higher and clung to them. "Makes sense. It's not the same, but if I could take off this cast for the night, I would."

He sat down on the opposite side of the bed and quickly went through his nighttime routine, keeping his back to her. Finished, he placed both hands on the bed to adjust his position and get some shut-eye. As he reached for the bedside lamp, a lingering touch brushed down his spine. He turned his head, and his jaw dropped. Katherine was naked, up on her knee, her casted leg jutting out to the side. Exposed. He could see every bit of her, and she was glorious. He licked his lips and recalled how to breathe. "You're beautiful."

"Take them off."

"What?" She was naked. What else could he take off her?

"Your pants. And anything else. I want to see all of you. Every sexy inch of the man who's been teasing me. Tempting me. I showed you mine."

"Perfect." Gabe tugged at his waistband, rolling it down to the mattress as he lifted his hips. "You're perfect." He slid his pants and boxers off in one shove. He then put his hands under his head and lay out fully so she could see the horror of his scars. The damage left by shrapnel and surgeries. The angry lines. The images he'd used to conceal some of the destruction. And the ridiculous cock he carried around, which at least had the decency to go down. He closed his eyes, because what if her face morphed into fear or, worse, disgust when she saw him? He wasn't sure he could bear it.

He sensed her shifting on the mattress, hip to hip, so close the heat of her body warmed his. Her fingertips brushed along his forehead and down his furred cheek, across his lips to his neck. She touched every part of his arm from the shoulder to the tips of his fingers and back up. Moving across his chest, she teased his nipple and made his abs clench at the unfamiliar sensation. He lifted his eyelids a tiny bit. Instead of revulsion, he saw desire. Her tongue trailed across her lips, and he couldn't help but smile.

"Better," she said and kept touching him lower, following the trail of hair that led to his reawakening cock.

Damn. That fucker was going to ruin—oh shit. Her hand covered his cockhead with a solid grip. Not tentative at all. She rubbed her palm against him and was rewarded with a bead of pre-cum. His balls filled, heavy with desire. He swallowed and held himself still. Her grip slid down his shaft, not quite enclosing it. God, she had long fingers. Perfectly formed, elegant hands that were driving him crazy. She released him, and he snapped his eyes open wide. She wouldn't leave him like—oh. She cradled his balls one at a time. His hips twitched, ready to slide inside her.

But she was gone again.

No, she'd kept moving her hand, trailing over his hip and down his good leg. She leaned back to reach his knee and lower leg. Gabe gave into temptation and trailed his fingers up her thigh to her trimmed pussy. "Can I?"

"Touch me. Anywhere. I'm going to touch you everywhere because you're the most beautiful man I've ever seen."

He bit his tongue. Refused to argue with her. It was a kind lie.

She sat up and raised the knee of her good leg, opening for him. He could lift her up and put that perfect pussy right on his mouth. Eat her up and distract her from—oh fuck. She leaned back and her mouth was on his erection. Her hands traced along the deep scars on what was left of his leg. She swirled her tongue, and every insecure thought fled from his brain. There was only her. He glided his fingers through her puffy lips and teased her clit. Her moan vibrated right into his spine. He pressed one finger to her opening.

Wet. She was wet for him. With the lightest pressure, he entered her using the tip of his finger. Tight. She'd never be able to take him. Heaven. His cock was in her mouth, and she was stroking him. He had his finger in the most beautiful pussy he'd ever seen, and all he could do was pout about not fucking her. Selfish bastard. He slid in and out of her slowly, learning every curve and ripple of her sweet flesh. He searched for the touches and moves that made her tremble or gasp and pressed his thumb to her clit. That earned him a moan and a hip thrust.

The reverberation down his dick called him back to his own pleasure. Her hair cascaded over his skin, soft as silk. He swept the curtain back. Her gaze met his, her lips stretched around his head. Fuck. He was going to come. But not before he took care of her. Using her reactions as a guide, he fingered her like it was his most important mission. His worth as a man depended on making her light up before he lost his mind. He eased in a second finger.

She released his cock from her warm, wet mouth. "Gabe. Fuck me."

He pumped faster. Deeper. She sucked him back in, hollowing her cheeks. A competitive glint in her gaze challenged him, racing him to see who could succeed first, finish last. He committed to coming out on top, even though there were no losers in their battle. His cock hit the back of her throat, and she worked him hard, her spit and his cum wet on his shaft. Fuck. He'd never been sucked so eagerly. He shook his head to clear the fog she'd created. Ignored the tingles in his spine demanding his release and narrowed his intentions to only her pleasure. But her vocalizations made the situation more challenging. He released her hair, losing the view but gaining the freedom to augment his strategy. With his free hand, he stroked her breast and pinched her nipple, still fucking her hard with his other hand and pressuring her clit. She had to come soon or he wouldn't be able to hold off any longer. His hips had joined in the fun. Her hand slid down his length and cupped his aching balls.

Done.

He was done.

He came with a roar.

But instead of spitting him out, she kept working him, shaking and swallowing. Humming with...pleasure? She wasn't pissed that he'd come in her mouth without warning? A vise closed around his fingers; rippling wetness flowed into his palm. He thumbed her clit as she released. She loosed his spent cock and wailed, then flopped backward on the mattress. Her spasms slowed, and he freed his hand carefully from her tender folds. Her eyes were locked on his as he mouthed the two fingers that had been inside her and sucked all the sweet cum from them. Next time, if he was lucky enough to get a next time, he'd be sampling from the source.

He had to say something. "You're gorgeous when you come."

"And you are the sexiest, most attentive man I've ever been with."

"More? Do you want more?"

"Not tonight. You wore me out. It's—it's been a while since I've... and like you said, we have a big day tomorrow. Let me work up the energy to turn around and get my head on the pillow because what I really want right now is to snuggle. Is that too—"

"Perfect. It's perfect." Gabe sat up and helped her get straightened out. "How do you—"

She laid her head on his chest, put her good leg over his. He tugged the comforter over them, and she pulled his arm across his body to her. He wiggled his other arm under her shoulders and clutched her tight. Closing his eyes, he muted his doubts.

Maybe she would stay.

CHAPTER 14

*T*he alarm on Katherine's phone chimed, and she reached for it. Soft morning light filtered in through the window. During the night, she'd rolled away from Gabe's heat, too warm to sleep. But he hadn't let her go completely. He clutched her calf close to his body, leaving her stretched and far too open. Resisting the urge to yank her leg free, she stretched and turned off the annoying reminder that there was work to be done.

"Morning." The growl of his voice slid up her thigh and settled deep inside.

She used her arms to push herself up, and he released her. She lifted the sheet to cover her chest. "Sleep well?"

"Yeah." He adjusted the comforter to cover his lower half completely, but not before she got an eyeful of his morning wood.

More like morning log.

The man was fucking huge. Attentive in bed. And attractive as hell. As much as she would like to indulge her desire and spend a day in bed with him, they—*he* had guests coming, and the lodge was still in disarray.

"You take the bathroom. I'll start the coffee." His voice had a harsh distance in it.

Her jaw tightened. Maybe he was just as uncomfortable with being vulnerable as she was. If she didn't do something, the distance and discomfort would grow, which would make the coming week of sharing the bed intolerable. She wrapped her hand around his, where he clenched the covers in a stranglehold, and leaned into him. Then she pressed a kiss to his tense mouth. He softened his grip and stroked his free hand down her naked back to the top of her ass.

"Later." She settled a half-lidded gaze on him, caressing him with desire. "First, we make the lodge ready for your guests, then—"

He tugged her close and kissed her again. "I'm holding you to that, Jadis."

She laughed at the ridiculous nickname.

After a quick cleanup and wrestling on her clothes, she thumped out to the kitchen, the scent of coffee calling her. Gabe wore loose cotton pants and stared at the coffee maker as it sputtered the last of the brew into the carafe. "Bathroom's all yours," she said.

He snapped his gaze to her. "Didn't hear you come out."

"Everything okay?" What had he been thinking about staring at the coffeepot? Them? The lodge?

"Amy called. Seb showed up at her place about twenty minutes ago. She'll be here around nine thirty after they have breakfast."

Maybe Gabe had been thinking about Sebastian? "I like him."

"He's a good kid."

"With a horrible family." And she had tons of experience with that.

He tipped his head briefly. "Happens. Lots of guys go into the military for that reason."

"Not a bad option, but I hope something changes for him so he has choices." She respected the military, but it could extract a terrible cost. Gabe's body was evidence of that. And it was only a choice if there were other options available. But what could *they* do? Especially when she was only there for a short time.

Gabe retrieved two mugs from the cabinet and filled them. "I'm going to clean up. What's first on the agenda?"

Thankfully, a question she could answer. "Finish the guest room. Clean, decorate, photograph. Paint the hallway. Any other B and B things you have planned. I'm going to work with Amy and Seb to freshen up around the front door. Make the entrance more welcoming."

"It's a front door." Gabe scoffed. "I mean, I guess I could buy a mat that says *Welcome*."

Katherine bit her tongue to keep from sharing her first impression of his place. Telling him the lodge was as warm as a military barracks wouldn't be helpful. "I'm not sure, but Amy will have ideas."

Gabe gave a curt nod and left.

Tension washed out of her in his wake, and she folded into a chair at the table. Gabe had been oscillating all morning, going from relaxed and open to tense and shuttered in a moment. The sex, even without intercourse, had been amazing. But their interactions were strained, and she didn't like it. Had she gone too far, tracing his scars with her hands? It had been intimate, but maybe he'd felt exposed. Did she need to apologize? Or was it something completely different? Sebastian? The lodge? Almost all of their conversation had been superficial. At some point, they would have to talk, to be as honest with their words as they'd been with their bodies. If not that night, certainly the next one when the guests were occupying the only other inhabitable room in the lodge. Katherine's throat tightened. She was much better at using words to keep people at a distance than inviting someone in.

Hours of hard work later, the sun was starting to set, and Katherine flopped on the couch, letting her crutches drop to the side. "Amy tried to kill me."

"I don't remember working this hard on the place with my uncle." Gabe set the pizza box on the dining room table and served up slices on paper plates. "If I had known…" He handed one to her and put one on the coffee table near Sebastian, who was flipping through the offerings on the television. The scent of hot cheese and pepperoni wafted over her.

"I'm starved." Katherine savored a bite. It was the best meal she could remember eating. "What are we watching tonight, Sebastian?"

He set the remote down and chomped the end off his slice. The opening to a science fiction series filled the screen. "I saw this show at Amy's once." Sebastian glanced back at Katherine. "The tech is cool, and there's a political triangle that could break out in war at any time."

"I've been meaning to watch this one." Gabe settled between them in the middle of the couch. "Jadis, you okay with sci-fi?"

"Sounds great." Katherine didn't care what was on. She was just relieved the lodge looked ready for visitors. At least better. Amy's brilliant idea to add potted evergreens to the entry and mount snowshoes, of all things, over the front door had made such a difference. That, and all the cleaning they'd done. If Katherine never scrubbed a windowpane again, it would be too soon. In hindsight, she should have hired a service.

Gabe rose and thrust out his hand for her empty plate. "Another slice?"

She shook her head. Gabe and Sebastian had been discussing all the special effects, the reality of faster-than-light travel, and the political intrigues in the show. Katherine pretended to watch, but her eyes were getting heavy, and her back was achy. If she could, she would stay and ask Sebastian about his schooling and how he'd become fascinated with science and what he wanted to study after high school. But she didn't have the energy to put together a question, much less understand the answer. She wrenched herself off the couch, positioned her crutches, and made her way carefully to the dining table and Gabe. "I'm going to bed. You two enjoy the show."

Gabe dropped a slice on each of their plates. "You sure?"

"Of course. See if he'll stay. The couch is free." The guest room was already made up with clean sheets and ready for the guests.

"I'll try. You all right with bunking with me again tonight?"

"I like *bunking* with you." She smiled at the flash of dimples on his face.

He leaned in and kissed her lips sweetly. "I'll take care of the kid. You get some rest."

His words teased the long-dormant dream she'd once had of having her own family. She tucked the old, unattainable hunger away. "Wake me up when you come in."

But he didn't.

The covers were crumpled at the end of the bed, and Gabe was wrapped around her. His heat had been enough to keep her warm all night. A part of her liked sleeping in his embrace more than what they'd done the night before. A part of her that needed to shut up, because they weren't a couple. She lived in New York. An uncomfortable ache gripped her heart, urging her to snuggle closer.

Ridiculous.

She lifted Gabe's arm, and he grunted.

"I'll make the coffee," she said in a soft voice as she freed herself completely and left his warmth behind.

Sebastian was wrapped in a blanket, asleep on the couch, blond hair splayed across a pillow. He looked small and young. The impulse to hug him flashed through her empty arms. At least he'd stayed the night. He shouldn't be living alone, waiting for his mother to care for him. A woman who clearly didn't understand what a gift that child was.

As quietly as she could, Katherine made her way to the kitchen and started things rolling for the morning. Snow had fallen overnight, and the pines were coated with a fresh layer of powder. The guests would appreciate it for the skiing, and the storm was likely why Sebastian had stayed. A list of tasks that had to be accomplished before the couple arrived scrolled through her brain. But they weren't her tasks, and it wasn't her B and B. It was Gabe's. She didn't really have a place, other than a condo in New York that was increasingly less compelling to return to. There was nothing, no one, waiting for her. But if she didn't go home, what would she do? Could she stay at the lodge? Would Gabe want her? She scraped the hair back from her face. It was too early for those questions.

~

GABE LINGERED IN THE BED, missing the heat of Katherine's body. Sleeping with her had been more intimate in some ways than what they'd done the night before. Both experiences made him crave more. But waking up to her had made the day shine brighter. The sound of her rattling around in the kitchen reminded him of being at home.

He sat up. The lodge wouldn't prepare itself for guests. He slid a clean protective sock over his stump. Surprisingly, he'd been more concerned about Katherine's reaction to his hard cock than his amputation. She'd been accepting of both, but her lack of reaction weighed on him. It couldn't be real, could it? He wouldn't know until her cast came off and she was free to run away.

Stowing his doubts, he finished putting on his sweats. A shower could come later, after breakfast and taking care of Sebastian.

In the kitchen, Katherine was at the stove with a spatula in one hand, surrounded by the familiar scents of breakfast.

"Whatcha cooking?" he asked.

She glanced over her shoulder before turning her attention back to the frying pan. "The only breakfast I know how to make. French toast."

"Smells good." Gabe kissed the back of her neck. "Bacon?"

"In the oven."

He poured himself a cup of coffee. "Refill?"

"Sure." She flipped over a piece of bread.

"Where's Seb?"

"Upstairs. He went to check the paint in the hall." Katherine sipped from her full mug. "You know, I just don't understand. He's an incredible kid. How could anyone leave him alone?"

"Not sure. But between us and Amy, he's got people now." Gabe waited to see how she'd react to *us*.

The corners of her mouth lifted as she slid the finished toast onto a plate. "He does."

A balloon of hope expanded in Gabe's chest. "What can I do to help?"

"Put this on the table and find the butter and syrup." She handed the plate to him and opened the oven.

After a few minutes, Sebastian joined them at the table and ate ravenously. "This is good," he said between mouthfuls.

"I'm glad you like it. Other than that, I'm a terrible cook. In New York, I eat out or have food delivered."

"You live in New York? What's it like? I've always wondered about the subways."

Katherine gave Seb a half smile. "To be honest, I don't really use the subway."

"Taxis?"

"On occasion. There's so much to see and do there. The Met. Broadway. Ice-skating in Central Park."

"Never been ice-skating." Sebastian swirled his fork through the syrup.

"Skiing?"

"Usually snowboarding. When I get invited."

"I'm officially inviting you to see New York." Katherine glanced up at Gabe. "Both of you. I'll show you all my favorite things about the city." She glowed.

"Yankees game?" Hope filled Sebastian's voice.

"No problem."

"That'd be epic." Seb's eyes were wide, and he fidgeted in his chair.

Gabe swallowed down the wishes that had bubbled up from his heart into his throat.

"What are we doing today?" Sebastian asked, almost like he was hoping they'd get on a plane.

"There's not much left to do inside." Gabe drained the rest of his cold coffee in one gulp. "I mean, we can't start more projects with the guests coming. Do you have time to hang out and help me outside?"

Sebastian nodded.

"I started a deck with my brother when he was here. Could use a hand with the measurements and the next cuts."

"Sure."

Katherine beamed at Gabe. "I'll work on the website after I take care of the dishes."

"Seb and I—"

"Can go outside and get to work. I can't help with the construction, so let me do this."

Sebastian took his dishes to the kitchen.

Gabe rose to follow. "Fine. But just this once, Jadis."

The sting of her hand across his ass made Gabe smile. He gave her a quick kiss and led Sebastian to the workshop where the lumber was stored.

Despite the cold air, Gabe and Seb made good progress on the deck Gabe wanted to have ready for summer guests. The whir of the saw interrupted the conversation he was chasing with Seb. The kid had no father. His mother showed up most weeks, at least for a night, but he hadn't seen her in about ten days. Gabe lifted the blade and let it spin to a stop. "What about school?"

"Online academy." Seb toed the snow. "They gave me a laptop and keep my internet connection going, but it's restricted."

"Do you like online school?"

"Yeah." Sebastian shrugged. "I can do the work anytime, and the teachers are nice. Mostly."

"What're your favorite classes?"

Seb tilted his beanie-covered head. "Math and science, I guess. But history's good, too."

"Math, huh? Should have known the way you rattled off those fractions. But what about friends?"

"I already know all the kids in the valley. We hang out. I like not having to get to school at a certain time."

With a flaky mom, Gabe was sure that made Seb's life easier. But who was making his life *better*? "You're a junior, right? Any plans for after high school?"

"Not yet."

Hard to have plans for the future when everyday survival was in play. Gabe unclenched his jaw. "You still got time."

They continued to cut the boards and screw them in place until Gabe's stomach growled. He checked his watch. "Let's clean up and get some lunch. I've got some baking and other stuff to do this afternoon."

"Can I get a ride home?"

"You don't want to stay? Help me bake?" Damn. That was a lame invite, but it was already out.

Sebastian shook his head. "Homework."

"Gotcha. I'll get you home. But after we eat?" Gabe wasn't about to let Seb go on an empty stomach. Hell, if he could, he'd let Seb stay at the lodge permanently.

"Okay."

Lunch was a quick event with sandwiches and chips before Gabe reluctantly climbed into the truck with Seb. It had been a productive morning. Katherine had made the website sparkle, but she seemed itchy to work on something else. If he could get the next two rooms set up before she left, then she'd have more photos and pages to work with. Anything to keep her engaged and willing to stay.

He dropped Seb off at home with more cash after checking that he had plenty of wood and food. Leaving the kid, even though he wasn't Gabe's responsibility, left a weight in his gut. Something would have to be done about the situation soon.

Gabe had barely returned to the lodge and cleaned up when a navy SUV pulled into the gravel parking space. His mouth went dry, and he glanced around. The place gleamed. That stay was going to go perfectly, and he'd get another great review. Two with Katherine's. But he had to start somewhere, and it beat zero. He put on his best welcoming smile, opened the door, and greeted the fit middle-aged couple as they made their way to the entry.

"Gabe Gallegos. Welcome to the Ponderosa. Can I help you with any bags?"

"Reverend and Mrs. Scott. But you can call us Bill and Mary." The tall sandy-haired man shook Gabe's offered hand. "And I'd be grateful for a hand with the luggage. Let me get Mary settled inside first."

"Of course." Gabe stepped inside, holding the door wide for the couple.

Bill followed his wife and then turned to where Katherine was standing near the dining table. "And you must be Mrs. Gallegos."

Gabe's balls shriveled. He stared at Katherine, his future hanging on her next words.

CHAPTER 15

"*K*atherine." She slapped her practiced business smile across her face and reached for the assuming man's hand. The inability to breathe at the thought of being married to *anyone* didn't matter in that situation—only Gabe's success. "Welcome."

"I'm Bill. And this is my bride of thirty-two years, Mary."

A woman who'd spent more time in the sun than the salon smiled at Katherine, and she liked Mary instantly. Odd. Katherine never had an immediate affinity to new people. Even Amy had been suspect at first. "Can I get you something to drink? Tea, coffee?"

"Herbal or decaf tea would be great. That road in here was a little harrowing."

"I know what you mean. I drove it for the first time at night. It took me days to recover." Katherine filled the kettle with hot water and set it on the stove. She took a slow, deep breath and willed her hands to stop shaking. A reverend. And his wife. Oh lord. Gabe moved up the stairs, chatting about the area and skiing, with Bill following. Mary sat in a chair at the table.

"How long have you been an innkeeper?"

Katherine paused before answering. "Not long. Gabe has all the experience."

"You two are newlyweds?"

"Mmm." The whistle of the kettle saved Katherine from telling a more explicit lie. She filled a cup and placed it on a saucer with a spoon. An assortment of tea bags in a small basket waited on the table.

"Let me get that." Mary was at her side, reaching for the cup. "I can't imagine you trying to carry hot water with crutches. What happened?"

Mary returned to the table, and Katherine retrieved a napkin from the sideboard. "An unfortunate incident on the slopes. I remembered being a better skier than I am."

A flash of confusion crossed Mary's face. "You don't go often?"

"Not as often as I'd like. You?"

"When we can. Since weekends are generally busy with our flock, we have to make time during the week. In the summers, we hike, but I love fresh powder. Utah has been unseasonably warm this year, so when I saw the snow that you've been having, I insisted we take our annual vacation now." A soft smile complimented her rosy cheeks.

"We're so glad you did. Is there anything I can help you organize? Lift tickets?"

"That would be wonderful. And I was thinking we could do some snowshoeing around here, too."

"The trails are great." Katherine hoped they were, at least. She'd seen a rental place in town when they'd been shopping that had a trail map in the window.

"Mary?" Bill crossed from the staircase to the table, Gabe in his wake. "How about a nap?"

Pink darkened on Mary's cheeks as she set her cup back on the saucer. "Lovely, dear."

"Gabe gave me a great suggestion for dinner. Already have a reservation." Bill waved his wife up the stairs.

Mary turned to Katherine. "Thank you for the tea, Mrs. Gallegos."

"Just Katherine. I'll reserve lift tickets for you and Bill for tomorrow."

"Do they have a five-day pass?"

"I'm sure they do, but I'll double-check." Katherine smiled. Bill was already pulling Mary away, and the pink hadn't left her cheeks. Their nap wouldn't involve much sleeping.

Gabe closed the distance to Katherine as the Scotts disappeared into their bedroom with a click of the door and a snick of the lock. How good was the soundproofing in the lodge? They were about to find out.

Gabe leaned down to Katherine's ear. "I wouldn't mind *taking a nap*."

Katherine held in a chuckle. "You have a happy hour to prep. And I have to do some concierge work."

"I didn't expect you to take that role." Gabe straightened.

"I offered. Besides, if I'm your *wife*, it only makes sense that I would assist with the guests."

"You're not mad about the 'Mrs.' thing, are you?" Gabe grabbed the back of his neck. "After he said 'reverend,' I…"

"It's fine. I mean, I don't like lying, but they assumed. And it's only for the week." The squeeze of her heart made less sense than her initial panic. But that was a different problem. A small moan called Katherine's attention to the staircase. Wow, the reverend worked fast.

"It can be our fantasy honeymoon, Mrs. Gallegos." Gabe nuzzled her neck and kissed her behind her earlobe. "You, me, a snowy Colorado lodge with nowhere to be…"

She shivered. Her gaze met his eyes, and his heat warmed her. "Okay, *husband*."

THE HUSKY SOUND of the word "husband" on Katherine's lips made Gabe's spine tingle with desire. He blinked down at her. For the first time in his life, that word appealed. Was it a product of his maturity? Or was it her?

Gabe suspected the answer wouldn't make the precarious situation any less dangerous. If the Scotts caught him in a lie, it would be disastrous. If it made Katherine uncomfortable, that would be worse. And if he was ready to settle down and Katherine was the one but she left —well, there were no words for that situation. Despite the risk, Gabe committed to playing his part of the charade to the fullest. Great risk meant great reward. Theoretically.

But first things first: his guests. "What should I prep for happy hour? They have reservations at seven in town."

"Light, but with some protein. They're likely to be hungry after their *nap*."

Gabe squashed the flash of jealousy that pulsed through him at the delay in his own *nap*. Katherine had left him craving more since their night of touching and the best blow job he'd had in his life. Not because of technique but because she'd taken her time, acted like she truly wanted his pleasure. As soon as she let him bury his face between her legs, he would return the favor.

But first, appetizers. He whipped together a recipe for spinach-and-cheese quiche filling and prepped the mini-tartlet pan with wonton wrappers before putting it all in the refrigerator. Some vegetables, cheeses, and a bowl of nuts and he'd provide a nice spread that wouldn't go to waste if they were holding out for dinner or didn't come down from their nap in time to enjoy it.

"Okay," Katherine said as she entered the kitchen. "Passes are set for pickup tomorrow. And I called the shop in town. They rent snow-shoes, and they'll give the Scotts the platinum treatment. I told the shop owners you'd give them a discount if they have relatives coming to visit."

"Good idea." Gabe loved how she didn't ask, just did what needed to be done—exactly what he needed in a partner. "I've done the prep I can do." He glanced at his watch. "What should we do now?" His cock twitched with an untimely answer.

"Would you come look at something with me? Amy mentioned some things about her website, and I need another set of eyes to make sure I'm not imagining a problem where there isn't one."

"Sure." He followed her into the bedroom. The pristine covers begged him to mess them up with Katherine. But she dropped her crutches to the floor, sat at his desk, and flipped open her laptop. "Let me grab another chair."

Their shoulders touched as he leaned in close.

"See this?" Katherine pointed to the address line of the website. "See how the Sunflower site is *Alabaster Bed and Breakfast Association* dot org, slash *sunflower*?" She clicked over to a search page. "I looked up other inns in the area. All the member inns have a digital badge on their site, so it's easy to confirm."

Gabe forced himself to pay attention to what Katherine was pointing at and saying instead of the way her leg pressed against his. The heat of her body traveled through him and went straight to his unruly cock. He clenched and unclenched his hands, trying to focus on what was important.

"Every site is an extension off the main ABBA domain."

"That means…"

Katherine sighed. "Amy doesn't really have her own website at all. It's just pages on ABBA's. And everyone is sharing *one* booking system."

"That sounds risky for Amy."

"I'll bet that Betty is getting a cut off every booking they make." Katherine glared, angry not with him, thankfully, because she was in full ice-queen mode.

Fuck, it was sexy.

"They might save money by sharing everything." He stroked his hand up her thigh, unable to keep from touching the magnificent woman.

"We'll talk to Amy. Tomorrow."

"Good."

He leaned in to kiss her neck, but she met his lips with her own, her soft heat and teasing tongue taking him far from the lodge, guests, and websites. He existed only in her. She stroked up his chest and around his neck, running fingers through his hair. He wrapped his arms around her back and pressed her close, the softness of her breasts against his chest adding to the need to strip her bare, fuck her deep.

She nipped his lip, and he released his hold slightly. Her breath was as ragged as his, but she managed to speak. "I heard footsteps on the stairs."

"Shit." Unsure how she'd partially balanced in his lap, he eased her back onto her chair.

"I'll go out first." She glanced down at his crotch. "Pull yourself together and meet me." Her eyes twinkled.

"Might want to fix your hair first." Gabe nodded at the loose tendrils and teased her with an eyebrow waggle.

She quickly re-pinned the loose tendrils, and it was all he could do not to pull it all free again. Having guests was a total cockblock. Too bad his "hammer" hadn't gotten the message. No time for a cold shower, but a few minutes away from Katherine and he should be able to get himself under control. "After they leave…"

She scooted her chair back, lifted herself up on the crutches, and moved around him. "We'll have all night."

Katherine smiled widely as the Scotts placed food on the small plates Gabe had placed on the table.

"Join us," Mary said.

Gabe poured sparkling water for everyone and sat. Katherine put a few things on a plate, too nervous to eat.

"Tell us how you two met." Mary popped a quiche into her mouth. A flash of disgust crossed her face, but she chewed and quickly swallowed. "Interesting," she murmured.

"I, um, was on vacation." Katherine glanced at Gabe, but his eyes were wide. He'd be no help. "Gabe was staying at the same place. When I arrived, there was a horrible storm."

"And she was dressed for a fashion runway." Finally, he found his voice.

"This bear came at me from nowhere."

"I hadn't shaved."

"And he growls at me about my lack of proper footwear and steals my luggage." Katherine flashed Gabe a grin, loving the way he'd jumped in to tell the story.

"You mean, I carried in your forty bags you'd packed for a weekend?"

"He's exaggerating." Katherine smiled at Mary.

"Only a little." Gabe nudged Katherine.

"You two are so cute together. It reminds me of when I first met Bill. I wasn't too sure about him either."

"Ah, Mary. You fell for me the moment you saw me." Bill winked at his wife.

"I tripped."

"Sure, sure." He stood and held out a hand. "Don't want to be late for our reservation."

Katherine waved the couple off. The Scotts' room key worked on the front lock, which meant Gabe was free for the night. Katherine's skin tightened uncomfortably. It had been years since she'd engaged in actual sex. Would Gabe still want to? Did she?

Warm arms wrapped around her middle, and Gabe pressed his chest to her back. "Still hungry?"

"A little."

Gabe picked up the wonton from her plate and held it out to her.

She took it and bit into the crispy-looking quiche with the perfectly browned top and froze. She grabbed a paper napkin and spit the gooey mess out.

"What's wrong?" Horror filled Gabe's face.

"It's, um, pasty." Katherine winced. "Did you follow the recipe? Could it be a high-altitude thing?"

"I followed it exactly, except for refrigerating before I cooked it." He tore one apart and frowned.

"The Scotts didn't seem to notice." If she ignored the brief look on Mary's face and how fast they'd left and that they hadn't eaten much.

"I should've tested the recipe." Gabe picked up the tray and tossed the rest in the garbage.

"Next time." She couldn't stand to see him so dejected. "We still have the entire night. Hand me my crutches?"

He helped her up, and, once she was steady, she nipped at his neck and then nuzzled him.

"Come to bed?" His voice was husky.

"I'll be there in just a minute." She pressed her lips to his. "Go get comfortable."

He released her. "I'll be waiting."

Katherine closed her eyes and took a couple of deep breaths. Fear. She recognized the thing that held her in place. But why? Gabe had seen her body and made her come with just his fingers. His body could inspire romance stories. The man was sexy as hell. Yet if he took command of the situation, she'd panic, just like she'd done with her ex, fearing the loss of control. And then she'd run.

She was overthinking. She'd led the other night, and he'd had no problem. Time to put her past behind her. She turned on her crutches and entered the bedroom. A small lamp on the far nightstand cast more shadows than light. But it was enough to see Gabe spread out naked in the center of the bed like a Renaissance artwork.

Oh. My. God.

Gabe stroked his cock with one hand, tattoos rippling along his arm. Tribal bands and intricate geometrics. The other arm, raised over his head and resting on the pillow, was inked in a full-color American flag. His gaze burned into Katherine's. "Like what you see?"

God, yes. Too much. But the slight hesitation in his voice buoyed her resolve. "You got started without me. Naughty."

He squeezed the head of his cock, and his abs tightened.

She dropped her crutches by the side of the bed and shimmied out of her yoga pants, then pulled her sweater and t-shirt off in one motion. Gabe's attention danced over her body. She freed her breasts and ran her hands over them, plucking her nipples.

"Come here." Gabe held out a hand.

She released one breast and slid her hand down the center of her body, inside her panties, and fingered her clit. Gabe rolled toward her. She tilted her head, letting her loose hair graze her back. The heat of his focus, the familiar touch of her fingers…she was going to come.

"Please," he rasped. "Let me take care of you."

She abandoned her pussy in its needy state, knelt on the bed with her uninjured leg, and painted her arousal across his mouth with her fingers. "Only if you're a good boy."

He licked his lips. "Just tell me what you want, what you need. Anything."

"Help me out of these." She maneuvered to lie on the bed. Gabe gripped the side of her panties, slowly shifting them down her lifted hips, and then took his time moving them over her cast before he flung them to the floor. He remained in place, waiting for her next instruction. "Kiss me."

Gabe shifted and brought his lips to hers, tongues tangling. She stroked her hands over his head and down his shoulders before pushing him back. "Lower."

His eyes widened for a moment, and then he was in motion, positioning himself between her parted legs. Moving her good leg over his shoulder, he nuzzled her clit with his nose, and she couldn't hold back the moan. "Yes."

He dragged his tongue between her lips, his beard teasing her thighs. She scratched her nails through his short hair, gripping his head tightly to her. "More."

The word unlocked whatever held Gabe back. He lifted her leg from his shoulder, holding it up and back as he dove deeply into her. His tongue moved in wicked flicks across her clit, inside her opening, building the arousal that she'd initiated on her own. Deeper and deeper he tongue-fucked her pussy, pausing to suck her clit, then right back in. She couldn't anticipate where he'd be next or what he'd do, and it drove her right over the edge. She arched her back and released a wail as every muscle in her lower body tensed and shook. Her heart raced as Gabe continued to slowly lick her clean. She moaned and pushed his head away. "It's too much."

Their gazes met, his sparkling with anticipation, her lids heavy with satisfaction.

"How do you want me?" Gabe asked. "I have condoms. And lube. Just bought."

"Come here." Katherine wasn't ready for that discussion. In

another minute or two, yes. But first she needed to kiss the man who'd made her come so hard her body was still singing. He pressed up on his perfectly cut arms and planked over her before she guided him to her mouth and kissed him like they were making love.

Love.

She was falling in love with Gabe.

Katherine broke the kiss and stared into his eyes as she caressed his cheek. If she truly loved him, it was time for some honesty. "I haven't been with anyone in...almost a decade." She took a deep breath and blurted the more difficult truth. "And I can't have children."

She froze, locked on his face. What would he think? What would he say? Would it change everything? He was a young man.

"Can't?" he asked softly, his gaze intent.

"Hysterectomy. And this is so not the conversation I want to be having with you right now, but—"

"We can talk about anything. Anytime. Doesn't change how I feel. How much I want you. If anyone understands losing a body part, it's me." He put his hand over the scar on her stomach. "It sucks. Bad. But it doesn't change who we are."

Tears pricked her eyes. "I want you so much, but I'm kind of scared. What if I've forgotten everything?"

"Don't be scared. We'll go slow. Stop if anything isn't right." Gabe caressed stray strands of hair from her face, never breaking their connection. "It's been years for me, too." He kissed her. "What do you need?"

"Lube. Use the lube. Because what I really need is your amazing cock so deep in me." So deep she could erase all the doubts and disappointments.

He rewarded her with a smile that shone with his soul. "Anything you want, Jadis."

She laughed, letting the tension of her truth release. The nickname tickled her the more often she heard it. She'd been called lots of things in her life, but none were as empowering as the ice queen. "Hurry."

After rolling across the bed and retrieving the tube from the nightstand, he lifted up on one knee. His heavy cock thrust forward at her. She rolled the head through her hand, and he slicked up his palms. He nudged her aside and applied the clear gel with the same strokes he'd been using when she'd walked in. That big fat glorious cock was going to be inside her, but not soon enough.

"I need you. Now." Her body ached for him.

He flashed a perfect white smile, then lined himself up with her opening, stroking the mushroom head through her lips, teasing her clit.

She lifted her hips and notched him in. "No teasing."

"You sure?"

Katherine gripped his hips and tugged him closer, his cock spreading her wide. "Oh fuck."

Gabe stiffened. "What?"

"It feels…amazing. So good." The connection, his heat, the intimate touch of his skin inside her body, the shift in her muscles to accommodate his entrance—it took her breath. She pulled at his hips, and he pressed in another few inches. A familiar echo of the sex she'd experienced before rattled through her brain, but so much more vividly. Like her past was a line drawing and suddenly color had been added. "Keep going."

He retreated, and her nails dragged across his flesh, trying to keep him close. Then he thrust forward, and the air in her lungs exploded out. "Yes."

His movements didn't falter. In. Out. Deeper. His gaze locked on her the entire time. Katherine widened her legs to allow him full entrance, as deep as he could go. Her throat constricted with the wail of pleasure. Not yet.

"I'm almost there. Should I stop?" Gabe's focus had moved to her pussy.

She looked between their legs, a couple of inches to go. "All of you. I want all of you."

He sucked in a ragged breath and pressed forward. Finally, his hips met hers, connected. They were perfectly united.

One.

Katherine's eyes stung with unreleased tears. She wrapped her arms around his shoulders and hid her face in his arm. "Do it."

Instead of the pounding she'd anticipated, he slid slowly back and forward, excruciatingly careful. The slow slide, the retreat, and stretch her only focus. "Harder."

His speed didn't change, but the intensity wiped away the world. There was only Gabe. Only her. Connecting in the shadowy light, reconnecting parts of her she'd ignored so long she'd forgotten they existed. The sensation of being too naked warred with the demand to get closer. Her body took over; clenching desire squeezed away her fears. Gabe's rhythm increased, his head back as he arched into her. His cock drove her past any insecurity and into an explosion of light and color and weightlessness. His roar as he came was muffled. Not even her ears worked. She clung to him as she returned to her body, and tears leaked down her face.

Gabe gripped her shoulders and forced her to face him. "Did I hurt you?"

"No." She swiped at her betraying eyes. "It was perfect."

CHAPTER 16

Gabe wrapped Katherine in his arms as he slowly withdrew from inside her. The ache of leaving her body stabbed his heart almost as strongly as her tears. She said he hadn't hurt her, that the sex had been perfect, but people didn't cry without a reason. He kissed her again, gazed into her eyes but couldn't unravel the mystery. "Why?"

"Why what?" She caressed his cheek.

"Why're you crying?"

She gave a tiny shake of her head. "I can't explain. It doesn't matter. You were wonderful."

He didn't feel wonderful. He was a heel, fucking her to tears when she'd told him it'd been so long for her. Instead of demanding more explanation, because it really wasn't that great a mystery, he rolled to his side and held her. As amazing as it had been to be buried balls-deep inside her, squeezed so tightly in her hot, wet hold, his selfishness had hurt her. There were all kinds of ways to bring a woman pleasure. He would show her every one he'd mastered and learn new ones. Just for her.

If she'd stay.

She shifted in his arms, her back to his front. He pulled the covers over them and held her tight as they slept.

The next few days passed in a blur. The Scotts were rarely around, especially in the evening. But Gabe was still responsible for breakfasts and cleaning. Katherine offered to help with washing the sheets and towels, but the scrubbing fell to Gabe. It was miserable, and he'd never had to do it when he'd helped his uncle. The man had been wise enough to hire someone for that part. Gabe gave one last swipe to the toilet, dragged off the yellow gloves, then dumped them in his cleaning bucket, determined to quiz Amy about how she handled that part of the business.

The situation with Katherine weighed on him, too. During the day, they discussed tasks around the B and B. At night, they were affectionate, kisses and holding each other, but no real sexual contact at all. His body throbbed with need, like she'd bruised his entire being with her emotional withdrawal.

The day the reverend and his wife were supposed to check out, Bill clapped a hand to Gabe's shoulder. "Can we take a walk?"

Shit. They weren't happy. They wanted a refund. Gabe swallowed. "Sure."

Once they were beyond the parking area, trekking along the curved road that led to the lodge, Bill finally spoke. "Mary wanted me to talk to you. Normally, I wouldn't get involved, but when the wife asks—" He shrugged. "I'm sure you know."

Gabe didn't, but he nodded anyway.

"She's worried about you and Katherine. Thinks there may have been a disagreement. She's worried we might have been the cause."

Gabe halted. "What?"

"You two seem to be just starting out. As innkeepers. And newlyweds. If you lived closer to us, I'd invite you to our couples' counseling sessions. Or maybe there's something I can help you with now?"

Counseling? Gabe gulped. "No. It's been great having you as guests. We've both enjoyed your visit. Tremendously." Shit, he was lying to a reverend. Their presence had made it impossible to address what had happened with Katherine, and after so many days, he couldn't bear to bring it up. "Uh, Katherine's from back East. They're a bit more reserved in their affection. In front of people." Was Bill buying that? "We *are* new to innkeeping. But I hope you enjoyed your stay?"

"We had a wonderful time. Love to come back in the future."

Gabe breathed a sigh of relief. He should have been elated, but the pressure to seek counseling with someone he was barely dating, no matter how much he liked or possibly loved her, knocked him on his ass. He followed Bill back to the lodge in a daze. The Scotts left soon after. Thank god.

Gabe dropped into the chair next to Katherine. "I think I should get started on the Jack and Jill rooms, but I want your ideas."

"Jack and Jill?"

"Shared bathroom. My uncle used to have two sets of bunk beds in one room and a queen and a single in the other. It was more for skiing groups where people are just trying to pack in and save rental money so they can ski more. But I don't think that works so well these days."

Katherine wrinkled her nose. "That sounds awful. But maybe a family option?"

"Put a king bed in the larger room and, what, two singles in the other?"

"It would give you options. You could rent both rooms or just one or the other with the bath."

Gabe scratched at the whiskers on his chin. "That only gives me two real rentals. I need three to be eligible for ABBA."

"I'm not completely convinced that matters." Katherine glanced up at the ceiling. "What about the attic?"

"What do you mean?"

"There's obviously a sizable space up there. You could change out the ladder that goes to it and put in an actual set of stairs. Maybe put a bathroom over one of the existing ones so you can leverage the plumbing that's already there."

"It's possible. Pricey."

"Something to think about. But you have to do something with the

Jack and Jill rooms, and you can't add another bathroom between them. Not enough space."

Gabe grunted in agreement. No room. No money. No idea how he would solve that problem or his situation with Katherine. But he knew how to do construction, thanks to his brother. So, he'd start there. He leaned over and kissed her, hiding his surprise when she tugged him closer and deepened the kiss.

She released him. "Get to work upstairs. I'm going to update your social media."

Gabe nodded, having no clue what she was talking about. Didn't matter. She'd kissed him. Maybe later they could reconnect and figure out the sex. Or at least figure out some orgasms.

KATHERINE COULDN'T TEAR her eyes away from Gabe's back as he left. If she could take back her tearful reaction to the sex days ago, she would. The tears had caught her off guard. He'd assumed she was in pain, and at the time, the words wouldn't come to fully explain what was happening. At that moment, she hadn't even been sure of herself. Her body, overwhelmed with all the sensations, the connection, the intensity of the moment, had exploded in a torrent of emotion that leaked out her eyeballs. No orgasm had ever knocked her so far off-kilter. And she was dangerously close to losing the man who had taken her there.

What would he do that night? The Scotts had vacated the upstairs room. Would he retreat? She still had several weeks before her cast came off. Not that she couldn't fly home... Her throat closed at the thought of leaving, but how could she stay if Gabe didn't want her?

Pushing her doubts about the coming night away, she scheduled some social-media posts. It was easy to show off the breakfast and happy hours Gabe had served. She added a couple of artistic shots of the snowy landscape, the discarded snowshoes on the front stoop when the guests had returned from their forest trek, and even one of steaming coffee in a handmade mug. Afterward, Katherine was at a loss for what she should do next. Talk to Gabe? And say what? *I want you. I'm pretty sure I'm in love with you. But my emotional baggage makes me look like a light packer.* Because that's what every man was looking for in a partner.

Instead of unraveling the tangled ball of feelings, she returned to what she was best at: working. At least she could benefit Gabe financially before he ended things with her. She sent Amy an email asking about the next ABBA meeting and if she could attend as her guest.

Noise from upstairs tempted her to climb up and see what Gabe was doing or even start cleaning the upstairs room. But if it remained dirty, he might stay with her. She poked around in the fridge for ideas for dinner and finally started some rice because that went with everything, and the machine practically made it for her. Tears threatened again. She'd never cried so much in her entire life. Disgusted with herself, she retreated to the bedroom for a nap.

KATHERINE WOKE, draped over Gabe. She'd slept the entire night, and he'd stayed with her, without sex once again, but it was something. She traced the lines of the muscles in his forearms—tanned, inked skin wrapped around strength and incredible tenderness. No matter how attracted to him she was, she wasn't meant for him. Not really. He deserved someone younger, someone he could have a family with. Someone less broken.

She slid from the bed and made her way to the kitchen as quietly as she could. Before she sat down at the computer, she brewed a pot of coffee and wrangled a mug to the table. The kitchen light provided enough illumination for her to work.

Amy had replied to her email. On an impulse, Katherine asked her to meet for lunch. If nothing else, it would get her out of the lodge for the first time since the Scotts had arrived. She clicked over to a popular travel site to check for their review. When the page loaded, her jaw dropped, and her gut roiled around the few sips of coffee.

There were eleven reviews where there had been none days ago.

One five-star dated the day before and the rest one and two stars. Had there been a mistake, a confusion with the links? No, several of the reviews were very specific, mentioning Gabe, the owner, or describing the lodge physically with less-than-flattering adjectives. One even accused the lodge of having "filthy, stained linens."

Flames exploded in her head.

Katherine took screenshots and dug deeper. Several of the accounts were brand-new, and the only reviews they'd posted were for the Ponderosa. Katherine marked the Scotts' review as helpful and then began searching the website for any recourse. She found the forms Gabe would need. Dread hit her. She opened every popular travel site she could think of. On every single one, the horrible reviews repeated like a bad wallpaper print.

Someone was sabotaging Gabe.

Betty?

If so, then Katherine bore the blame. She'd attacked Betty in front of Amy. And that snake of an association president had hit back with excruciating exactness. Rustling came through the bedroom door. How would she tell him?

Gabe poured a cup of coffee. "I have some muffins left from yesterday. Want one?"

"Sure." Katherine wouldn't be able to stomach a bite.

A few minutes later, Gabe placed a plate in front of her, along with a dish of butter and a knife. He sat next to her and slathered his reheated pastry. Katherine studied every move, avoiding the ugly situation. But that never worked in business. Better to face the issue head-on with as much objectivity as possible. She took a slow breath and lifted her chin. "I have to show you something."

"What's up?"

She turned the laptop toward him. He set the remaining piece of muffin on his plate and wiped his hands on his napkin, leaning toward the screen. His fingers hovered over the touchpad, and then he swiped once. Minutes passed. He swiped again. His jaw was tight when he looked up at her.

"They're trolls, fakes," she said.

Gabe pressed his lips tight together, rose from the table, and threw away the remains of his breakfast. He stared out the kitchen window for a long moment.

"What can I do?"

His voice was so deep and low, she'd almost missed the question. "We can protest. I have the forms and can fill them out. But it has to be from your email address."

"Will that fix it?" He returned to the table, picked up her pen, and wrote his email address and password in her open notebook.

"I'm not sure."

He nodded once and then stomped up the stairs. Construction noises filtered down after a few minutes. Katherine filled out the protests, sending them logged in as Gabe. She checked her phone. Time to get moving. After a quick shower and a little more time spent on her appearance than she'd done recently, she found Gabe coming down the stairs.

"Where are you going?" he asked.

"Lunch. With Amy."

"Need a ride?"

"I should be fine in my rental."

He grunted and moved past her to the kitchen. She searched for something to say. Anything that would take the sting out of the attacks. But nothing would change the situation, so she left.

The restaurant was warm and lively; the scent of toasted bread and spice filled the space. Amy waved her over to a table, and Katherine gave her a grateful hug. "Thanks for meeting me."

"Of course. Everything okay?"

"The Ponderosa got trashed on the travel sites."

"What?" Amy's face was likely a mirror of what she imagined her own had looked like when she'd found the false reports. Shock and horror.

Katherine held out her phone and let Amy read for herself. A short while later, Amy handed it back. "That's horrible."

"Do you think Betty could have had anything to do with it?"

"I don't know, but some of the aliases look like they might be other members of ABBA. But I can't believe they'd do that. Maybe someone used their information. I can ask around."

They ordered lunch from the chirpy server. Amy gave Katherine the information on the next meeting and confirmed she could attend as a guest.

"You're married, right?" Katherine asked after the food had been delivered and they'd started eating.

Amy paused with her soup spoon partway to her mouth. She ate the bite and then answered, "Yeah?"

"But you said he travels a lot."

"He does. We chat on the phone at least once a week."

"When he's in town or when you first got together, have you ever…" Could she even ask Amy the question burning inside her? She'd never talk to her friends in New York about Gabe, but Amy was different. Katherine trusted her not to weaponize their conversation later.

"Ever what?" Amy's soft smile invited Katherine to continue.

"Cried?"

"You mean like I'm happy to see him or I miss him?"

"No. During." Katherine leaned closer. "Sex."

"Oh. Have I ever cried during sex?"

Katherine nodded, pushing down the urge to take it all back.

"Not with—not recently. But yeah. It's normal on occasion." Amy patted her arm. "Wait. Did you and Gabe…?"

"Once."

"Damn. He's fine. Was it awesome?"

"Overwhelmingly awesome. But then—it was too much. My emotions."

"It's no big deal."

"He's acting like it was."

"Seriously? Sit him down and tell him, 'I like sex with you a lot. Tears are just overflow valves when women feel too much.' Or will that freak him out worse?"

"I don't know." Katherine had to change the subject. That was more honesty than she'd shared with anyone in as long as she could remember. "How's Sebastian? Have you seen him?"

"I fed him dinner last night. I think he shows up when he's lonely after he's sure his mom won't be home that night."

"I thought she left for good." The memory of her own mother's abandonment squeezed her heart.

"He holds out hope like any child, I guess. They want to have a home."

"Could someone take him in? I mean, now that his mom hasn't shown up for days?"

"You mean like a foster parent?"

Fostering. A legal pathway to taking care of Sebastian that hadn't occurred to Katherine. "Well, he needs one. And he gravitates toward spending time with you." It was horrible to pressure Amy, but since Katherine didn't live in Colorado, she couldn't take the child in. She didn't have a permanent address.

"My…*husband* would never approve. With his travels and the B and B, I don't know that I'd be eligible to foster Sebastian anyway."

The questions swirled around Katherine as she finished her lunch and half listened to Amy's small talk. What did fostering entail? Could she do it alone? Would Sebastian be willing to move to New York? Or could Gabe foster him? Would he want to?

If he did, where would Katherine fit, or would she?

CHAPTER 17

Katherine was right on time for her first ABBA meeting. She followed Amy into the local library's community room and patted the twist of her hair for a third time. A historical home had been converted to serve the purpose, with shelves in every nook and cranny. An upstairs room lined with encyclopedias, dictionaries, and other reference books acted as the meeting space. Several wood tables had been pushed together, and the association members, looking like a murder of crows, were already seated in the mismatched chairs. She and Amy took the last two open seats.

When she'd asked to attend the meeting a few days back, she'd been focused on the outcome, not actually having to attend. Katherine steeled her spine and lifted her chin. She'd give anything to be wearing her stilettos at that moment. Betty arrived and tapped her gavel on the podium, bringing the meeting to order.

There was no agenda, no speaker, and no interaction. Betty rattled off information about the funds in the organization, a surprisingly low number for a business group. Then she shamed a few members about nitpicky property issues, like snow buildup and signs in need of repainting.

And, finally, she reviewed their reviews.

"Deborah," Betty called out sharply, and a gray-haired woman paused her knitting to look up. "Your latest review said your towels were threadbare and your linens were dingy. Guests in Alabaster don't want to sleep on filthy, stained linens and use worn-out towels. We have standards to maintain *if* you're going to keep the ABBA badge on your website."

Katherine narrowed her eyes at Betty, who had turned into the spitting image of her father. And what an interesting turn of phrase, so familiar…

Deborah curled over, shoulders slumping as she nodded. "I'll order new ones."

"Today," Betty said with an arched eyebrow. "The association is here to support you and make sure we have the best standards in the area so that we get those returning guests. One bad inn reflects on all of us. And since we aren't located directly on the slopes, we have to be diligent about everything else we offer. Right?"

The poor beat-up crows cawed in dejected agreement. Were the meetings always like that? After several more shame sessions, the meeting was adjourned, and Betty promptly left with a couple of old birds flapping after her. Several of the innkeepers stayed and looked at Amy.

"Are we going for coffee?" one asked.

"We should go to a *bar* after that butt-chewing," another woman replied.

Katherine couldn't remain silent for another second. "Are all the meetings like this?"

"Pretty much," the bar woman said.

Amy touched Katherine's shoulder. "This is my friend Katherine. She's helping the new owner of the Ponderosa."

"Helping him with what?"

Katherine wasn't sure who asked but raised her chin. "His internet presence and reservation system. I have a marketing degree from Columbia, and I've traveled all over the world. You have such a unique opportunity here, but you're being bullied."

Several people nodded, but there was a wariness to the group.

"Why do you put up with it?" Katherine didn't own a B and B, wasn't a member, and was ready to quit the group.

"We need her," Deborah said.

"What we need to do is talk, because what I saw here is abuse. And I should know." Katherine stood on her crutches. "Where can we go to chat and not be overheard?"

A short drive later, they pulled up to a single-story log building with a sign that had faded to the point of almost being unreadable except for the word *shaft*.

How appropriate.

The inside was dark; wood tables rested on wood floors, and a bar ran the length of the building. After giving her eyes a moment to adjust, she glanced around the open space. Several of the ladies from the meeting had already pulled tables together in a far corner and waved her over. Katherine maneuvered her way between the haphazard chairs, her crutches sticking to the floor in spots. "Nice choice."

"Betty would die before coming in here," Amy said with an evil grin.

Katherine settled in the chair at the head of the table, where her cast and crutches were out of everyone's way. She gazed over the group. Did they have enough business acumen to recognize what tied them to Betty? "What do you think you need from ABBA that you can't do on your own?"

On cue, they replied as one, "My website."

Perfect. Not that fixing it would be easy, but the first hurdle was clear. They understood the problem at least at the high level. "How much do you pay for your sites?"

Before they could answer, a waitress wandered over and took orders for coffee and iced tea and baskets of fries and chicken fingers. Katherine ordered ice water with lemon and retrieved her phone to take notes. As the answers rolled in, the women were surprised to learn there was a wide disparity in cost and all of them were getting the same service. Then came the discussions about what didn't work on the site. Katherine let them ramble, shocked they hadn't compared their experiences before then.

As the complaints wound down, likely because of the fried food arriving, Katherine posed her next question. "Do any of you put reviews up on other properties?"

"We shouldn't," Deborah—the one who'd been eviscerated over old linens by Betty—said. "If we get caught cross-promoting properties, exchanging reviews, we can be dumped from the travel sites."

"Then I can assume you didn't leave this review." Katherine held her phone out to Deborah.

As the woman read the words—the review that had the bit about "filthy, stained linens"—her mouth dropped open and eyes went wide. She sputtered, "I—I never. I can't believe…"

"Betty has access to your email accounts on your websites." Katherine had no concrete evidence, but it wasn't a guess any longer.

"That *witch*," rang out over the other sounds of disbelief and disgust.

"But what can we do?" Deborah asked, the sound of defeat heavy in her tone.

Katherine plucked a french fry from a nearby basket and pointed it at her. "You can move your cheese."

"What does that mean?"

"Basically, it means quit relying on the perceived authority for your rewards. Take control of your outcomes." The explanation resonated through Katherine. She should have taken her own advice years ago.

The babble started up again as Katherine munched the greasy potato. Once they had settled, she continued. "First, you can contact the travel websites and let them know your email accounts were hacked by a troll and get them to take down the bad reviews."

They nodded. Good, because if they hadn't agreed to that first step, Katherine wasn't helping any of them.

"Next, I can help you set up your own websites under *your* control. That's what Gabe's doing."

Panic broke out.

"That's so expensive."

"I'd have no idea what to do."

"What happens if it breaks? I can barely work my computer."

Deborah's voice rang above the rest. "We'll lose our badge."

Katherine scoffed at the last one. "That badge is promoting ABBA. It's not giving *you* anything. Your B and Bs aren't found because of the organization site—that happens by word of mouth, travel sites and search engines. That's what's driving your visitors. I know because I just did a search to find a place to stay less than a month ago. And I *didn't* find the Alabaster Bed and Breakfast Association."

"She's right." Amy had been quiet up to that moment. Katherine was grateful for her soft but powerful agreement. All the heads had turned toward her friend. "We don't need Betty. I talked to Gabe, and he's spending less on his software and site annually than what our membership in the association costs."

"It all sounds good, but I don't know the first thing about setting up my own website, and I can't afford to be offline during the busiest season." Deborah crossed her arms.

"Of course you can't. That's why I'm going to help anyone who wants to move their site. We'll get everything set up, and then the last step is to redirect your existing web name to the new hosting company and the new software." Which could be tricky since they didn't have independent domain names, but Katherine would find a solution.

"I'd have to pay you," Deborah said.

"I'm very affordable," Katherine answered. She'd work for free to pay Betty back for the stress she'd caused Gabe.

Deborah leaned forward. "How soon can we do this?"

Katherine smiled at Deborah and the others, who were nodding in agreement, and started filling up her calendar with appointments. It struck her as she drove home that she finally had her first job that didn't involve her father.

～

GABE GLANCED out the front window for the hundredth time. After so many days of Katherine disappearing in the morning and being gone all day, he should be used to her absence. But the ache of desire hadn't eased a bit. The nights they spent together didn't help. He hadn't moved back upstairs, and she hadn't asked him to. But the only things happening in the bedroom were chaste kisses goodnight and some cuddling. Something had to give.

Katherine thumped into the kitchen dressed like a runway model if he ignored the cast and crutches. "Coffee. Thank god. I'm going to need it today."

"What's on the schedule?" Her schedule was closer to her heart than an evangelical preacher's Bible and more rigidly adhered to than reveille at boot camp.

"I have two new innkeepers who want help converting their website. And I need to get two others to go live. Word of mouth is taking off. I'm getting B and Bs that aren't in Alabaster."

"You better raise your rates."

"I did. It's not slowing down. I'm fielding a bunch of basic calls. Most of those I'm having the owner contact the site host just so they get used to getting their support. And if that doesn't work, then I help them. But I'm still getting calls."

Gabe placed her breakfast on the table at her spot. She had her own spot at his table. And a side of his bed. And she owned his heart. Did she care about any of that?

"Thank you." She ate a bite of his vegetable-laden scrambled eggs and reached for the salt.

Gabe said nothing. He sipped his coffee and stared out the kitchen window. How long could that go on?

"Gabe?"

He turned toward her.

"I know I haven't been around much. I'm not trying to take advantage of you. Is there anything I can do?"

He didn't feel taken advantage of. He felt abandoned. But he wouldn't be a big baby and cry about it. She didn't owe him anything. "Nope. I'm good."

"Dinner and a movie tonight?"

At least they'd have some alone time together.

"I can pick up Sebastian on my way back into town," she added.

Or not. "Sure. Sounds like fun."

"Pizza? Or maybe Chinese? I can phone it in. No cooking. I know you've been working your ass off on the Jack and Jill and the deck."

"Pizza. It's Seb's favorite."

She opened her mouth like she was going to say something else but closed it. Too soon, he watched as her car left again. How would he tell her he missed her, missed making love to her when they'd made love once and it had ended in tears? He wouldn't. That's how. Because even though things weren't ideal, she was still there. If he risked asking for more, he might lose her completely.

He barreled out of the lodge and resumed working on the railing for the deck. The work was challenging without his helper. Maybe Seb would stay the night and help him the next day.

The sound of a car interrupted Gabe's work. He glanced over his shoulder, shocked to see Katherine pulling in. Sebastian was in the passenger seat, staring at her and laughing. So at ease, they could have been family—his family.

Katherine called out to him, "I got done early. And look what I found." She held up a pizza box. "Take and bake. Finally, hot pizza instead of reheated. When should I put it in the oven? Should take about twenty minutes after the oven heats up."

He checked his watch. It was already late afternoon, and he'd worked through lunch. "Now. I'm starved. Sebastian, can I get a hand after you help Katherine get inside?"

"No problem," Sebastian said and followed Katherine as she worked her way into the lodge. Her excitement about a simple pizza gnawed at him. Why was he so uptight? Right. Sex. He hadn't even masturbated. They were going to fix the situation that night. Quietly if Sebastian stayed over, but no more waiting.

Sebastian reappeared a few minutes later.

"Hey, buddy. Glad you're here. Missed having the extra hands."

"Yeah." Sebastian's smile conveyed far more than his typical teenage speak. He'd missed Gabe, too.

"Help me restack this wood, and we'll do one last cut. That's about all we'll have time for before dinner's ready."

"'Kay."

"You doin' all right?"

"I'm good." Sebastian shrugged.

"You know you can stay here as often as you like or—"

"My mom called the other day. Think she might come back soon."

The pitiful tendril of hope in the boy's words wormed through Gabe's guts. It was past time to do something real about that problem. He'd call someone in the morning—the county or a lawyer or someone.

They finished installing a piece of handrail and put away the power tools for the evening. Gabe sent Sebastian inside to wash up while he locked the storage shed and tarped his wood. As soon as he entered the Ponderosa, he was met by the sound of Katherine slapping her hand on the dining room table. He hurried over. "What's wrong?"

"My credit card is blocked," she screamed. "I'll kill him."

"Whoa." Gabe stroked a hand over her shoulder. "What do you mean, blocked? How do you know? And who's 'him'?"

"My father. He's a signer on the account that I've had for over twenty-five years. I've never bothered to get a different one. Dumb."

"Do you need something? I can help you out."

"No. I was trying to help *you* out. I wanted to get the mattresses for the rooms upstairs. But the card was declined, and when I called, they told me my card had a hold put on it. He's the primary on the account, even though it's in my name. I pay the bill. He's had nothing to do with it."

"Wait, what?" Gabe removed his hand from the angry woman, no longer caring if she was upset. "What do you mean, you were helping me out?" He took a step back and crossed his arms. "I don't need your help to get stuff for the lodge. I'm not a fucking pity case."

Katherine rose from her chair, using it like a walker, and spun on him. "It wasn't pity." Her voice rose, and her face was turning red. "I was trying to do something nice. I know I've been gone a lot. Working jobs that I wouldn't have had if it hadn't been for—"

The doorbell rang, cutting her off. Gabe turned his back and opened the unlocked door. A man in a blue coat with an official patch sewn onto one shoulder stood on the stoop, holding a clipboard. Gabe's gut tightened further. "Can I help you?"

"County inspector." He held up a badge. "I understand there's some construction going on here. I'm here to check your permits." He glanced over toward the unfinished deck.

"I—" *Shit*. Gabe cleared his throat. "Permits?" His brother had mentioned something about that, but at the time, they'd been doing minor repairs and not actual construction. "I didn't realize I'd need them."

"Construction. Outside structures and major renovations require the work to be reviewed by the planning office and a permit issued. Before work begins. I'm assuming you don't have a permit for this deck?"

"No."

"And I understand there have been some modifications to the bathroom upstairs?"

Only one way he'd know that. Betty. "Nothing major. I closed off a door to the hall and opened one to a bedroom."

"Any other construction going on?" The man placed his foot on the threshold.

Gabe considered clotheslining him and locking the door, but it wasn't one of his brothers harassing him. Or the enemy. Just a guy doing his job. Gabe stepped back and opened the door. After a quick tour, the man handed Gabe a bunch of paperwork, including information on where to pay his fines and apply for the proper permits. As he shut the door behind the inspector, the fire alarm in the kitchen rang out.

"The pizza." Katherine grabbed her crutches, but Gabe made it to the kitchen first and removed the burnt pie from the oven. He turned on the fan and used a kitchen towel to wave the smoke away from the alarm.

A few minutes later, it finally shut off, and he could think again. Besides the blackened crust, most of dinner was salvageable. He called out to Katherine and Sebastian.

She appeared a few moments later. "He's gone."

"The inspector? I know. I let him out."

"No, Sebastian."

CHAPTER 18

*I*f she could've rewound time and kept her anger about her finances to herself, Katherine would've. She'd let her frustration wreck their evening, and then the inspector had shown up. Again, her fault for not holding her tongue when Betty had visited. In all of that anger and drama, she'd lost track of Sebastian, proving she was not foster-mother material. Or girlfriend material.

"I'll go look for him. He can't have gotten far." Gabe punched his arms into his coat and grabbed his keys.

"I'll go with you."

"No."

The single word stabbed into her chest. He was right, though. She'd caused enough trouble.

Gabe whipped open the front door, letting in a blast of cold air. "The center of the pizza is edible. I'll call you when I find him." He left without a glance back.

Her hunger had vanished when she'd realized Sebastian was gone and the county was going to fine Gabe for work she'd convinced him he should do. She cut out the edible part of the pizza and put it in the refrigerator. The rest she scraped into the trash.

Gabe's life was upside down because of her. In some ways, her quest to control was just as toxic as her father's. If she cared about Gabe at all, she'd get the hell out of his life before she hurt him anymore. But she couldn't even book a flight home with the hold on her credit card.

There was one thing she *could* do, though—call the jerk who'd complicated that mess.

After three rings, her father's voice grated across her raw nerves. "Katie, what a surprise."

That nickname was the final straw. "Richard," she snapped. "What do you think you're doing putting a hold on *my* credit card?"

"Technically, I own that account. I told you if you didn't return within the month, there would be consequences."

"Take the hold off. Now."

"I'm not discussing this over the phone. I've already scheduled a flight. We'll talk when I get to Aspen."

"No, we'll talk—"

He'd hung up. That bastard. There was no way she'd meet with him. But if she didn't, how would she help Gabe? And if Gabe demanded she leave after the mess she'd created—and he had every right—how would she get home? The small amount of money she'd made with the websites wasn't enough to book a last-minute flight. Even if everyone paid their invoices, it wouldn't be enough. And it sure wouldn't enable her to clear the fines the inspector had levied. She owed Gabe that, at least.

Richard had her cornered. And the one person she craved to share her pain and rant about her father's manipulations was gone, looking for the boy she'd scared out of the house. She rubbed her fist against her chest where the ache of his rejection still lingered. She should never have screamed about her credit card. He'd taken her effort to help him as pity. Pity was the last thing she felt for him. But he had no way of knowing that because she'd shut him out. The mattresses had been her attempt at reconnecting. Her apology to build the bridge between them—and an abject failure. What if the purchase had gone through and the new beds had been delivered? She shuddered.

Gabe's anger over the mattresses defined just how different they were. Yet she'd seen clues. In the stores, she'd been tempted to offer to pay for the linens and artwork. But something about the way he held himself, had his wallet at the ready, told her it would be unwelcome. He'd even paid for lunch for everybody that day. At the time, she'd been so focused on Sebastian she'd missed it. But she hadn't paid, and neither had Amy. Shame washed through her like a shot of acid. She'd totally screwed up, ignoring his boundaries, doing what was "best" for him.

Much like her father always did, using his money as a control and running over her objections. But she'd allowed it, encouraged it, even. She'd spent her entire life running back to "Daddy." When things got difficult in her marriage to Andrew, she'd flown home. She'd avoided finding a job in her field because it was easier to rely on "Daddy." She'd blamed Missy and Ned and everyone else for the chaos at her grandfather's law firm instead of looking in the mirror. But she could no longer avoid the reality that she'd exacerbated every dark moment in her life by taking the easy path, the selfish path. She'd even shunned her mother, refusing to spend time with her after she'd left Richard.

The one person she'd connected with, she'd been avoiding. Gabe had cracked through her shields, and, under the guise of working, she'd avoided him ever since, unwilling to have the honest conversation. In reality, she could have spread out those meetings or done some of the communication by email or phone. But she'd been running. Just like she had with Andrew when their sex life had exposed her vulnerabilities.

Why would Gabe want her for a girlfriend?

Why would Sebastian want her for a guardian?

Beyond some marketing skills and monetary assets, she had nothing to offer. Gabe's website was done. If she resolved the issues with her father and agreed to return home, she'd be able to fix the messes she'd made in Gabe's life before she left. Leave him in at least as good a situation as she'd found him, possibly slightly improved. He would protect Sebastian better than she ever could. At least then she wouldn't have to add their names to the list of people she'd disappointed.

~

GABE CIRCLED THE PARK AGAIN, then drove along the road to Amy's. He'd called her twice, and she hadn't seen Sebastian.

Damn, he'd let his ego get the best of him, barking at Katherine when she was only trying to be nice. The thing was, he didn't want her money. He wanted her time. And he wanted her touch more. Their intimacy was the type of thing people wrote books about, and she'd given him a glimpse and then frozen him out. She hadn't even been comfortable accepting his friendship when he'd brought her home from the hospital. Instead, she'd deposited a crap ton of cash in his account. He'd caught her at the store, trying to pay for his things. Even the cash she'd given Sebastian, on top of what he'd paid for Seb's work, had been a sign. And most clearly, her out-of-control anger at her father over a credit card, which was probably just a bank mistake.

Somewhere along the line, she'd learned to associate money with love, and intimacy with risk. He was sure of it, but there was no obvious way to fix it. And Sebastian had been caught in the middle of Gabe's epic fail. He slammed his hand on the steering wheel and turned his truck toward Seb's house. Maybe he'd gone home and Gabe had missed him on the first pass.

He came around the bend and found a silver sedan in the driveway with a gray-haired man behind the wheel. Who the hell was that? The hair on the back of Gabe's neck bristled—something was off. He parked and approached the cabin, ignoring the old dude. The front door was ajar. Gabe poked his head inside, scanning the interior. "Sebastian?"

"Who are you?" A blond woman, the picture of Sebastian but with lines around her eyes and mouth, appeared from one of the back rooms. She posed with her hands on her hips.

"Gabe Gallegos." He entered the house. "Is Sebastian here?"

"No. And why would a grown man be looking for my son?"

It was the same question he'd had about the man parked in the driveway until she'd shown up. "He's been helping me with some projects at my lodge."

"Well, I'm sure he'll be back. And I hope you're paying him." She disappeared back into the room only to immediately reemerge with a huge duffle bag. She staggered to the door and dropped the heavy bag with a thud. At the table, she plucked a pen from the pile and opened one of Seb's notebooks. Gabe read the note as she scrawled it across the page.

"You're moving out?" He had to be misinterpreting. "What about Sebastian?"

"He'll be fine. Sometimes he disappears, especially if he's upset. But he'll come back. Always does."

"I meant, what's he supposed to do if you're moving out? Aren't you taking him with you? He's a child. Your child."

"Seb's fine. He's as old as I was when I got pregnant with him and my family kicked me out. And he knows more about running this house and paying the bills than I do. I'll keep money in the account. And it sounds like he's got a job with you." She crossed her arms and glared.

Gabe tried for a softer tone. "If you got kicked out at his age, you know how hard it's going to be for him. A lot of necessary doors remain closed until he's eighteen. Are you okay with him suffering like that?"

"He's a free spirit, and he's fine taking care of himself. Even doing good in school. In fact, he spends too much time worrying about me. This will be better for everyone."

"What about his dad?"

She snorted. "That loser. Never even knew his real name. Found that out after my family kicked me out. It's easy being the guy. You can walk away. *We* get stuck."

It was on the tip of Gabe's tongue to tell the woman if she was old enough to fuck, then she was old enough to use birth control and be responsible. The point was moot. And he wasn't prepared to have the adoption argument with her. He couldn't imagine his family kicking him out for having a kid. If anything, they would have rallied around and taken care of everything. Just like they had when he'd lost his leg. Just like Katherine had tried to do. Who was he to judge that woman? Except that Sebastian was going to be the one to suffer. Gabe sighed.

She pushed past him. "Can't keep my man waiting too long." She giggled.

As if there were something to laugh about. As the silver car pulled away, Seb's mother didn't even glance back. Gabe's chest tightened around his heart as he rattled around the empty house. He checked the wood supplies and the pantry. Everything seemed okay. Not that it would matter for long. Child Protective Services couldn't ignore the situation any longer. He dialed the number and left a message as instructed.

If he hadn't fought with Katherine, he wouldn't have seen Seb's mom leave. Wouldn't be compelled to take action. And there was a good chance nothing would be done. Again. Seb would hate him for doing it—calling in the officials—betraying him. Katherine likely wouldn't be too happy either. But he didn't know how in the world to take care of either of them. He couldn't even take care of the lodge. How could he be responsible for living people? For a family of his own?

He waited a couple more hours. Drove around town again, peering through the crowds of tourists with zero luck. Neither Amy nor Katherine had called with good news. Gabe hoped wherever Seb was, he was happy and cared for. When he pulled into the lodge, the front light was on and one light in the main room. Maybe Katherine would be at the kitchen table waiting for him, but she wasn't. All signs of the burnt pizza were gone. As quietly as he could, he crossed to his bedroom door, rested his hand on the knob. Should he—?

No. There was nothing left to say. He'd failed to find Sebastian. It was clear she didn't have any faith he could run the lodge on his own. Better to avoid her disappointment until the morning. He turned and went upstairs to the red guest room with the en suite bathroom. Soon, Katherine would be back home in New York, finding a new job and going to art museums. Sebastian would likely be in foster care, and Gabe would adjust to living with a revolving door of strangers. If he should be so lucky.

CHAPTER 19

*K*atherine wrapped her arms around her knees, alone in an empty bed. Gabe's approaching footsteps the night before had promised relief from her guilt until he'd walked away. He'd come back to the lodge, not her. She hadn't slept the rest of the night.

Her phone vibrated on the nightstand. She checked the screen.

Daddy: *We'll land at 10:30 your time. Meet at the Grant @ 11.*

No need to reply. The order had been issued, but she took a moment to edit his entry in her contacts. He might be her father, but he no longer deserved the childish moniker. She checked the time— already nine. She flung off the covers.

After a quick shower, she wrapped her hair in a tight twist and applied her full makeup as if preparing for battle. Too bad she had to be practical instead of polished in her clothing choice. The cast was unforgiving that way. She settled on all black with silver jewelry to draw the eye up and then hobbled into the kitchen. A half carafe of coffee was still warm but not hot. Katherine gulped down a cup as she scanned the ice-cold note Gabe had left for her on the counter.

Gone to find Seb. G

In a perfect world, she'd be *with* Gabe searching for Sebastian, planning a fun night once they found him and apologized for the upset. She and Gabe would've already cleared their misunderstanding. But she didn't live in a perfect world. And Gabe wasn't interested in talking to her. But that didn't mean she couldn't fix a few things before she ultimately had to leave. She checked her handbag for her keys. She found the pouch that Madam Tiana had given her first, along with a folded-up twenty.

How odd.

Katherine had forgotten all about the purple crystal, but she tucked it in her pocket along with the cash. The stone would serve as a physical reminder about her decision to change things even if she had to tear them down and rebuild. With a resigned sense of confidence, she got in her car to go battle the dragon.

The luxury hotel where her father was staying wasn't any more special than the Ponderosa. In fact, it was colder. Impersonal. The fabric-covered benches didn't invite anyone to settle in for a good read or a movie. There was no fire in a fireplace waiting for someone to add another log. There was no Gabe waiting at the door to help her in or take her bags. If she didn't have business there, she'd never stay. Thank goodness the holiday skiers had filled the town to capacity when she'd been booking her room.

She asked a passing bellhop for directions to the restaurant, and he barely paused to point. Nice manners. The polished floors made using her crutches treacherous, but she finally got to the hostess stand and was guided to a back table where her father was seated, along with another man she instantly recognized. Katherine lifted her chin and gave an icy smile. "Richard, Marcus. How unexpected."

Marcus was attractive for a man nearing sixty. Well-kept silver hair, impeccably dressed in perfect business-casual slacks and a pullover. He rose and leaned in for a kiss as he gripped her elbow. She turned her head, allowing him to brush her cheek with his lips before freeing herself from his grasp. He wasn't a bad guy, just boring and safe.

"Katie, what have you done?" her father said in a condescending tone.

Why had she come at his command? She should have made him

wait, taken control. If only she'd thought of that two hours earlier. She let out a resigned breath. It wasn't the best place to start a negotiation from, but it wasn't a disaster—yet. "I had a skiing accident."

"When?"

"Right after I got here."

"All the more reason for you to come home. You should have called."

She clenched her jaw. Was he really going to pretend they'd been on speaking terms? Marcus pulled out the chair for her, and she sat, leaning her crutches on the table within easy reach. She browsed the menu. Eggs Benedict. As in Arnold. Perfect.

A server came, and she ordered coffee along with her meal.

"That's a lot of food. Sure you want to eat all that?" Richard asked. Between the nickname and the shot at her weight, it was clear he planned to bait her.

She sipped her coffee.

"I'm so sorry about your injury." Marcus's hand fluttered toward her, and she glared at him. He dropped his hand. "Will you be in the cast long?"

"Another two weeks. Thank you for asking."

"I'm sorry you were injured as well, Katie. I'd be happy to pay for you to see a specialist in New York. You should have the best treatment. Why wouldn't you have flown home immediately? Don't you want your leg to heal properly? I'll have you home and in the best care by Monday."

She blinked at her father. His formulaic manipulation fell completely flat. Curious. He'd once been her everything, but in the time she'd been gone, he'd been reduced to a mere mortal. No longer the god she'd worshiped to her own detriment. Perhaps it was the overall loss of his power at the firm that had diminished him and left him as compelling as a three-week-old balloon.

Richard crossed his arms. "What do you think you're going to do if you remain out here? You won't have any money. I made sure of that. Come home. I'll restore your access to your accounts."

"I'm working. Thank you for asking." She smiled sweetly at her father, swallowing her real response at his pompous assumption that he could give her something that was already hers.

"Doing what?" His voice rose. Clearly, he hadn't expected her to have other sources of income.

"Marketing, of course." Her degree was useful once again.

"What, websites for little B and Bs?"

How did he know that? "I'm sure we don't want to bore Marcus with trivial details. How are you, Marcus?"

"I miss you."

The waitress served their meals, saving Katherine from responding to the answer that had left a horrible taste in her mouth. Miss her? He didn't even know her. They'd barely dated before he'd proposed. But she'd known Gabe even less time, and she had so many feelings for him. "I'll need a box," Katherine said before the server could get away. "I just remembered I have someplace else to be."

The waitress scurried off.

"Don't be ridiculous, Katie. Eat your food."

"I'm not negotiating with you. My bank account, my credit card, my condo, and my trust fund are just that: *mine*. Your mistake, Richard, is in thinking you can manipulate me."

"And your mistake is thinking you have any control over this situation. You're needed at home. You *will* be on the plane when I take off or you're going to starve. And I will ruin anyone who tries to help you out here. So whatever clients you have, I'll know, and I will crush them. That lodge where you're staying, the Ponderosa—I'll put Mr. Gallegos out of business. You don't have an option. You. Are. Coming. Home."

The server placed the box to her side as bile rose in her throat. Posting Gabe's picture, his story, on his site had seemed so smart at the time. She blanked her face and shifted up onto her crutches. "Why are you so adamant about this?"

"I love you, Katie girl. You need to be at home. By my side."

If he loved her, he'd quit using the nickname she detested. "Are you dying?"

He paused and finally met her eyes. It wasn't just his outside that had withered. His eyes were weaker, his gaze less fierce despite his attempt to hide it. "No. But the firm is. And even though I can't directly employ you, this is your grandfather's firm. This is your legacy. You can't abandon that."

A heaviness settled in her chest. She stuffed her hand in her pocket and gripped the amethyst. "I'll think about it."

"We're leaving Sunday. Noon. Do the right thing."

She stifled her sassy response about how *he'd* know what was right, and left. Marcus trailed her. He finally spoke when they reached her car. "I'm sorry things are difficult with your father, Katherine. He's been struggling ever since the board removed him as chairman."

A chill raced through her. "I didn't know."

"I think he's embarrassed. You did a lot for him—maintaining relationships and his image."

Katherine sighed. More like she'd provided Richard with all the dirt he'd needed to bury anyone who opposed him, while smiling next to him. The perfect picture of a family, hiding the truth of how broken they were.

"I think you should have this." Marcus held up their engagement ring. "I bought it for you. When you come back, you don't have to be alone."

"Let me think about it." Because "no" would mean she'd be without a potential ally.

Marcus tucked the ring into his jacket and then reached into his back pocket, retrieving a stack of bills from his wallet. "Here. To tide you over until Sunday."

She opened her mouth to protest, but he placed a finger over her lips. "Let me do this one thing. I know this engagement didn't start off on the right foot, but I think we could be okay together. And either way, I don't want to think of you going without. Your father is in a difficult situation. But that doesn't mean it can't come out all right for us. I'll always take care of you."

"Thank you, Marcus. I'll...think about it." She let him open the door for her and help her with her crutches as she navigated into the driver's seat.

"Call me. For anything."

Katherine drove to the lodge, holding back tears. The entire conversation with Richard had been one big manipulation. If she left, she could take care of Gabe, protect him, even if he didn't want her to. She had to make sure he'd be okay. And it wasn't like her life would be awful. It would be mostly what it had been up until a month ago. Client meetings and supporting her father. Marcus wouldn't be demanding. Sex once a week or less. Her skin crawled.

But if she stayed, she and Gabe would struggle. Neither of them had an established career or a steady income. He might own the lodge property and have an income from the military, but there were taxes and maintenance. Banks weren't going to loan them money when there was no obvious method of repayment. The lodge wasn't going to provide the resources they needed to live, much less care for Sebastian. Besides, it was unclear if Gabe *wanted* her to stay at that point.

GABE'S PHONE RANG, and he pressed the button on his steering wheel to answer as he continued his search for Sebastian. "Ponderosa Lodge. Gallegos."

"Mr. Gallegos? This is Ms. Blackwell with the Colorado Department of Human Services. I'm following up on a report you filed?"

"Yeah, I called about Sebastian Tidwell. He's a minor, and his mother moved out of their home yesterday. And he's missing."

"And what is your relationship with the minor?"

Damn, the tone in her voice made Gabe's entire body tense. "He does odd jobs for me at my lodge."

"So, you're his employer?"

"Technically?"

"Is the residence adequately heated? Does he have food and refrigeration for perishables?"

"Yes. He says his mother puts money in an account for the house."

"But she's not living there?"

"Correct." He scowled. What was the woman getting at?

"This is not the first report we've had. Every time we've made a site visit in the past, either the guardian was present or the minor's location was unknown. You said the minor is missing?"

"I've been looking for him. I'm not sure he knows his mom left for good."

"All right. I'll follow up in the next few days. But the child is sixteen as of a couple of days ago."

Sebastian had a birthday and hadn't told them? Gabe's neck burned, and he rubbed it. He hadn't asked Sebastian enough about himself.

"If he's in a safe environment, has a job, and is attending school—I have to be honest, he won't be at the top of the list for foster care. We have almost eighty children on the waiting list right now. Most of them are in dangerous conditions. We have to prioritize by risk. It sounds horrible, but if you knew the stories of some I haven't been able to pull yet... We just don't have enough licensed foster families to place them."

"I understand." Gabe didn't. He couldn't understand how anyone could harm their own flesh and blood or abandon them. He'd had the privilege of growing up in a house where his parents' love and support were never a question. The idea that his experience was universal had been trampled in the military as he'd gotten to know his peers. But to see it up close and personal—it broke his rose-colored lenses and stomped them into dust. And Sebastian's story wasn't horrific enough for him to rise to the top of the at-risk list.

"If something changes, especially adversely, please call me immediately."

The woman cared, but her constraints were legit. There were only so many places to put these kids, and the ones in dire situations had to come first. He couldn't fault her, and a touch of shame washed over him.

"Thank you for all you're doing for the kids. I'll try to make sure Sebastian's okay until something can be done," he said, ending the call.

With no place left to look for Seb, Gabe drove to the county offices to address the other disaster in his world—the red-tagged construction. Ninety minutes later, he was broke and fucked. He'd paid his fine for the bathroom remodel and the deck, but he couldn't afford to apply for the required permits to continue construction. Materials had eaten up most of his savings. And while Katherine had given him a huge deposit when she'd broken her leg, he'd never touched the funds. It hadn't felt right at the time, and after they'd slept together—just no. The inspector would come by to clear the red tag inside sometime in the next few weeks. Until then, Gabe was stuck.

Back at the lodge, he didn't expect Katherine's car to be in the drive since she was always gone, but there it was. He sat in his truck long after he'd turned it off. He should talk to her. Or call his brothers or Nick. But the situation had rolled into a ball of suck that was too big for words. He closed his eyes, but he didn't even know what to pray for.

A knock on the window snapped him upright. Katherine.

"You coming inside?" She tugged on the door handle.

He pressed the button to unlock it. Cold air wafted into the cab. "No Sebastian?"

Gabe shook his head and slid from the truck.

"Amy said not to worry yet. Give it a few more days and she's sure he'll turn up."

"Hope so." He followed her inside. A fire burned in the fireplace, and the warmth cocooned him. He loved that place, but he wasn't sure how to make it work. He glanced at Katherine. Story of his life.

"We need to talk," she said.

There were few words that could universally make a man's dick shrink, but those four worked. She wasn't wrong, but, damn, he dreaded that. Couldn't they skip right to make-up sex? "Okay."

"Let's sit by the fire."

Gabe followed her and took a seat on the couch, close but not touching. Silence weighed in his gut like a boulder, but he didn't know what to say. He lifted his chin and met her eyes.

"You've been avoiding me since we had sex," she said.

Heat burned his cheeks. "I'm so sorry."

"For what, exactly?"

Not the words he'd expected. "Making you cry."

"It wasn't you." She stroked her fingers down his arm. He craved so much more. "I mean, it was, but not in the bad way you took it. Gabe, I told you I haven't had sex in years, not since my divorce. But the last time with my ex-husband? That was the reason we got divorced."

She rolled her lips between her teeth and stared into the corner.

Gabe took her ice-cold hand in his. "Can you tell me?"

She closed her eyes. "He invited another man to watch us. And I felt dirty and slutty, and I hated the rush I got from it, and it—" She squeezed Gabe's hand and blinked. "It felt like something bad and dangerous and that I wouldn't be safe if I didn't get out of there."

"He put you at risk?"

"No. That was just my reaction. But the situation was all about Andrew. I didn't know about his desires. There were signs, of course, but I ignored them. Just like he ignored what I needed."

"What do you need?" Gabe ran his free hand down her shoulder and held her.

"You." Her gaze locked on his. "You made me feel so beautiful and cared for and safe. Everything we shared was exactly how I imagined sex should be, and it was overwhelming."

She'd stolen all his words. What could he say except that he might possibly be falling in love with her? But he was too much of a mess to go there or take her there. Instead, he released his hold on her and opened his arms. Luckily, she fell into them. He wrapped her tight against his chest.

It was his turn to be honest. He swallowed hard, opened his mouth, and tried to let the truth fall out the way she had done so easily.

"I *paid* for sex the last time."

She stiffened in his arms.

"It was years ago." Fuck, it wasn't coming out right at all. "Women don't want to be with me. And I got so lonely. My scars were fresh, and I was still in rehab, and it was clear I would live, but what kind of life? I didn't yet believe that I could ever have anything close to normal. And I just wanted someone to hold me. To touch me and pretend I didn't repulse them. And I didn't trust anyone to do that, honestly. So I paid. The woman who, uh, who took my money. She was really sweet about it, even invited me to come back anytime."

"Did you go back?" Katherine's voice was tender.

"It wasn't real." The memory made his lungs ache. "I just want something real."

Katherine put her hand over his heart.

Could she feel how hard it was pounding? Admitting all of that could push her away for good. He sucked in a ragged breath because he still had to say the hardest thing. And if he didn't say it, he would regret it forever. "What we have is—well, I mean, you're leaving, and we've only known each other a short while—but it was the closest thing to real I've ever had."

"For me, too." She cupped his jaw and met his eyes. "I wish our lives were more in sync. But besides our ages…I live in New York, and you live here."

Gabe nodded and clutched her tighter. "I'm not ready to give you up yet."

She molded to him perfectly. "Me either."

Her words whispered through his shirt and into his heart. A heart he'd have to put in a protective box to survive their parting when it came.

CHAPTER 20

Katherine shifted in Gabe's embrace. She couldn't see a future with him, but she wasn't ready to give him up. "Let's go to bed."

He led her to his bedroom, and she studied him, trying to hold on to every second they had left. They undressed. Gabe, sitting on the bed, set aside his prosthetic and then lay back with his gaze locked on her.

Katherine slipped into his arms and relaxed in his hold. He smelled like cut lumber and snow. But as close as she was, a distance settled between them. The separation was like a paper cut compared to the amputation that was coming in a matter of days. "Make love to me."

Gabe's lips were on her neck in seconds; his hands cupped her naked breasts, gently squeezing. But gentle didn't match the tension that thrummed through her. The storm swirled in her chest, demanding everything Gabe could give. She'd take it all, absorb his love, destroy her heart because afterward, when she had to go, there would never be another man. She'd found the one. She just couldn't have him. She pressed him into the bed and shifted her hips, tugging the damn cast with her.

That was one thing she wouldn't miss once it was cut off.

The only thing.

Katherine took a slow, deep breath and tried to contain the ferocity of desire roiling in her.

Gabe lay out flat, arms overhead. "Take what you need, Jadis."

The restraints broke, and she covered him with her body, kissing everywhere she could reach, tugging his hair and dragging her nails down his skin, lines recording her path. The marks fed her need to possess him, to impress herself on him the way he'd done with her. She nipped his neck and sucked, repeating the process and leaving a trail of round red marks leading right to his flat coppery nipple.

His hands dug into her hips, and he groaned. With his support, she lifted her injured leg over him and rose on her knees. Flames danced in his brown eyes, and the veins of his neck pulsed. She stroked her hand over his huge fucking cock that made her pussy wet with anticipation. A bead of cum appeared at the tip, and she swiped it off, then slowly licked the length of her finger. His hips jutted up.

"Lube," she rasped.

Gabe released her and twisted to retrieve the gel. He gave it to her, and she grabbed his hand and loaded up his palm.

"Show me. I need to see exactly how much you need me."

Gabe pressed his hands together, smearing the liquid between them before grabbing his erection in both hands and working its length. She met his gaze, his movements visible in her periphery, but not nearly as important as what was happening between them. Passion. Love. Futility.

Anger pulsed through her, but she pushed it down. Saved it for later.

Because he'd covered every delectable inch, his cock was shiny and ready. She threaded her hand between his legs and caressed his balls, loving the groan he released. His hands moved faster up and down his shaft. She knocked them away and took control, guiding him to her opening and then dropping onto him with a slow, steady pressure, giving neither of them quarter until he was fully inside her. The stretch forced her to pause, wait for her body to adjust. She braced herself with her hands on his chest, and he wrapped his fingers around her wrists, holding her in place.

With the power of her thighs, she lifted up and then mimicked the pace he'd set when he'd masturbated for her. "I'm going to take such good care of you. Leave an imprint of my body forever on your beautiful cock."

Gabe's hips bucked, and she increased her pace, giving her hips a thrust at the base and rubbing her clit on his pelvis with each meeting. She locked her gaze to his, his eyelids at half-mast, his mouth contorted as he bit his lower lip. She pressed her nails into his chest, and he squeezed her wrists.

"I want you to explode inside me." She wasn't just imprinting herself on him, she was wrecking herself for anyone else. No one would ever be able to fill her, complete her, be her "one" after Gabe.

His mouth dropped open, and he released her wrists to hold on to her hips. She tightened her knees, keeping herself connected to him, raised her hands, and pinched her own nipples. When her back arched, she took him even deeper. His cock stretched her, and his hips thrust wildly while she kept the challenging pace, driving him to orgasm.

With a roar, his eyes snapped open, and he slammed her hips down as he launched himself up from the bed and into her. His gaze bored into her as he came in a shuddering eruption. He'd barely relaxed onto the mattress before he began working her clit, making sure she came as hard as he had. She allowed herself to fall over into the weightless bliss and collapsed onto his chest, panting and mindless. He traced his hands along her back, soothing and possessive.

Once she had her breathing under control, she kissed him with every wish she had for their future, and every apology that it could never be. He held tight to her, as if he could keep her, and that made it hurt even more when she pulled away.

KATHERINE STEPPED from the steamy bathroom, wrapped in a towel, to find Gabe holding out a mug. She took it and inhaled before taking a sip.

"How about some breakfast?" he asked.

"Sounds perfect, but I have meetings today."

He tilted his head to gaze at her. "Get dressed. It'll be ready when you come out."

At the table while they ate, Gabe caught her up on everything that had happened with Sebastian and CPS and the fines he'd paid, and that the county should clear the red tag any day.

"Good. You'll be able to get back to work on the remodel," Katherine said. Gabe didn't respond as enthusiastically as she'd expected. He was holding something back, but she didn't press him. "What are you going to do today?"

"Probably call some of the vets and get some skiing in." He cleared their plates.

"I can clean up."

"Nope, I got it. Need to stay in practice for innkeeping." He flashed her a smile, but it was as fake as a socialite's D cup.

"All right. I should get going." She got her crutches under her, went to Gabe, and kissed his cheek before heading out the door. As soon as she got on the road, she called her dad on speakerphone. He answered on the last ring before it would go to voicemail, a stupid game he played. But she ignored it and set a meeting for later that day. She might have to let Gabe go, but she was going to take care of a few things before she went, and Gabe could be as angry as he wanted to be, because she'd be two thousand miles away. The fact that she'd taken care of him before she left might be the only drop of peace she'd have to hold on to.

She met with two of the B and B owners together. They were best friends and seemed to agree to everything Katherine suggested for each of their sites. Especially since she could create the new sites for the same money they were paying ABBA to host. Their monthly savings would be a bonus. The best part was she'd be able to finish the work remotely.

The drive into Aspen to see her father gave her plenty of time to strategize. She could tie many of her past impulsive decisions to the immediacy of her travel. If she'd had to wait to book a commercial flight, she wouldn't have been able to run away from her messes so easily. She might not be divorced. She might not have taken the actions that led to the unraveling of the law firm. And she might have skipped a couple of failed engagements. But that was water over the runway. Before she hopped on that plane with Richard, she'd resolve her issues. She'd leave with everyone she cared about in as good a place as possible. No regrets. Exactly as the medium had foretold with the Judgement card. As a reminder to stay in control and focused on the result, she once again placed Madam Tiana's amethyst in her pocket.

"Hi, Daddy." She kissed her father's cheek. "Marcus. So good to see you. Sleep well?"

Marcus nodded and narrowed his eyes. She was overplaying her hand. Better dial it back. She tucked her hand in her pocket and toyed with the purple crystal.

"Katie," her father said. "Glad to see you're in better spirits. We ordered a couple of appetizers. Would you like a drink?"

It was barely after noon, but she could play along. "White wine. You pick."

He perused the wine list while she made idle talk with Marcus about his health and the weather. "Katherine," he said quietly while Richard ordered, discussing the quality of the by-the-glass options with the server.

"Yes, Marcus?"

He held out the ring again. "Would you wear this?"

She gave him the softest smile she could. "Not yet. I think we should spend some more time getting to know each other. See if this is right for us, not everyone else. Don't you?"

"I don't have any doubts, but it has been fast. I'm more than willing to give you all the time you need." He tucked the ring back in his suit-coat pocket.

Katherine breathed a muted sigh of relief.

"So, Katie," her father said as the server placed a half-filled glass of wine in front of her. "What have you decided?"

She swirled the glass, sniffed, and took a small sip. "I'll go home with you on Sunday."

"Good girl. I knew you'd come to your senses. Right, Marcus? Didn't I tell you?"

Marcus nodded.

"I'm sorry I made you wait for the answer. And for making you fly out here." She placed her wineglass on the table. "It was so kind of you to join my father, Marcus."

"Think nothing of it." Marcus waved his hand nonchalantly.

"But, Daddy, with you cutting me off without a cent, you've left me in an incredibly awkward situation. I made commitments to the people caring for me after my injury. And now I'll have to explain why I can't honor them. Embarrassing, really. For both of us."

Richard's back stiffened. "What?"

"I need access to my bank account and credit card to avoid breach of contract."

"Why both?"

Got him. "Well, at least my card."

He said nothing. She blinked up at him but kept silent. After another long moment passed, Marcus broke. "Rich, Katherine needs her funds. She's agreed to come home…"

"Of course, Katie *girl*." Her father plastered a huge fake smile across his face for Marcus's benefit. Katherine wasn't fooled at all. He'd purposely added "girl" to set her on edge. That moniker holding any truth had passed long ago. Bastard. But she'd won the battle. Points to Marcus for backing her up even if he was terrible at negotiation. Rule one: first one to break the silence loses.

"Can you call the company now?" She smiled sweetly as she called his bluff.

He blustered about the number, but she pulled out her card and read it to him off the back. After he'd made the call, she relaxed into her chair and adopted the persona her father had leveraged for innumerable business meetings, an air of nowhere else to be despite every tick of the clock's second hand weighing on her. Finally, the men were ready to leave, and the server brought the check.

"Let me get this." Katherine placed her reactivated credit card inside the leather folder. Everyone at the table held their breath to see if the transaction would clear—the final test of the agreement.

The server returned with smiles and platitudes. Katherine added a generous tip and scrawled her signature with an unfamiliar awareness of the power money actually wielded. It had always been plentiful, like air. Gifted in expressions that mimicked love. Used to carve a path through any resistance. But losing it, even for a few days, had given her new clarity.

Money was still a powerful tool, but it wasn't air, and it wasn't love.

Just like she had very little understanding of the science that created a breathable atmosphere, she also had very little understanding of healthy expressions of love. Her heart compressed under the weight of that realization. Too bad she wouldn't get a chance to learn from Gabe, who seemed to know all about love.

But Gabe deserved a life with someone who could give him a family. Someone who would enjoy running a B and B and building their dreams around his. For once, she wouldn't be a self-centered bitch.

Katherine stood. "I'll see you Sunday, Daddy."

"We're wheels up at noon."

She nodded and left. As fast as she could, she backtracked to the county offices, praying to get there before they closed for the weekend and ruined her plans.

CHAPTER 21

Saturday morning, Katherine nibbled on the delicious blue-corn blueberry muffin Gabe had set in front of her. "These are perfect."

"I finally figured out the recipe. Maybe I should get started on a second one. Can't have too many good breakfast foods when you run a B and B." He filled her coffee and dropped into the chair next to hers. "What are you doing today?"

She scrambled for the small talk that had come so easily the day before. But Gabe mattered to her. She should tell him about leaving, and she would, but not yet. "I need to take some pictures at the B and Bs that have contracted me for the website redesigns. I gave them assignments to make their places more inviting in the photos. Maybe you could come with me?"

"I could do that. Since my own projects are on hold."

"You cleared up the permit issues?" Would he tell her about the outstanding permit fees?

"Mostly. The *fines* are paid, and they're going to clear the red tags on Monday. I started the permit process, even submitted some simple sketches. The build-outs are minor. I'm not moving any supporting walls or anything, so my hand drawings should be good enough."

"I didn't know you had drawings. Can I see them?" She could take the impression of the redone lodge with her when she was gone, and maybe Gabe would update the photos on the website afterward. Not that she would stalk his site. Not at all.

He came back and laid the pages in front of her. "My brother drew the deck, and I did the two of the attic space."

Katherine perused the plans, wishing she would be there to see them brought to life. But she didn't belong in his future. "This deck is going to be spectacular. And I love the way you folded the attic stairwell to save space."

"After the deck's done, I'll see about adding some outside doors from the bedrooms. But that will be later."

"One step at a time. This is a lot to accomplish as it is."

"When we drink that first cocktail, watching the sunset over the valley, it'll all be worth it."

Katherine swallowed down the loss of that moment that would never be. "You know, some of the other owners aren't as handy as you. Have you considered contracting out to supplement the guest income?"

"I hadn't, but since I'm going with you anyway, I'll see what they have to say. That means more permits." Gabe fake shivered. "Thought I left all that government paperwork behind when I retired from the military."

Katherine laughed with him. It was a lame joke, but she'd take anything to lighten her mood.

After several hours of driving around, talking to the other innkeepers, and taking tons of pictures, Katherine was ready for a break. "Can I buy you lunch? Or, well, it's late enough—dinner?"

"Sure." Gabe grinned. "Although I think I should pay, since I have enough work lined up to keep us fed for the foreseeable future."

"Fine, you can buy early dinner. And a glass of wine. I'm exhausted from all that talking."

"The owners love you. You're like the pied piper leading all of them away from ABBA."

"I don't want to ruin their organization, but I don't think it's serving them. Maybe they can reorganize after the power is stripped from Betty." Much like the firm's board had done with her father.

They parked the truck and walked down the main street. At the hardware store, Katherine froze mid-pace. "Sebastian?"

A blond head lifted from the shelter of the doorway. His eyes went wide. "Hey, Katherine. Gabe."

Gabe moved in close. "We missed you, buddy. We were just about to get some dinner. Want to join us?"

Katherine's heart pounded. Gabe was right to play it casual, but she ached to grab the boy in her arms and squeeze him while demanding to know where he'd been. But he wasn't hers, and the day after next, she wouldn't be around to take care of him anyway. Part of her heart shredded at the loss.

Maybe she could set up a college fund for him? But first, he had to accept their offer to feed him.

Sebastian's wary gaze bounced between them, but then he nodded. The tension in Katherine's spine that she hadn't been aware of released.

After getting seated, they talked about the menu. Katherine was content to avoid the real issues. The place was efficient, and full plates were set in front of them a few minutes after they placed their orders. The burgers were juicy, and the fries were hot, and she used eating as an excuse for silence. But the elephants in the room were preparing to stampede.

Katherine took a sip of white wine to clear her throat and gather a drop of courage. "Sebastian, we owe you an apology."

"For what?" Seb's face was a picture of confusion.

"Arguing in front of you," Gabe answered as if they'd planned the conversation. "We made the situation uncomfortable. And we're both sorry. We've been looking for you since that day."

"Sorry about that." He lifted one shoulder. "I didn't leave because you were fighting. I left when I saw the badge. They keep trying to take me from my mom."

"That was the county inspector for the construction," Gabe said.

"Where were you?" Katherine couldn't imagine how scary it was for Sebastian to feel like he had to hide from the people trying to protect him.

"I hung out with my buddy Colin. His mom works shifts at the ER. She's cool with me staying when she does the overnight ones."

"I'm glad you're okay. But there's something else." Katherine glanced up at Gabe. It was his story to tell, but Sebastian needed to know his mom had moved out.

"Have you been by your house?" Gabe asked.

"Not yet. Going there tonight." Sebastian rubbed the fuzz on his jaw. "Colin's mom is off for the next four days."

"I went by there a few times, looking for you," Gabe said. "I ran into your mom."

"Yeah?" Sebastian straightened in his chair and glanced at the exit.

"She was packing her things, buddy." Gabe's tone was gentle, but Katherine could see the wound the words created as soon as they hit Sebastian's ears. Her own body reacted with a tightening around her chest and a spike of pain between her shoulders that surged into her head, exactly how it had been years ago when she'd found out *her* mom had left.

"Packing?" Sebastian's voice carried the same shock in his widened eyes.

"Yeah." Gabe gripped Seb's shoulder briefly. "But you're welcome to stay with us."

Katherine masked her wince at the word "us."

"Maybe." Sebastian wiped his hands on his napkin. "But I should go check on the place tonight. Don't like to leave it too long."

"Of course," Gabe agreed. "But let's finish these burgers first. They're too good to waste." He took a big bite as if to prove his words. It worked. Sebastian finished his meal. Katherine choked down a few more bites while the conversation she still had to have with Gabe sat like a lead weight in her stomach.

As they were leaving the restaurant, Katherine paused on the side-walk. "Guys, can we hit the grocery store before we drive you back?" She planned to buy Sebastian some fresh food and take care of him at least a little. "I think I saw some prepaid cell phones there, too. That way, you can call Gabe if you need him?"

Sebastian nodded, and Katherine released the breath she'd been holding. So far, so good.

In the store, she wheeled a tiny cart around, adding fresh fruit and vegetables for both households. "Milk?"

Sebastian nodded and took the half-gallon carton from her to place it carefully next to the bananas, in front of the packaged cell phone. Katherine had the clerk add on ninety days of unlimited service. It would be enough for him and Gabe to decide what to do long-term.

"Anything else?" She glanced from Gabe to Sebastian as they both shook their heads.

Gabe reached for his wallet, but Katherine stayed his hand. "I'm getting this."

He clenched his jaw but, with a quick glance at Sebastian, nodded. Katherine hoped the rest of what she had to tell him went as easily, even though that was impossible.

"Can you take me home?" Sebastian asked as soon as they left the store.

Any other time, Katherine would try to talk Sebastian into staying at the lodge, but she and Gabe were likely to have another fight when he found out what she'd done. She dreaded the moment she had to confess she was leaving.

Gabe parked the truck in front of Seb's house. It had the air of abandonment already. A fresh wave of guilt washed over Katherine. "Gabe, if you check the firewood stores, I'll help Seb get this food in the refrigerator and set up his cell phone with our numbers."

"Of course." Gabe handed the bags to Seb, and Katherine followed him inside.

Seb dropped the sacks on the counter and quickly placed the perishables in the small refrigerator. The light turned on, so the appliance was still working. After Sebastian found a pair of scissors, they broke into the plastic packaging that held the phone. With the help of the internet, they got the basic service set up. She sent Sebastian a text so he would have her number. "You know you can call me anytime. For anything. No matter where I am."

"You're going back to New York?"

"I have to." The space between her shoulders tightened. "I have a home there that needs my attention, just like this one needed yours."

"Gabe's gonna miss you."

"I'm hoping you can keep him distracted. Help him finish the deck?"

"Yeah." Sebastian toyed with the phone. "You ever coming back?"

She could, but would Gabe want to see her again? Would he have already moved on? "I hope so."

Gabe stomped his feet outside the door and then joined them in the kitchen. "All done. You got plenty of wood."

"Thanks."

"Come for dinner tomorrow?" Gabe asked.

"Okay." Sebastian stood.

Katherine hesitated at the door before they left. "If you need anything…"

Sebastian launched himself into hugging her. She held him tight for the brief moment he was there. He dropped his arms almost immediately, but his form had branded itself into her skin, into her heart. Her eyes stung. "Call me."

Sebastian nodded, and Katherine staggered out to the truck, where Gabe was already unlocking the doors.

GABE HELD his tongue as they drove back to the lodge while Katherine fidgeted. Something clearly weighed on her mind. Finally, as they turned onto the road that led to their driveway, Katherine shifted in her seat to face him. "I'm so relieved Sebastian is okay and that we found him in time."

"In time for what?"

She glanced away. "Before he was hurt or anything."

Gabe narrowed his eyes at her, but she clamped her jaw shut.

Something was definitely up. He parked the truck and led the way into the front room. Every time he crossed the threshold, he was torn. Part of him was relieved to be home, and part of him dreaded the responsibility of owning the lodge. Maybe there was something else he could do with his life, but he didn't know what. The construction gigs would be challenging and fun, but there were only so many improvements innkeepers could afford. And if he'd planned to work construction for the rest of his life, he could have stayed in California with his brother.

He helped Katherine with her coat. "Want some wine?"

"Wine would be perfect. Gabe…I have some things I need to tell you."

The hamburger soured in Gabe's gut even though he'd known that was coming in the truck. "Sure. Let me get a fire started, and then I'll grab a bottle and a couple of glasses."

"I can start the fire."

Gabe turned for the kitchen as Katherine thumped across the living room. By the time he'd uncorked the bottle and returned, she was already on one end of the couch. He took the middle seat and poured, handing her a glass before settling back, dreading what came next.

"I have to apologize."

A weight landed on Gabe's chest. "For what?"

"I did something for you."

He sipped the red wine, letting it wash over his palate. "Oh yeah?"

She twisted the wineglass in her grasp. "I paid your permit fees."

Flames erupted in Gabe's brain, but he kept his voice modulated. "Why would you do that?"

"To help. You have such a hard time letting me help you. It's like you don't even—"

"Don't even what?"

"I'm not saying this right." She shook her head. "I don't want to manipulate you."

"And I don't want your money. It makes me feel like I'm a fucking charity case or, worse—your whore." Gabe set the wineglass down and paced over to the fireplace. There wasn't enough air in the room. "If all I wanted was your dough, I would have spent the money you paid for the room."

"What?" Katherine set her own glass down. "Why didn't you use that?"

"I'm in a relationship with you, Jadis. I've been attracted to you from the moment I saw you. And, yeah, I had to get past that New York...*directness* of yours, but now I love it. I love you. I don't want a sugar momma. I want someone who believes in me. Someone who wants to spend time with me, give me their love."

Katherine gasped and seemed to shrink into the couch. "You love me?"

"Yeah."

Her heart expanded in her chest so hard it might burst. "I love you, too, Gabe. That's the reason I've done everything I have. Why I've made some really difficult decisions. I want you to have your dream."

"What about *your* dreams? What if I can't see myself doing this without you?"

Tears ran down Katherine's face. "We...we don't always get what we want."

"Then maybe I should just sell the place and go back to California."

"Maybe you should. Because I have to go back to New York."

"I know you have a place there and things to take care of, but—"

"I'm leaving tomorrow." She blinked up at him with teary blue eyes.

"No." He dropped back onto the couch and grabbed her hands in his. "It's too soon. Your leg. And...I'm not ready."

She swallowed hard and gripped his fingers. "My father's in Aspen with my ex-fiancé."

"What?" Gabe freed himself from her grasp.

"He flew out after he cut off my accounts. I met with him and negotiated getting my credit card back so I could pay for the permits before I left. As a gift to you. For everything you've done for me. You changed me, Gabe. I wish—"

"I never asked you for any of that. I told you to stop buying things.

And now you have the audacity to sit here and tell me you agreed to go home *tomorrow* for me?" Gabe stood. "You don't get it. I. Don't. Want. Your. Fucking. Money." He brushed a hand through his hair, anger renewing. "And what the fuck with your dad? He has the authority to cut you off? You're a grown fucking woman. Don't people like you know lawyers or something? Or is this all just an excuse to pay off your boytoy and run away?"

"Gabe...I love—"

"Don't. You throw words around like weapons to get your way. Just like you use your money. Do you even know the definition of the word *love*? Do you even know *how* to love someone? Do you even *want* to?" He clutched the back of his neck. The situation was so broken. He dropped his hands in defeat. "I can't do this with you." Gabe stomped up the stairs, away from Katherine's fake sobs and her pitying looks.

Fuck.

Losing her, the idea of her he'd built in his heart, hurt worse than the loss of his leg ever had. He'd fallen in love with someone who couldn't love him back.

CHAPTER 22

Katherine stayed awake all night, hugging her good leg to her chest and wishing Gabe was in bed with her. Their final night together had been a total loss.

"I don't want your fucking money." He'd hurled the words like rocks as he'd distanced himself. He didn't want her money, he wanted *her*. And her money couldn't fix that.

"Do you even know the definition of the word love?*"* The truth of his words stung. She hadn't. But he'd been teaching her.

Gabe had also given her the solution with a glare in his eye, so accusing, so disappointed: *"Don't people like you know lawyers or something?"*

She did. A huge number of them, in fact. All of them connected to her father. And the thought of taking legal action against Richard grated against everything she'd been raised to believe about family. Even her mother had never called a divorce lawyer.

A chill washed over her. She should have contacted a lawyer as soon as Richard had interfered with her accounts. Despite her aversion, she would. But as she considered all the attorneys she'd ever met or worked with, only one stood out—Edward Strauss.

Ned.

And he hated her. Had every right to hate her for what she'd done to him and the people he loved, especially because one of them was her ex-husband. If she called Ned, what could she possibly say to convince him to help her? She continued to brood over the problem, turning it in her mind like that classic colored-cube puzzle. Her situation was nearly as impossible to solve. She fell into an uneasy sleep, trying every combination possible.

With the dawn came clarity, resoluteness, and an unfamiliar sense of humility. She would take whatever she had coming and beg, starting with the best apology she could formulate. And not as a precursor to manipulating him. An honest atonement.

No scent of coffee or movement in the house, and the clock told her it was hours later than she'd guessed. But that was Gabe's home, and he'd be back. Before she could find an excuse, she dialed Ned's number, hoping he'd remember the time, so many years ago, when he'd told her she could come to him for anything. Technically, he'd never taken back the offer.

The call connected. "Edward Strauss."

"Ned? It's Katherine. You told me once if I ever—" She struggled for air and took a second to breathe. "I need to apologize to you and your family. And I need your help. I know you don't want to hear either of those, but I hope you'll find it in your heart to listen."

"Katherine, slow down."

The sound of Ned's rich, warm voice through the phone broke her control, and her eyes released a flood of tears. "I'm sorry. I'm so sorry," she choked out between sobs. "For everything."

"What's happened?"

"Everything. Everything's happened. I didn't have anyone to help me. And I came to Colorado. And I fell in love with Gabe. Which is stupid. No one falls in love that fast. And Amy. Amy is my only friend. And Sebastian. He is such a great kid, and he needs a mom, and I could try, at least. But Richard is demanding I go back to New York, and he brought Marcus. If I leave, I'll lose everything. And if stay, Richard will ruin everything. I don't know what to do." Tears streamed down her face. She didn't care.

She couldn't regain control. She'd been in control for weeks, or at least faking it. The only person she'd ever asked for help in her life was her father, yet he was the cause for that phone call—a call and an apology she should have made long ago. That made her cry harder. "And you hate me." She took a deep, shuddering breath. "I owe all of you, each of you, an apology. It seems so inadequate after everything that happened."

"Where in Colorado are you?" Ned asked, kindness coloring his voice.

"Near Aspen, in a little town called Alabaster. Richard fired me on New Year's Day. And the last place I remembered being happy was Aspen. I only planned to visit for a couple of weeks, but I broke my leg skiing, and then Gabe—" Her breath caught. "He's wonderful."

"Leaving the firm leads to great things." His smile resonated through the phone. That gave her pause.

"I need a lawyer, Ned. One that won't be influenced by my father's company." She braced herself for rejection.

"For what?"

"Richard cut off my trust fund, my credit card, and my bank account to blackmail me to go back to New York. The bank is stonewalling me, probably because he's on their board. I could put my condo up for sale, but I have no way of knowing when it might sell. The only credit card I have was on his account, and he blocked it. Well, he took the block off, but when I don't get on the plane at noon today—"

"I see."

"I know I have no right to ask you for help. But..."

"I can't commit to that. I'd have to discuss it with Jack and Missy. I know that's not what you want to hear, but their feelings matter to me. Can I reach you at this number?"

"Yes."

After reaching out to Ned, she considered calling her father, but why? There was no way she was getting on the plane. Ned would probably turn her down, but he might recommend another attorney. Maybe Amy knew someone. But the last thing Katherine would do was return to New York. Gabe might still evict her. At least she had an open-return ticket on a commercial flight. But if she left at her father's insistence, ran once again when the situation became difficult, she'd spend the rest of her life regretting the loss of Gabe. And Sebastian. And Amy.

Amy.

Amy had to have some advice. That's what friends did, right? Supported each other in the midst of a disaster. Katherine had never had a true friend. She winced. Before she froze with doubts, she hurried to her car, ready to test the bounds of her new friendship.

GABE STARED AT THE CEILING. The paint looked good. The mattress was incredibly comfortable. The lodge was taking shape, and he didn't give a shit. He waited for the sounds of Katherine leaving, unable to bear the idea of saying goodbye. And, really, what point was there to getting up? He couldn't take a shower if she was still in his room. Eating sounded like a horrible plan. Sebastian had asked for some time alone. The construction projects were frozen. He dropped his forearm over his eyes, blocking out the light that beckoned from a beautiful blue sky. He could go skiing, but even that would require too much effort. Why couldn't it be overcast and raining?

He shouldn't have been so harsh since Katherine had finally opened up and been honest. But it hurt that she would dump him with almost no warning. He'd been reconsidering his entire future, and at no point had his possible plans included leaving her. Why was it so easy for her to abandon him?

Fuck. He couldn't continue to wallow in bed without losing the last shreds of his self-respect. With a grunt, he dragged himself out from under the covers, put on his leg, and tossed on the clothes he'd been wearing the day before. At the top of the stairs, he paused. No sounds rose. She must still be sleeping or packing. Hell, she might already be gone. He screwed up some courage and trod down the staircase.

Nothing. But his bedroom door was shut. Her coat was still on the peg near the front door. He slid on his jacket and knit cap and faced the bright Colorado day.

The tightness in his throat eased—her rental car was still there, too. He shuffled to the side of the house that faced out over the hilly valley. If he lived a hundred years, he'd never tire of the view or the air or the lifestyle of being in the Colorado Rockies. Despite his threats, he had no intention of returning to California except as a last resort.

But what the hell should he do?

Even the perfect view didn't fill the aching space in his chest. A sensation that took him back to living in the hospital—to the last time he'd faced a terrible loss. That was a slippery mental slope.

He retrieved his phone from his back pocket and dialed the one man who would understand the intensity of his confusion. His former captain and good friend.

"Thor. Long time no talk." Nick's cheerful voice matched the weather, dragging Gabe a small way out of his emotional hole.

"Saint. How's married life?"

"The best, man. Noelle's got another show in Florida soon, so we'll go see my parents and maybe hit up Disney World. She's mastered stick shift and is scaring the life out of me with that car."

"Should have got her a Humvee."

Nick laughed. "She, and most of Tucson, would probably agree with you. But she just looks so damn sexy in that red hot rod."

Gabe forced a chuckle. "I bet."

"What's going on with you? How's the lodge? Did that long-term rental work out?"

Nick's uncanny ability to pierce directly into the pain point of his team was still in effect. "That's why I called."

"We can come back out as soon as we get back or on the way back from Florida."

"Nah." Gabe yanked the zipper on his coat higher and paced. "It's nothing like that. My renter, the one who booked for two weeks, she stayed."

"She?"

"I fell in love with her."

"Good problem to have. Usually." Nick had experience with falling in love with the perfect person who was also the completely wrong choice. He would understand and maybe have advice.

Gabe spilled out everything that had happened with Jadis and how much he didn't want to run the lodge as a lodge. "I don't know what to do. About any of it." The front door clicked shut, and he spun in time to see Katherine pick her way across the pea gravel to her rental car. Gabe's throat closed as she pulled away.

"Gabe? You still there?" The urgency in Nick's voice snapped Gabe back enough to speak.

"She left. She just got in her car and left."

"Slow down. Breathe with me."

Gabe focused on the sound of Nick counting and breathing slowly in and out, matching his pattern until the adrenaline rush subsided.

"Good," Nick said. "Now, did she have luggage with her?"

"No, but she's got money. She could just buy new clothes."

"Pause. Think. Women might buy all new clothes, but they don't leave their toiletries behind. Especially someone like you described."

"She *told* me she's leaving this morning." In response, he'd blown up. Walked away. Broken up with her.

"If she's not back in an hour, call her or text her."

Gabe agreed and told Nick he'd call after he found out anything. But there was no question in his mind: Katherine was leaving him. When she'd responded in fear to her father's threats, instead of working through her options with her logically, Gabe had attacked. His own insecurities had torn them apart. Deep down, he couldn't believe a woman like Katherine could love him. She'd said she did. Had no reason to lie. He scrubbed his hand down his face. Damn, he'd been a bastard.

CHAPTER 23

*K*atherine carefully navigated the narrow sloped roads down from the lodge toward the town. Snow piles lined the edges. She came to a stop sign next to a park with an empty playground.

Her phone rang. Probably one of the B and B owners. Katherine tapped the green button on her cell and then pressed speaker. "This is Katherine."

"Katherine? It's Ned."

"Hello." Thirty-pound butterflies flapped in her constricted stomach, waiting to hear what he would say. Instead of driving on, she pulled into the parking lot for the park.

"Wanted to let you know we're coming up today."

"We? Here? Today?" Hopefully, the squeak in her voice hadn't been clear over the cell.

"Jack and Missy are concerned about my mental health, but yes. I explained to them this may be the opportunity for you to divest yourself from the toxicity of Richard Wallace."

"Things are so different." She pressed her hand to her chest briefly. "I'm different. I have had weeks to think about...well, everything.

Getting Missy fired. All the dirty work I did for my father. I have to get free of him." Shame stole her voice.

"I think he's had far too much control over you for far too long. So, this *one* time, I'm going to get involved."

"I understand. I know I don't deserve your help, but I'm grateful."

"We need to move fast before he permanently hides or destroys your assets."

"But you don't have to fly up." If he stayed in Santa Fe, she wouldn't have to face Missy and Andrew. Or Jack, as Ned called him.

"It's been a while since we had a vacation, and Missy's never skied. It's on her bucket list."

"Oh." Katherine swallowed hard. "Well, the skiing *is* amazing. I haven't done much, obviously. But there's fresh powder."

"I'll call when we land."

"Thank you, Ned." Katherine noted the time after ending the call. If he was flying from the airport in Santa Fe, he'd be in Aspen in a matter of hours. Her hands locked on the steering wheel like it was a life preserver and she was in danger of drowning.

At the restaurant, Katherine fumbled into the chair across from Amy. The crutches were getting beyond old. When they cut that damn cast off her leg, she'd be dancing in celebration. "Thanks for meeting me."

Amy handed her a menu. Once Katherine set it back on the table, Amy asked, "What's going on?"

Katherine glanced away as if the right words would be found in the corner of the plastered walls. "I hurt Gabe."

"What? Why?" Amy's hand went to her chest.

"Accidentally. And his feelings, not his body."

"Good thing. The man has a nice body; no need to go ruining it." She relaxed back into her chair with a smile.

An answering smile teased Katherine's lips. "My father flew out with my ex-fiancé to blackmail me to come home. I was going to do it, so I told Gabe I had to leave today and why. And, well—"

"And you didn't tell me?"

"I've kind of been a wreck over it. And Gabe. I'm not used to having a good friend. Sorry." The regrets kept compiling. Katherine would have to become a much better person to remain in Colorado. "But I can't go."

"So you're not leaving."

Katherine shook her head.

Their waiter appeared, his long hair tied in a man bun and a small black apron wrapped around his trim waist. He rattled off the specials. Nothing appealed to Katherine, who had heavy-hitting butterflies cage fighting in her gut. She ordered a salad. Maybe she could choke down a few bites.

"So what about the fiancé?" Amy asked. "Did he *know* he was an ex when you came out here? And why am I just now hearing this story? We need more girl talk. With a bottle of wine."

"I broke it off before I left New York." Katherine flapped her hand to wave away the drama. "And for that talk, we'll need more than one bottle. I've been engaged several times. None of them meant anything —the men who asked me were business associates of my father's, and that's also the only reason I was dating them."

Amy frowned. "You know that's creepy, right?"

"Now I do. At the time, when I was in the middle of it, everything just happened. Who knows, I might have even married this one. He's nice."

"That's not a reason to get married."

Katherine shrugged. "Why did you get married?"

Amy echoed Katherine's earlier hand flap. "Lots of reasons. None of them any better than yours. But we're talking about you and Gabe. What happens if you don't go?"

"I'm basically going to be broke until I sell my condo. Especially since I just hired a lawyer."

"A lawyer? For the blackmail?" Amy's brow wrinkled.

Katherine winced. "My father's on my bank account, my credit card, and my investment accounts. I'm embarrassed to admit I never altered the ownership after my trust matured."

"And your dad is holding up the funds." Amy nodded. "Good thing you knew who to call."

"He's my ex-husband's lover." Katherine couldn't believe she was telling Amy everything, but she had to talk to someone. Her dad had always been her sounding board when life got complicated. Gabe was in no mood to listen to her. And if she was really going to stay in Colorado, be Amy's friend, then she had to trust her with the truth.

"What about the condo you want to sell? Is that in your dad's name, too?"

"No, mine." Thank god her maternal grandmother had willed the money directly to her instead of doing all the crazy trust stuff her paternal grandfather had done.

"You sure it's a good idea to hire the guy who's sleeping with your ex?"

"He's the best there is at contract law. But it's going to be...complicated since he's flying up today with my ex and their girlfriend."

"Oh. *That's* a story."

"You have no idea. And I didn't handle any of it well. Not my divorce, and definitely not my ex-husband becoming involved with another woman and another man." Katherine took a sip of water.

The waiter returned and placed their plates on the white table-cloth. Katherine poked a fork into the artichoke heart on top of romaine leaves.

"What are you going to do if you stay?" Amy asked.

"I have a couple of ideas. The websites for the ABBA members first. If that goes well, I'll have references, and then I can market to the other hospitality businesses in the area. And I'd like to help with Sebastian. But mostly, I plan to assist Gabe with the B and B if he still wants to do it."

"If?" Amy's eyes were wide.

"I get the impression he's not enjoying it as much as he thought he would. He hasn't asked me to turn the reservation system back on."

"We all have those days." Amy half shrugged. "But if you don't love it, it can wear you down."

"Whatever his dream is, I want to support him."

"Does he know you love him?"

Katherine flinched. "I told him. Not sure he believes me since we were talking about me leaving at the time. And then there's the issue of Sebastian. We've become so attached to him."

"You know, if you stayed, you could apply to become foster parents for Sebastian. With Gabe."

Katherine froze with her fork midair. Could she?

Could they?

Would Gabe want to do that with her?

She stuffed a bite of tomato in her mouth and tried to figure out how to change the topic. Luckily, Amy veered off onto promotion plans for Valentine's Day, decorating trends, and a mystery book she'd been reading set in New Mexico. The conversation flowed easily, and Katherine finished her salad, more relaxed than she'd been in days. She adored having a real friend who believed in her. The decision to stay was the right one.

As soon as she returned to her car, her phone rang again. *Richard.* Might as well answer. She straightened her spine. "Richard."

"You're late."

"I'm not coming." Katherine slipped her hand in her pocket and wrapped it around the smooth amethyst.

"Game playing? This is so beneath you."

Richard's confidence was foreboding. Katherine steeled her spine for what was coming.

"But not unexpected." Richard chuckled. "I've had a private investigator trailing you for the past week. Your friend, Ms. Davis, did you two have a nice lunch?"

Katherine glanced around through the windows of her rental car. Followed? Her father was insane.

"And that teenager you're so fond of, it'd be a shame if he were arrested for shoplifting."

Ice ran through Katherine's veins. Her father had done far worse than setting someone up for shoplifting. But it would devastate Sebastian, potentially ruin his future. "You unmitigated bastard."

"On your way, then?"

"I'll be there in one hour." She hung up.

Katherine released the amethyst and started her car.

～

THE ASPEN AIRPORT nestled against a mountain covered with patchy snow. Rows of private jets rested under a crystal-blue sky dotted with puffy clouds. Katherine turned right off the main road into the town and found the lot for the private plane terminal. A brown pitched-roof building with a stone facade. Islands of pines, interrupted by bare aspens, kept the airport from looking like what it was, a giant pavement parking lot for the elite to drop in and ski. She'd traveled through a lot of private airports. It was one of the nicest in appearance. But none of that mattered, because she was there to face the man trying to steal away her happiness. Again.

She entered the building and scanned the room. A flight concierge sat behind a raised round counter. An empty lounge with low-slung leather furniture invited the passengers to rest before the arduous task of climbing the stairs to the body of their planes. On the edges of the room, desks held sizable monitors attached to what Katherine assumed were the most modern of computers. A few of them were occupied, but none by Richard. Toward the back wall of windows was a bar. Of course. Richard and Marcus occupied two stools, highballs in their hands. Two old men day-drinking while they attempted to ruin her life.

Katherine clenched her jaw and forced the crutches to move her in their direction. Marcus noticed her first and rose.

"You're here. Do you need me to get your bags?"

"I don't have any." She shifted onto the stool closest to Richard.

"An excuse to buy new?" Her father curled his lip. The smug glint in his eye demanded she kick him with her cast. But she refrained.

"Should we call the pilot?" Marcus asked. "Let him know the last of our party arrived."

"No." Katherine's voice was louder than her father's yes. "I agreed to come to the airport. I didn't agree to get on a plane."

"I think I made it clear what would happen if you didn't." Richard swallowed the last of his drink.

As he set it down, Katherine gripped his wrist. "Richard—"

"You used to call me Daddy."

"You *used* to take care of me. But that hasn't been true for longer than I cared to admit. I've been taking care of you. You fired me, and the board still removed you as chair." Katherine narrowed her eyes. "Why is that?"

"That's not public knowledge. There's been no announcement." Richard whipped his head toward Marcus.

"I'm surprised it wasn't more than that. Haven't they completed the audit?" Katherine was stabbing in the dark, but with confidence.

Richard flinched. Bull's-eye.

"I imagine the losses associated with the failed merger to the Simmons' law firm stung for the partners who are so heavily invested in *our* firm." Katherine paused. Smiled. "Imagine if they knew how much you paid Simmons under the table." She shook her head.

"I don't—you have no proof of that," Richard sputtered.

"Are you sure?"

Richard scoffed. "The amounts were negligible. If you even think about talking to the auditors, I'll have your little friend, the boy, arrested for something far worse than shoplifting."

"Your trademark move. Destroy the other side with false drug charges, prostitution stings, or even loading their computers with child porn. Very effective. In the past. But you forget, *Daddy Dearest*, I know everyone you've ever used to do your dirty work. Who knows, I might even have...receipts."

"So what? Whatever you have only indicts them."

"Not if the documents are emails from your *super-secret* private account. Did you think while I was digging up legitimate dirt on everyone else I wouldn't bother to look into you as well?"

"You don't know what you're talking about." Richard's face was red, and his hand shook as he raised his empty glass toward the bartender. "You don't have any evidence."

"I might not. But then again, I might. I've never wanted to hurt you. It never even occurred to me because you're my dad. But if you push this, if you hurt the people I love—I will put every resource, every devious trick I ever learned, every bit of dirt I have toward the mission of destroying you."

"Who do you think taught you all those devious tricks, Katie girl?"

"You merely put me on the path, Richard. The pupil has far exceeded the teacher."

"Won't stop me from incarcerating, what's his name, Sebastian. Or ruining Gabriel's business. Or Amy's. Or Deborah's. Shall I continue? I know every person you've met with while you were playing out here. Pretending to be the big-shot web marketer with a degree from Columbia. What a waste of money that was."

"Maybe for you. Just like *my time* with the firm feels like it was wasted. Now."

"Hey, uh...maybe we should just let this go for now." Marcus bobbed on his chair, trying to get her attention as well as her father's. "It's a long flight. Tensions are high. But, Katherine, you're flying home with us, right?"

"No." Katherine crossed her arms.

Richard's face tightened, his mouth screwed up, and she braced for the next vile onslaught. Then he gulped, his neck shaking with it, and his eyes went wide. Katherine turned on the barstool. Behind her stood Ned, Missy, and Andrew, her ex-husband, who everyone called Jack. Tension pulsed so hard Katherine expected a window to break. The bartender slapped down Richard's drink and quickly retreated.

"Katherine." Ned's deep voice shattered the roaring silence. "So good to see you. But you didn't have to meet us here. I thought we were catching up at the hotel later."

Katherine could kiss Ned. So fast to grasp the situation. "Serendipity." She fake smiled. "Richard asked me to come to the airport so he could explain how he wasn't just stealing my money. He was going to frame a teenager for a felony and have him arrested. As well as ruin several people's livelihoods. I can't imagine what might prompt this level of motivation. Can you?"

"I have a few ideas." Ned put his arm across the back of Richard's stool and bent close to his ear. "Richard. You and I talked about some of the things I know when I left the firm. The more...innocuous. But you should be aware, I've been retained as Katherine's lawyer, and I'm going to do everything necessary to get her access to her funds. If you make it difficult for me, I'll return the favor."

Richard sucked his back tooth and then pursed his lips. "A misunderstanding. Katherine is confused. You know they held her for observation for a concussion."

"What?" The question burst out of Katherine, but Ned stayed her with a hand.

"Her accident was weeks ago. She was medically released. I suspect you may have been confused about that detail. And now that you've seen with your own eyes, with an independent *witness*—" Ned nodded to Marcus, who shrank into his barstool "—all your concerns have been cleared up, and you *will* release Katherine's funds." Ned leaned closer.

"Fine." Rage burst in that one word.

Ned straightened but didn't release the barstool.

"Call the pilot," Richard snapped at Marcus.

"Ned, can I give you a lift to your hotel?" Katherine asked. "My rental is right out front, and I have plenty of room for luggage."

"How kind of you to offer. We can have a late afternoon snack and get caught up." Ned's eyebrow was raised, and Katherine understood that would be the part where she convinced Ned that she'd changed and he should follow through with helping her. After how he'd dealt with Richard, she could stomach some groveling.

"Katherine, I'll fix your accounts tomorrow," Richard said in a choking voice. "You should call your mother. She's worried about you."

His skin had a gray tone, and Katherine worried whatever he faced back home might be beyond anything she could have helped him with even if she had returned. She should tell him to get a lawyer. Tell him to stop playing games. Instead, she gave him something he'd never asked for before—a drop of honesty. "I still love you, Dad. Always will. No matter what."

She secured her crutches and left with her head high to go face the sins of her past.

CHAPTER 24

Katherine's spacious SUV shrank when it was filled with three people who had every reason to despise her. Ned sat in the passenger seat, holding her crutches out of the way. Andrew—no, Jack—sat directly behind her and Missy behind Ned. Every time Katherine swiveled her gaze to change lanes, she caught sight of the woman that could have been a younger version of herself if Katherine ignored the scowl. Should she tell Missy that would cause wrinkles?

Probably not.

In a few minutes that passed like hours, they were at the hotel, and valets were swarming the vehicle, helping everyone out and gathering the bags.

"Check-in isn't for another hour," Ned said with a glance at his watch. "Let's catch our breath in the restaurant."

Katherine inhaled deeply and slowly released it, then followed the united trio, dreading what would come next. They were seated near a bay of windows that looked out over the picturesque town with the snow-covered mountains in the distance. Ned ordered wine and four glasses and some appetizers. She had to break the ice for the real conversation. The one they'd flown up for.

"You look good, Ned. Retirement agrees with you." It was a lame start, but nice. Nice was better than fighting.

"I think New Mexico and love agree with me. And I'm still working, primarily for Jack's company. And the occasional contract for a friend. Missy and I started a practice. She passes the bar next month."

"Ned means I'll take the bar and try to pass." Missy brushed her hair behind her ear.

"I agree with Ned. There's no question you'll pass." Katherine examined the woman she should have been. The woman her father wanted her to be. The woman her ex-husband had fallen in love with. She was beautiful, but from the inside not just superficially. Katherine had only found that side of herself since coming to Colorado. The lack of jealousy reassured her she really was changing for the better.

Katherine voiced the question that had been looming over her since they'd left the airport. "What do you think Richard will do?"

"If he's smart, he'll do as he promised—restore your accounts. I won't have to do anything."

"That reminds me." Katherine reached into her purse and retrieved the folded twenty that had been keeping her amethyst company when she didn't have it in her pocket. "A trivial down payment on your retainer and fee. But at least it's official."

Ned took the twenty with a gracious chuckle.

"I expect to see you bill me for this trip. At least the airfare and hotel." Katherine owed Ned and his found family much more.

"Let's see what Richard does first."

"I know your billable rate, Ned. The phone call alone—"

"Don't worry. Missy handles that end of the business. And my rates no longer include the overhead of the firm."

Katherine nodded. But it was only fair that she pay for his time.

The server returned and did the ritual with opening the wine and having Ned taste it, then pouring the glasses. The distraction gave Katherine a moment to compose herself. If she was going to be a better person, the person Gabe deserved, she owed these people a genuine apology.

"Missy?"

Soft brown eyes connected to hers.

"I owe you an apology. I went to my father with a story I knew would get you fired." She looked down at her glass, unable to maintain the eye contact. "I took great satisfaction in handling your exit myself. It was inappropriate on so many levels. I'm sorry."

"It was awful." Missy's soft voice held a note of pain. "But probably the best thing that could have happened. I was so caught up in sticking with my plan to be a New York lawyer that I would have sacrificed the love of two incredible men to continue my stubborn pursuit. If you hadn't blown that up, I'd still be chasing that tired dream."

"You make my nastiness sound like a gift."

Ned laughed.

"Maybe providential," Missy said.

"It was jealousy. You were outstanding. Everyone could see that. And you and Andr—Jack—" Katherine tucked her hand in her pocket and gripped the cool stone, her talisman. "I'm so sorry."

The trio of appetizers arrived, and Ned and Jack worked as a team to make sure Missy had a plate. Jack handed Katherine a plate with a few morsels on it. Her hand shook as she took the offering. There was no way she could eat. Her mouth was sandpaper. And she still had more work to do. She sipped her wine.

"The irony in the situation," Katherine began when she had her shaking under control, "is that the moment I turned on you was the moment I doomed myself."

"What do you mean?" Missy asked.

"Once you were gone, the merger fell apart." Katherine glanced at Ned. "Rightfully so. But because the merger didn't go through, the board became aware of just how strapped for cash the firm was. And that led to Richard firing me."

"You're not wrong." Ned raised his glass. "But I think leaving was just as good for you as it was for Missy."

"I hope so. That remains to be seen."

Katherine glanced at Jack. Up to that moment, she'd been avoiding his gaze. And he'd been avoiding her, too, staying silent and removed.

She had more work to do. An uncomfortable silence settled between them. Katherine steeled her spine. "It's a little awkward sitting here with my ex-husband and his partners, knowing I'm the villain. Especially after you flew up here to rescue me. I don't think I've ever been so quite at a loss as to what to do or say."

"So you're going to run away again?" Jack asked with an accusing bite in his tone. Missy put a hand on his arm.

"No. Not now." A flash of how she'd run from their marriage, emotionally run from her mother, and had been about to run from Gabe made the accuracy of his question sting. "I did. In the past, I ran." She paused, searching for the truth. "You never should've married me. I didn't know what love was. It's only recently I've learned. And I could blame youth or your dazzling beauty, but I wanted to escape, to run from my family. You provided that for me."

"I wanted us to be happy in our marriage." He gazed at her, and his crystal-blue eyes were softer. "But I wasn't completely honest with you either."

Katherine saw her ex-husband clearly for what might've been the first time. A man who wanted love but needed more than one person because he was so much larger than life. So filled with love and sex and passion.

"I tried to be the victim," Katherine admitted, "and make you the monster. But it was just a story to make myself feel better because I couldn't be what you needed."

"We both made mistakes."

She took another sip of wine, looked directly at Missy. "He looks happier than I've ever seen him."

"I take some credit for that," Ned said with a sexy chuckle.

"What have you been doing out here for a month?" Missy gestured to the view. "It's so beautiful."

Katherine was grateful for the purposeful change in subject, to talk about something other than her failures. The bridges weren't completely rebuilt, but at least there was the start of some scaffolding. Something to build from. That was enough for their first time talking since Katherine had blown up their world.

"I've started a business. I'm helping the Alabaster innkeepers with their marketing, refreshing and redecorating the accommodations, and implementing the latest reservation software on their redesigned websites."

"You always had an incredible talent for marketing," Jack said with a tone of approval.

"And I...met someone." With any luck, Katherine hadn't ruined that relationship, too. Or could at least fix it.

KATHERINE SETTLED into her rental car. Meeting with Ned, Jack, and Missy had gone far better than she'd anticipated. The fact that they seemed to accept her apology and were willing to help her gave a lightness to her heart she hadn't had in years.

She had one important stop to make on the way back to the lodge—to check on Sebastian. He let her in and returned to the table where a small computer was open to a website with math equations. She arranged herself in the seat beside him. "School?"

"Yeah, getting it done early. Colin invited me over for some gaming later. His mom picked up a shift."

"Oh good." Katherine searched for a way to ask him the important question, but it would be so easy to have it come out wrong. "Everything here okay?"

"Gotta find a new place to live."

"What?"

"The landlord's kicking us—me—out. Wants to do some remodeling and turn this into a short-term vacation rental."

"Does your mom know?"

"Yeah. I called her. She asked if I could move in with Colin."

The sadness in Seb's voice crushed her heart. "You know, I was coming to ask you a serious question that seems fortuitous now."

"What's that?"

"First, do you want to live with Colin?"

"Not really. He's cool, but his mom's kinda weird. I like being there when she isn't. They wouldn't want me there all the time either."

"What if someone did want you to be with them all the time? Would you be willing to consider it?"

"I can get a place of my own. Now that I'm sixteen, I should be able to get a part-time job…"

"What if you didn't have to?"

Seb shrugged. "That'd be all right, I guess."

"Don't go looking for another job too quickly. Gabe still has work to do on the lodge, and he's lined up some projects with the other innkeepers." She had no right to speak for Gabe, but Sebastian shouldn't take any action without at least discussing it first.

Seb nodded. Even if it didn't work out between Gabe and her, Gabe would want Sebastian around. He loved the kid as much as she did.

"How long did the landlord give you?"

"Last day of February."

Three weeks. Her gut said it might be against the law to give such short notice, but Seb's mom wasn't going to stop it. "You have a place to live. With me. No matter where I am. If you want it."

"Really?" He leaned back in the chair and gaped at her.

"Absolutely. Always." She promised him with her eyes as well as her words.

A small smile lifted the corners of his mouth, and the air in the room was lighter.

"You keep working on your studies. Do you need a ride to Colin's?"

"Nah."

"Pick you up for movie night Tuesday?" Hopefully, with Gabe. Hopefully, at the lodge.

"Yeah."

She squeezed Sebastian's shoulder before she left to deal with Gabe.

CHAPTER 25

The raging butterflies were back, and Katherine regretted the few bites of food she'd eaten in the hotel. At least the drive gave her time to rehearse what she would say to Gabe. And to dread his response.

The lodge was dark when she arrived. She glanced at the time. It wasn't *that* late. After carefully making her way across the treacherous parking area, the handle to the front door turned easily. He hadn't locked her out—that had to be a good sign. She locked the door behind her and hung up her coat.

Katherine turned on the entry light, and it was enough to see into the dark room. A bottle of Jack Daniels sat on the table next to a large manilla envelope, Gabe's phone right beside it. The back of Katherine's neck itched. Gabe sat in the center of the couch, unmoving, bent over, elbows on his knees. She'd never seen him like that. It screamed of the big ball of emotions that were tangled between them. She begged whoever might be listening and powerful to help them work it out.

She came around the couch. Her beautiful man's focus entirely on the items he had in front of him. Sitting beside him, she stroked her hand down his shoulder. "Gabe. I'm here."

He flinched. "Thought you were going back to New York."

The resignation in his voice cut her. "I couldn't."

Gabe sat up and wiped a hand down his face.

"I'm so sorry." Katherine touched his knee briefly. "But I listened. I met with a lawyer, and he's going to fix everything."

"You found a lawyer. On a Sunday?" His tone was thick with disbelief.

"He's a friend." Katherine cleared her throat. "Not a friend, exactly, but I've known him a long time, and he's in a relationship with my ex-husband."

Gabe blinked a few times, then nodded. "You told me part of the story the night we met."

"Right. I did. Surprisingly, he was still willing to speak to me. And he's going to help."

"Gonna be expensive."

"It'll be worth it to be free of my father's toxic control. To be able to keep building a life out here." She hesitated to say the "with you" part of the statement, unsure if he would be receptive to her planning a future with him. "What's going on?" She pointed at the table.

"Been trying to make some decisions."

"In my experience, Jack is a bad decision." It was a terrible joke and only her nerves talking.

"Mine, too. That's why the bottle's still capped." Gabe rubbed his hands down his denim-covered legs. "I'm closing the lodge."

"What? But this is your dream." She'd planned to make it *their* dream. Did she have to move out? Was he going back to California and leaving her? No.

"I don't want to run this place as a B and B. It wasn't all that fun having the Scotts here, even though they were great. What happens when I get crap guests? When I have more rooms and there are strangers running all over the place? I'm a terrible cook." Gabe's red-rimmed gaze locked on her, hooking right into her heart.

"You're going to sell?" The shock in her voice came as a surprise.

"You keep saying your life is in New York." He wrapped his hand around hers. "I realized the only reason my life is in Colorado is this lodge. If I sell it, I can be wherever you are. Even bought a plane ticket so I can go with you." Gabe swallowed hard. "I mean, if you want me to."

"No."

"Gotcha." Gabe removed his hand from hers. "It's refundable."

She shook her head. "No, I mean, I don't want you to go to New York. I won't be there. I'm going to be here. In Alabaster."

"Thank god. Because I couldn't figure out how to make that work with Sebastian. And I want a family. With you."

Katherine took a shaky breath. "With me?"

"Yes. Here. The three of us." He picked up the envelope and handed it to her.

Katherine fiddled with the clasp and released the papers. She skimmed the top page. A list of classes. "You're going to become a foster parent?"

"If you're staying, you could, too."

"I want to stay, and I absolutely want to take care of Sebastian. But I want to be your partner. Help you how I want to help. Even if that means spending money."

Gabe nodded. "I've been an ass about that. I took it as pity or a sign you didn't think I was capable of doing everything on my own."

"My parents only ever showed love by buying things or paying for trips. Money was held over my head as a tool to make me behave. I wanted to give you what I had freely. To never make you beg for something I had the means to give. No strings."

"Movie nights. Talking with you over breakfast. Going with you to meet the other owners and see how damn impressive you are. That means more to me than any amount of money."

Katherine dropped her head to his shoulder. "I love those times together, too. But can I still buy you things?"

Gabe laughed and wrapped his arms around her. "If you must. I'll try not to be ungrateful."

"I'll try not to be extravagant. But no promises."

"You know we're going to have to watch our expenses, especially if Sebastian moves in with us. I'll do all the construction jobs I can, and I know you'll be successful with your websites. But it's going to be tight. Colorado's expensive."

Katherine smiled. Until she had all the details wrapped up, she wouldn't confess how much she was worth. It really didn't matter. She'd stay and work hard with Gabe even if they had nothing. "We'll make it work. I know we can."

Gabe wrapped her in his arms and kissed her lips, the tip of her nose, her eyelids. "I love you, Jadis."

"I love you, too." She pressed her lips to his and teased them apart with her tongue. Their shared breath filled her lungs. She paused the kiss. "Come to—"

Gabe's phone rang, interrupting her invitation. The display said *Saint*.

"I have to take this." He kissed her briefly. "I'll be in right after."

Katherine made her way to the bedroom as Gabe's hot-chocolate voice filled the room. Hurdles remained, but she could see the future with Gabe. And she was willing to fight for it.

KATHERINE PUT the finishing touches on her makeup. Meeting with her father—and Ned and Jack and Missy—had been emotionally exhausting, but she still had barriers to clear. Driven by the possible solutions, she had quietly rushed through her morning shower and dressing. Just as she left the bathroom, a brisk knock echoed through the entry. She glanced at Gabe, still in bed, his dark eyes gazing at her. "I'll get it," she said. "Shower's open."

Katherine thumped her crutches to the front door and flipped the lock.

An older man with a clipboard and a broad smile stood on the concrete stoop. "Lloyd Puckler, county inspector. Here about some permits."

"Of course." Katherine moved back, opening the door in welcome. "So glad you're here. Can I offer you some coffee? I was just about to make a fresh pot."

She chatted with the inspector as she moved around the kitchen, covering all the important topics like weather and the ski report and how long he'd lived in the area. Gabe appeared right as the brewing finished. She poured three mugs and handed them out while Gabe served the cream and sugar.

"Gabe, I have some errands to run and the follow-up appointment for my leg. I'll be back this afternoon, might be late."

He pressed a kiss to her lips. "See you then."

The two men went out the front door, and Katherine gathered her things, sucked down the cup of cooled coffee, and drove into town. She called Amy to meet her for breakfast, suddenly starving.

Waiting in the parking lot, she made a call to a New York realtor. After an informative conversation, she learned that property values were down, but she should still be able to get nineteen million for her apartment. Katherine called a moving agency and contracted with them to pack everything she owned that the selling agent didn't want for staging and ship it to a storage facility in Colorado Springs. She held her breath as the movers processed her deposit. When the credit card cleared, she let the air flow from her lungs.

Her father had, so far, kept his word.

Amy rapped on the window of her SUV, which she really needed to return—later. Katherine grabbed her crutches and wrestled her way out of the car, praying the doctor could tell her good news at her appointment.

"What's up?" Amy asked.

"I've got an idea, and I need your help."

"Sure, with what?" Amy held the door of the coffee shop open.

The warm scent filled the earth-tone-painted room. Couples sat at small bistro tables. A built-in bench with pillows ran under a block of windows. "This is cute. You should have brought me here before."

"I can't share all my favorites in one day. What are you having?"

Katherine ordered a large latte and a croissant breakfast sandwich. Amy duplicated the order. Then they found a spot tucked in a corner.

Katherine leaned toward Amy. "I had an idea about ABBA."

"Oh, really." Amy's smile had a touch of evil villain, and she laced her fingers under her chin. "Spill."

"We need to have an emergency meeting and take a vote. I've been turning around the financial report from the last meeting in my mind. And after getting the details on the dues and the hosting, I think there might be missing funds. I'd have to see the expenses, of course. Like I don't know what you pay for the meeting room."

"Nothing. It's free."

"What about speakers? They cost."

"We have two a year."

Katherine tilted her head. "So you see my point."

Amy leaned back. "Shit. I can*not* get involved in another one of these."

"What do you mean?"

She flapped her hand. "A story for another time. So, an emergency meeting. A vote. For what?"

"Vote of no confidence in Betty. And elect a new board."

"Could that work?"

A girl in an apron appeared at their table. Katherine thanked the runner for the coffees and sandwiches. She paused long enough to take a bite of the croissant. She moaned. It was the best thing she'd tasted in Colorado. Maybe ever.

"I know. Best breakfast in town. Except for mine." Amy chuckled.

After putting away half the sandwich and most of the coffee, Katherine asked, "Does your organization have bylaws?"

"Has to. It's a 501c6."

"I'm going to translate that as yes." Katherine grinned.

"It's a tax designation. But, yeah, to get it, there have to be bylaws."

"Can you get a copy? I'm sure it will have wording about elections and such. When's the last one you had?"

"Two years ago, maybe?"

"Might be overdue."

"Oh, I like how you think."

They made plans to reconnect after Amy did some digging and

talked to some of the other members. Katherine didn't care what it took. Betty was going down.

Katherine had just enough time to make her doctor's appointment. After seeing her for two minutes, her doctor sent her for X-rays and made a new appointment for two weeks, when she would remove the cast and possibly put Katherine in a walking cast, depending on what the images showed. Katherine tried to put the information in the positive column, but the doctor's offhand comment about her age and healing pricked her. With a headshake, she pictured the colored cube and recommitted to her plan.

One more stop before she could return to Gabe. The barriers between them, around them, were falling. It felt like everything was possible.

The shop she found was near the Aspen art museum. A single artisan's work filled the space. Katherine paused outside and inspected the pieces in the window. A pair of amethyst earrings caught her eye. The design showcased the variation in the crystals secured to the posts with delicate silver wires.

She might make two purchases.

A wisp of certainty filled her lungs as she breathed in the slightly metallic air in the glass-case-filled room.

GABE SLURPED his second cup of coffee as he led Mr. Pickle, or whatever the inspector's name was, up the stairs to see the remodeled bathroom.

"You're gonna have quite a place here when you build out these plans," Mr. Pickle said as they came down the ladder from the attic. "Want to show me the deck and then I'll finish the paperwork and clear out of here?"

"Uh, thanks. Sure." Gabe led the way down the stairs to the front door. The lodge would be spectacular when he finished with it. If he could find the funds and the time to finish it. If they could afford to keep it. Gabe held up his cup to the inspector. "Refill?"

"Don't mind if I do."

Gabe poured the coffee and turned off the burner. The cold outdoor air hit his lungs and blasted away the last of his doubts. He loved the lodge. He loved working with Sebastian, teaching him. And he loved Katherine. And she'd said she loved him, too. But would she be able to live on a tight budget? He should have clarified what her expectations were. He should have ignored the call from Saint. But his friend had insisted Gabe better answer every call after he'd confessed how depressed he was. Gabe didn't want Saint to worry enough to initiate a wellness check. And even though he'd let the critical moment pass, no matter what, he would do whatever it took to make his dream of their family happen. He would earn the love Katherine had granted him.

Gabe finished the tour and noted the advice to make sure the construction would meet code during the final inspection. He took the paperwork and glanced at the name. "Thank you, Mr. Puckler."

"Call me Lloyd." He shook Gabe's hand. "And let me know if you need any advice. This old place is really going to shine again."

As soon as Lloyd left, Gabe opened his laptop in the bedroom and did what he could to keep the two people who mattered most to him, besides his birth family, in his life. If any of his plans worked out, it would be more than he deserved. Hours of emails and FaceTime meetings with his family later, he looked up.

Katherine was in the doorway. Fuck, she was breathtaking. Blond hair tight in a twist, diamonds twinkling at her ears, icy blue eyes locked on him. He shivered with desire combined with dread. If he truly lost her, there would be no recovery. No fake heart the doctors could install to help him survive.

"What happened with the inspector?" Katherine asked.

"I'm cleared to restart. The attic permit was approved, too."

"That's great." Her smile brightened the room. "I arranged to sell my home in New York this morning. The agent thinks it will take less than ninety days since I told her to price it aggressively. We don't need every dime out of the deal."

"Are you sure about staying?" Gabe clung to the last drop of doubt like a drowning man with an anchor.

"In Alabaster?"

Gabe nodded. "With me."

"Did you misunderstand when I said I love you?" She took a couple of steps toward him and froze.

"You meant it." Gabe struggled for breath. "And you're really staying—"

"That depends." Katherine reached in her pocket and arranged herself in a strange half-kneeling position, her cast making her awkward. "Gabriel Gallegos?" She held out a small square black velvet box.

The air caught in his lungs.

"Oh god." Katherine clutched the box to her chest. "I'm not sure how to ask this. I never considered what I should say, but I want to be with you. I want us to be married and take care of Sebastian and be a family. And I know I drive you crazy and you think I'm the ice queen and it's far too soon, but—will you marry me?"

CHAPTER 26

Katherine rushed on: "Because I thought about it, and—"

Gabe pressed a brief kiss to her lips, stealing her breath. "Are you always going to out-plan me and be six moves ahead?"

Heat flamed her cheeks, and tears welled in her eyes. "Probably."

"Are you sure you want a broken warrior? A failed innkeeper who isn't sure what he's going to do with his life?"

"You're not broken or failed, and you're going to build a business around construction for the other innkeepers. Are you sure you want a bossy, controlling old lady?"

Gabe stood and lifted her back up. "You're not old."

"I'm ten years older than you."

"You know I've been assigned a lot of numbers in my *short* life: a birthdate, a social security number, a driver's license number, even an ID number from Uncle Sam. And you know what all those numbers have in common? They don't tell you one goddamned thing about me. They tell you nothing about my heart, my soul, my dreams, or my disappointments. Your age or my age doesn't say a thing about us that matters. I've seen your heart." He grazed his fingers down the center

200

of her chest. "You've shared your dreams." He pressed his forehead to hers, his gaze melting with hers. "I know your disappointments." He placed his hand on her lower abdomen.

Tears spilled down her cheeks.

"I love you, Katherine. All of you. Exactly as you are." His lips touched hers in the softest kiss. "I even like that you're bossy and controlling." His smile spotlighted her with its brilliance, and she couldn't help but smile, too. Damn, the man was sweet. The perfect balance to her bitter.

"But I do have one question." He plucked the white-gold ring from the box and slid it on his left hand, fingering the two stripes of yellow gold and three inlaid diamonds. "I get the ring, but why the diamonds?"

Katherine sniffed. "They're traditional for an engagement ring." She clutched his hand where the ring sat. "The three diamonds are for each of us. You, me, and—"

"Sebastian." His deep voice rattled through her. Gabe laughed. "I filled out the forms online while you were gone this afternoon."

The nerves she'd been battling the past days finally settled. She was exactly where she was supposed to be. "You're perfect, Gabe. I love you so much."

He kissed her again, over and over, slipping his tongue between her lips. He tasted like forever. But he hadn't committed. She tilted her head back. "You didn't answer me."

"Yes. I'll marry you." He nuzzled her neck.

Peace. That was the unfamiliar sensation that settled deep inside. Peace, wrapped in happiness and joy. "Thank you," she whispered.

The words weren't enough. But they were a start, and she'd have years to convey how much she cherished having a space where she belonged, in his home, his heart, his family.

"I should be thanking you. You just made me the happiest man on the planet. And saved me a great deal of stress since I wasn't sure how or when to propose to you. Only that I wanted to."

"We don't have to get married right away. It shouldn't affect our application to foster."

"Are you saying you're just marrying me to get Sebastian?" The teasing tone made her smile.

"Nope. I'm marrying you for that great big cock." She grazed her hand over his rising erection.

"You're lying."

"It's true. I'll prove it." She placed her hands on his solid chest and pressed, but he didn't move at all.

"No. This time, I'm taking the lead." He freed her hair, dropping the pins on the desk by his laptop. Then he ran his fingers through her locks.

She arched into him like a cat. For him, she could give up control for a little while. He ran his hands down the sides of her neck to her shoulders and shifted her coat down her arms. Before she could wrap her arms around his neck, he pulled her shirt up and over her head. She moved her hands to cover herself, suddenly vulnerable.

He gripped her wrists and kissed the top of each breast. "You are so perfect."

The twinge of insecurity dissipated into the twilight, and she let her hands go to his shoulders. Let him remove her bra and the rest of her clothes. Let herself relax onto the bed as the amazing man who'd agreed to marry her slowly removed his clothing, exposing his chiseled body, his sexy ink, and his unbelievable cock.

"I want to suck you." She reached for him, but he stepped back.

"Not yet."

She draped her arms across her chest and stomach.

"So." He lifted the arm from her middle, drawing it over her head. "Fucking." He moved her other arm from her chest. "Perfect." He sat to the side of her and ran his calloused hand slowly up her leg along her inner thigh, parting her legs and lightly teasing her slick pussy.

"Now." She grabbed his arm. "Please."

Gabe laughed. "You're the only person I know who can make 'please' sound like a command."

"It was supposed to sound like begging."

"Right." He turned his back to her and released his prosthesis. Then he was over her, between her legs, sliding down. "Don't move."

He gripped her thighs and lifted her legs as he spread them obscenely and dove into her, his tongue whipping through her slick folds and teasing her desperate clit.

"Oh fuck, Gabe." She twitched with the compulsion to grip his hair and drive his action. But he'd told her not to move, and she had to prove to him she could compromise. She could be his partner. She could let him lead.

He breached her with two thick fingers and sucked hard on her clit. Her orgasm ripped through her like a gale-force wind blowing away every bit of restraint. She screamed and rode out the storm untethered except where her lover held her, anchored her in his safety, and gave her exactly what she'd been afraid to want.

Finally, the storm subsided. She lay boneless on the bed as he shifted and pivoted toward her. His kiss sealed their commitment more than any ring. His cock pressed at her entrance, and he slowly slid in, eased with her cum. She stretched for him, pressed her hips up to take him as deeply as she could. The barriers that had lived inside her for so long were blown away by the powerful man who loved her and didn't want her to change.

She wrapped her arms around him, stroking his skin in time with the strokes of his thick cock. His gaze locked on her, and time ceased to exist. It didn't matter when they officially married. They were forever.

GABE GLANCED AT HIS RING, the unfamiliar weight heavy on his hand, the perfect reminder of how much had changed. How much bigger his world had become. He looked forward to the day when the ring became such a part of him he'd only notice when he took it off.

He brought his fiancée a fresh cup of coffee. They'd made love all night long and finally dragged themselves out of bed because, although the earth had moved, it still continued to spin, and they had more to accomplish to create the family of their dreams. "Sebastian is at Colin's?"

"He's coming for movie night tonight. I told him we'd pick him up. I figure we can propose to him then."

Gabe chuckled. "Propose?"

"It's a proposal of sorts. Him moving in here. I still want to go through the official foster process and call his mom, but there's no reason he can't live here now. The landlord wants them out by the end of the month, but why wait?"

"Good plan." Gabe lifted the top of his laptop. "Speaking of plans. We should mark the lodge website as under construction or something. I don't want anyone *planning* to stay here. Except you and Sebastian."

Katherine pulled the computer to her, tapped away on the keyboard, and then announced, "Done."

"You know, this might impact our ability to get approved as fosters. I'm not sure website and construction gigs are going to paint a picture of financial stability." Gabe rubbed his chin.

"About that—once the condo sells, and I don't know when that's going to be, money won't be an issue for us. Actually, it's not now with my accounts freed up."

"You still have to pay off your mortgage. And a few hundred thousand sounds like a lot, but it can go quick. Especially if we run into any medical issues." He glanced pointedly at her cast.

"I own the condo outright, and the agent thinks she can get nineteen million easily."

Gabe spewed coffee over the table. Good thing the laptop was still in front of Katherine.

"Did you say nineteen *million*?"

"I haven't checked in a couple of months, but my accounts are worth at least four times that."

"What the fuck are you doing with me?" He waved a hand down at his flannel shirt, blue jeans, and work boots.

"It's a number, Gabe. It doesn't tell you anything about my heart, my dreams, my disappointments."

His words from her lips wiped away his concern. He stood up and pulled her into a full-body kiss. "Wise words."

"I heard them recently from a really smart man."

"He sounds brilliant."

"I think so." She smiled up at him.

"I'm still going to do construction jobs."

She gave a quick nod. "I'm still going to redesign websites."

"Okay." He released her and retrieved a rag from the kitchen to clean up his mess on the table.

"But our honeymoon is going to be epic." Katherine crossed her arms.

He paused and took in the challenge resonating from the way she held her body. If he fought her every time she spent her money, their marriage would be one long battle. It was hers to spend how she wished. Her money didn't make him less of a man, any more than losing his leg had, unless *he* let it matter.

He crossed his arms, too, hiding his grin, and added a glare. "Okay."

She pursed her lips and then softened into a slight smile at his joke. "Which foster-parent orientation class should we go to?"

"There's a chance we could be selected to foster more kids."

Katherine glanced at the ceiling. "We have the room. The Jack and Jill could have bunk beds if we needed. And you're still going to convert the attic, right?"

"Got the permits approved."

"Then we'll play it by ear. I don't have much experience, but I wouldn't mind more kids."

"I'm used to a big family." And Gabe should call his mother. Wasn't every day her children got engaged.

"I'd like to get used to that."

"Good." Gabe adjusted the computer and scooted his chair closer to Katherine. "We can start by video calling my mom."

Katherine's hands went to her hair.

"You're perfect, Jadis. She's going to love you."

GABE FOLLOWED Sebastian up the stairs. Seb had been hesitant to pack a few days' worth of clothes but finally relented when they promised he could check on the rental house any time he wanted. Maybe Katherine could take Sebastian shopping for different decorations. Make the red room his. "You can put your things in the dresser. And the towels in the bathroom are clean."

"Thanks. I won't mess anything up. If you get a guest—"

"This is *your* room if you want it." Gabe resisted the urge to explain. Not until they were all together. "Come downstairs when you're ready. I'll tell you all about it." Gabe left Sebastian to settle in and returned to Katherine in the kitchen.

Katherine closed the oven door and turned to him. "Pizza's in. Twenty minutes."

"We should talk when Sebastian comes down."

The thump of footsteps on the last few stairs signaled it was time.

"Grab a drink, and let's sit in the living room," Katherine told the teenager as he stared into the refrigerator.

Gabe let Katherine tug him to the couch. As soon as Sebastian joined them, he said, "What's up?"

Katherine glanced at Gabe. Gabe sucked in a breath. Apparently, he would have to propose. "We've decided not to run this place as a lodge. Instead, Katherine is going to do websites for local businesses, and I'm going to do remodeling projects."

"Like the deck?"

"Yeah. And we want you to live here. With us."

"For as long as you want to," Katherine added.

Sebastian tilted his head. "Live here?" His gaze traveled the room. "What about my mom?"

"The landlord gave her the eviction notice, right?" Katherine's hand fluttered to her hair.

"Yeah. But, I mean, what if she wants to come back?"

Gabe leaned forward. "She'll still be your mom. If she gets a place and you two want to live together again, we won't stop you. You'd still have a place here. And if she just wants to see you, no problem. As much as she wants."

"You wouldn't have to worry about money or food. You could focus on school. Maybe think about college?" Katherine's voice was soft, inviting.

"College?"

Katherine reached for Seb's hand. "You're smart. We want to support your dreams. And you have time to decide about where to live. You don't have to answer tonight."

"I don't want to wait. It's yes, but I have one condition."

"What's that, buddy?" Gabe would grant any request unless Katherine beat him to it.

"I get to pick the movie."

Katherine laughed. "This time or every time?"

"I'll let Gabe have a turn. But your picks—"

The ring of Katherine's phone cut off Seb's teasing. She glanced at the screen. "It's my lawyer."

"Answer it," Gabe said.

A moment after she'd answered, she asked, "Can I put you on speaker? I want my family to hear this." She pressed the button and held the phone out.

"Richard called me to confirm your accounts have been restored. He's started removing his name entirely." The lawyer's voice resonated with confidence.

"So easily?" she asked. "Why didn't he call *me*?"

"I'm your attorney. And I think you rattled him. He asked to speak with you when you're ready. I think he wants to apologize."

Katherine's face scrunched. "I will. But not tonight." The timer buzzed in the kitchen. "We're having a movie night."

"Sounds like a good way to spend the evening, Katherine."

"Ned, thank you. For everything. And send me a bill."

"When we get home. One other thing—Jack suggested you could help us with a website for our firm. He said we'd be fools not to at least ask you. Are you interested?"

Katherine's chest constricted. She hadn't been sure where she stood with Jack when she'd left them at the hotel. It was his version of a peace offering. "I'd be delighted."

"We're still in town for another few days."

"I'll call you tomorrow. We can meet to discuss ideas." They were giving her the opportunity to make amends and build on that scaffold of friendship.

"Bring your family. I want to meet them."

Gabe nodded to Katherine, and they turned to Sebastian. He gave a thumbs-up.

"I will," she said and ended the call.

Gabe and Sebastian whooped. "You got another job."

"I did!"

Sebastian gave her a hand slap of congratulations. Gabe tugged her into his arms for a hug.

They sliced up the pizza and then negotiated which action flick to watch. Sebastian sat on the floor and snagged several slices. She snuggled into Gabe as the opening scene erupted with fire and gunplay.

Gabe placed a soft kiss on her lips. "I love you."

The warmth of belonging, of being simply happy, washed over her. "I love you, too."

EPILOGUE

September the following year

Katherine lifted the platinum lace overskirt and let it fall over the matching silk dress. It fell in line perfectly, unlike everything else about that day. Her dream wedding was devolving into a nightmare.

The flowers had frozen in the florist's cooler overnight due to an equipment malfunction. Amy had left to find a solution.

Rain saturated the grounds of the hotel where she and Gabe had planned their dream wedding.

Sebastian, home for the weekend from his first semester in college, was dressed to be the best man. So what if the ties and cummerbunds she'd ordered for their tuxedos had come in a pale blue instead of the matching platinum shade she'd paid for?

None of it mattered. She spun in the mirror. The vintage lace that covered her bare back tickled but looked divine. Her amethyst earrings perfectly matched Madam Tiana's crystal that she'd had the same artist set in a necklace. Katherine embodied the romantic version of the ice queen Gabe had fallen in love with. Exactly as she'd planned.

So what if she'd have to take off her matching silk heels and be barefoot instead of ruining them in the puddles? They were finally getting married. And she was more in love with her soon-to-be husband than when she'd proposed almost two years ago.

"What are you doing here?" Amy's voice penetrated the room Katherine was using as a dressing room.

"You didn't return my calls. That's not what we agreed to. After forty-eight hours with no contact, I followed protocol," an unfamiliar deep voice said.

"I've been busy with this wedding. I'm *still* busy."

"Busy with the treasurer's job for ABBA?"

"It's a tiny organization. No one's going to notice."

"*I* noticed."

"You're supposed to. Leave or take a seat. I have to take care of this bouquet."

"I'll save you a seat."

"I'm the bridesmaid. I mean, matron of honor. I won't be sitting."

"If you don't join me as soon as the ceremony is over, you're damn right you won't be."

"As if. Those days are over."

"Not for me."

Amy burst through the door, clutching a bunch of flowers. Katherine fiddled with her earrings and pretended she hadn't over-heard the odd conversation.

"I can't believe him."

"Who?" Katherine widened her eyes, still trying to pass off the ignorance.

"My hand—husband."

"He's here, in town?" Katherine had believed the man didn't exist.

"Unexpectedly."

"At least you have a date for the reception now."

Amy blinked at her and then held up the bouquet. "An original arrangement, courtesy of the hotel garden."

"It's beautiful. Thank you." Katherine took the late-season sunflowers, mums, and asters that were tied with rough jute. "You're a lifesaver." It wasn't the white roses, lavender, and eucalyptus handheld with a satin tie that she'd planned, but it was gorgeous. At least she had a bouquet to cling to as she walked down the aisle.

"Not quite the perfect match to that dress. I'm still sorry I wasn't in LA with you when you found it."

"Gabe's mom and sister were wonderful. I would never have found this designer without them." And neither one had commented on her age. They'd just gushed at how wonderful it was that Gabriel had found his person. His older brothers had been a little more standoffish, but not rude. It was enough. They had all flown in for the ceremony two days earlier. She'd booked rooms for them at the hotel, and she was glad they'd come early, because if they'd had the bachelor night the day before the ceremony, Gabe might be laying down at the altar waiting for her.

A shadow passed over Katherine. The seating would be packed with Gabe's guests. Katherine didn't have anyone since Amy was standing up with her. Natalia had RSVP'd her regrets, and neither of her parents had replied at all.

A knock at the door interrupted Katherine's pity party. Amy peeked out through the small opening she'd allowed. "It's Edward Strauss?"

"Ned? Let him in." The breath caught in Katherine's throat. What was he doing there?

There was a bit more gray in his hair than the last time she'd seen him, when she and Gabe had taken Sebastian to New Mexico. His charcoal suit was perfectly tailored, and his tie matched his deep sapphire eyes perfectly. She could see why her ex-husband had fallen for him.

"Katherine. You look beautiful. Absolutely glowing." Ned's smile warmed her to her toes. "Gabe invited us."

"He did?"

"Missy, Jack, and Mia are already seated. But Gabe thought you might allow me to escort you down the aisle."

Mia—their child, whom she'd only seen in pictures but whose golden beauty made her a miniature twin of her mother. Tears threatened her makeup. "I didn't plan to have an escort. But I would be honored to have you walk me down the aisle."

Piano music lilted in from the garden through the window. Gabe's youngest brother, the virtuoso, had offered to play, and a grand piano had been wheeled out to the covered patio.

"It's time," Ned said and winged out his arm.

Katherine kicked off her satin stilettos, hitched up the lace overlay and the corner of her gown, and slipped her hand through Ned's arm. Amy handed her the bouquet and rushed over to the door. When she flung it open, Richard Wallace stood poised to knock. Katherine's stomach clenched. "What are you doing here, Dad?"

"Came to see my daughter get married. Thought I might walk you down the aisle."

Words rolled through Katherine, none of them in order, and none of them making it out of her mouth. Ned's arm opened, but she gripped him tighter. "I'm glad you're here, but I have an escort."

Richard nodded.

"Meet you out there." Amy darted out of the room, her wispy dress, with watercolored roses, fluttering in the breeze.

Ned leaned down and whispered in Katherine's ear, "He's still your dad."

There was a war in her heart between wishes and regrets. Katherine met Ned's eyes. She released her grip on his arm.

Ned kissed her cheek. "I'll see you out there."

As the door closed behind Ned, Katherine studied her father. His shoulders had rounded, and his hair had thinned, but he still had a glimmer of that inner power that had made him so formidable in the courtroom.

"How did you get permission to leave the state?" she asked.

"I begged. I have to fly back tomorrow."

Katherine sighed. "I'm glad you're here."

"Your mom's here, too. With that woman." He took a few steps into the room. "Can I kiss the bride?" Katherine nodded, and her father kissed her cheek. "You look beautiful. I'm happy for you."

Before Katherine could respond, he held out his arm to her, and she placed her hand in the crook of his elbow. The feel of him was familiar and foreign at the same time. He no longer fit the images she'd always held of him. But she still loved him.

"You can change your mind. I can call Ned back."

"Not for the world." She took a deep breath and let him lead her out of the room.

Amy led them to the opening of the garden, still wet from the recent rains and shimmering in the fall light. Katherine's heart rate slowed. Peace flowed through her veins. She was exactly where she should be.

Amy proceeded slowly up the aisle between the rows of chairs and took her place at the front.

"Ready?" her father asked.

"So ready."

More people than she'd expected filled both sides of the aisle. Gabe had insisted he could manage the guest list but hadn't shared that the B and B owners would be attending. His big smile and twinkling eyes told her he'd gotten one over on her. She'd been complaining for days about the mismatched attendance, and he hadn't said a word. She narrowed her eyes threateningly, and he tossed back his head and laughed. She couldn't stop the enormous smile that broke out. He'd said he owed her a lifetime of surprises, since she'd popped the question and knocked him for a loop. She looked forward to every single one.

Richard kept pace with the stately beat of the music, tugging her slightly when she started to race to the love of her life. Sebastian stood at Gabe's side, perfectly poised in his tuxedo. Nearly a man, but he would always be a boy in her heart. Finally, they arrived at the front where the officiant stood, ready to make their love official. After Amy took the bouquet, Richard placed Katherine's hands in Gabe's.

"Take better care of her than I did," Richard said as he released her.

"Always." Gabe's eyes were locked on her.

The next moments passed in a blur. Words were spoken and repeated, but she could only focus on Gabe's face, his heat, the beating of her own heart. That, and his kiss. He tilted her in his arms, whispered "Jadis" in her ear like a promise more real than the ones they'd just made, and then kissed her like no one was watching. His love surged through her. A roar and applause broke their connection before the kiss went too far. Their honeymoon couldn't come fast enough.

They dodged mud puddles on the way to the tent where the dance floor and tables were set up. The tables looked almost plain without the floral centerpieces. But someone in the hotel had put out tall urns filled with lemons and limes. The platinum bows tied around the silver cane-back chairs and the matching tablecloths looked as elegant as she'd imagined, and as the sun began to set, someone turned on the strands of Edison lights. The photographer they'd hired bounced around, getting candid shots of them and their guests. It was her dream wedding because she was marrying the man of her dreams.

They took their seats. Amy was joined by a tall man with dark bronze skin and a strong jaw—the husband Katherine had never met. Sebastian sat with his mom at his side. She and Sebastian had started to restore their relationship once he'd graduated from high school. Katherine was happy for the young man she loved as if he were her own.

As the guests settled, the wind rose, and the sides of the tent rippled. Waitstaff rushed plates out to the bridal party and the guests as the tablecloths billowed and several of the urns tipped. Quick-thinking servers lifted off the precarious decorations, and the flaps of the tent openings slapped against the rattling walls. The stringed quartet could barely be heard above the cacophony of Mother Nature and the uncomfortable guests.

Katherine leaned into Gabe so he could hear her. "We have to end this quickly. I think we should skip the dances."

"Good call."

"Did you conjure this storm to get out of it?"

"God took pity on me and our guests." Gabe flashed her a toothy smile.

"You'll owe me a dance," Katherine teased. Gabe had hated the dance lessons they'd taken and only agreed after some spectacular sex.

"As long as it's without an audience. And clothes." He winked.

She gave him a sultry look filled with promise.

"We should cut the cake." Katherine glanced over at the three-tiered confection. Ned and his family were seated at the table closest to it, calmly eating their dinner and passing their adorable toddler back and forth.

A gust blew through and knocked an open bottle of champagne into the waiting glasses, shattering them.

Gabe rose. "Cake, now."

Katherine followed him, but as they neared the small round table, something from outside battered the tent wall and tilted the table. The cake slid in slow motion, the tiers separating from each other. Nick, Gabe's former captain, lifted his hands and caught the top tier in his open palms right before it could hit his wife's gorgeous red hair.

"Nice save, Saint," Gabe called out.

"Always got your back, brother."

Nick's service dog barked sharply as the remaining tiers crashed onto the muddy ground, splattering Ned's and Jack's suit pants.

Katherine brought her hands to her face. Everything was a disaster. Every. Single. Thing. Gabe tugged at her wrists. Except him. Them. Nothing that happened really mattered. The corners of Gabe's mouth lifted, and in moments they were both laughing hard and holding on to each other to keep from collapsing. Servers bustled around, hands wringing as they attempted to deal with the destruction.

Jack held out a dinner knife. "You two should probably cut the cake and get out of here before an asteroid lands."

"Good call." Gabe took the knife and guided Katherine to the place Noelle, Nick's wife, had set the salvaged cake.

They cut into it together. Katherine carefully fed Gabe a small bite. Tingles went up her arm as his lips met her fingers, and the heat in his gaze promised all the naughty activities he planned to do with his mouth later.

Gabe dragged his finger through the frosting and painted her lips. Before she could object, he pressed his mouth to hers and kissed her.

The guests clapped and cheered as though everything was perfect. And, in reality, everything was. She'd married the love of her life, surrounded by people who loved them and cared for them. And hadn't they said for better or worse? At least those were the words they'd planned to say. She couldn't recall.

They returned to the head table, accepting the congratulations of the guests, who were all standing and clearly ready to leave. Katherine handed her bouquet to Amy. "Thank you. You went to so much trouble to get these flowers for me, you should have them."

"Breaking the tradition of tossing the bouquet?" Amy asked as she took the arrangement.

"I think the only single woman here is Gabe's sister, and with her five brothers, that's going to be her status for a while."

Amy hugged Katherine as they laughed. "Have a wonderful time on your honeymoon. Call me for anything."

Katherine squeezed her friend once more, then moved around the table. She kissed Sebastian on his cheek and told him she loved him. "I'll see you at fall break. Amy will be here. I'll keep my cell phone on. And be careful on the drive back to school."

"I'll be fine." He stood and gave her a hug. "Love you, too."

Tears pricked Katherine's eyes. He wasn't the scrawny boy she'd seen huddled in the doorway almost two years ago. He was nearly a man and on the path to becoming an engineer. His mom grabbed Katherine's hand. "He sure is something, our Sebastian."

She smiled warmly at the woman who'd trusted Katherine to finish the job of raising their son. "He is."

Gabe tugged her toward the exit. "We should go now before this tent falls down."

As she ran barefoot by Gabe's side out of the tent, her mother and father blew kisses at her. They burst out of the tent and into a rainstorm. Torrents of water poured over them as they retreated to the hotel and the suite they'd reserved for the day.

"There is no way we're flying out tonight. This weather is too rough for the private jet the agent booked." Katherine pressed Gabe against the door and slid his sopping jacket off his shoulders, letting it fall in a wet heap. "But I'm sure we can think of something to keep us occupied." She tugged his shirt free of his pants before slowly releasing each stud and parting the no longer crisp fabric.

"What would that be?" Gabe pulled the remaining pins from her hair as she kissed him along his neck and down his chest.

Katherine stepped back and turned. Gabe released the clasp at her neck, lowered the zipper, and let her ruined dress fall. Katherine turned to face him. Gabe sucked in a breath. A warm thrill rolled through her belly. She might be older than him, might not be what people thought of as "in her prime," but she could still take her husband's breath away with a little platinum lace lingerie. Very little.

He tugged her close and took control of their kiss while she undid his belt. His body begged her for freedom. She wrapped her hand around his hard cock, and he flinched out of her grasp.

"Jadis, your fingers are ice." He cupped her hands within his and blew hot air on them. "Let me warm you up, my love."

"I'd planned to heat you up first." She pouted.

"I'll meet you on the bed, and we'll warm each other up."

"Fine." She dragged the tip of her icy finger over his nipple before darting away.

Her husband finished removing his clothes; his slow unveiling captured her attention completely, exposing each tattoo she knew better than her own. The newest, a crown of snowflakes over his heart, had inspired the tiny snowflake she'd had inked on her own hip.

He sat on the edge of the bed as he removed his prosthetic. She traced the lines left along his thigh up to his hip. The proof of just how resilient he was. Everything about him made her want to wrap him up in her arms, take him deep into her body, and never let him go.

FROM THE FAR side of the bed, a digital chime sounded, waking Katherine from her sex coma. She wasn't sure how many times or ways they'd made love the night before, but her body ached with delicious memories. Gabe snored as the chime sounded again.

Katherine flicked on the table lamp. "Is that your phone?"

Gabe rolled, the covers exposing his chiseled bare chest. She would never tire of looking at him. If their flight was delayed again, she couldn't be sad.

"It's Ms. Blackwell." Gabe answered and remained silent for a few moments. Then he held his cell phone out and pressed the mute button. "They have an emergency placement. Siblings. We're the only fosters with capacity."

"Now? What time is it?" Katherine asked.

"Twelve-year-old twins. Their parents were in a car accident last night. Didn't make it. They need us to keep them until they track down any living family members."

Katherine flipped back the covers and went to her suitcase. "Are we picking them up or will she drop them off?"

"You sure?"

Katherine met Gabe's concerned gaze. "Bora Bora will still be there. We can go anytime." She pulled clothes from the case and placed them on the end of the bed. "These kids need us."

Gabe told Ms. Blackwell they would pick the kids up in an hour.

Katherine dialed her travel agent and canceled their honeymoon. "I'll let you know when we can reschedule."

Peace rolled over Gabe's expression. "I love you, Jadis."

"That's *Mrs. Gallegos*. And I love you, too." Katherine dropped to the mattress and wound her arms around him. Their life wasn't the one she'd imagined as a little girl, or even a young woman, but it was perfect, and she wouldn't change a thing.

ACKNOWLEDGMENTS

First I have to thank my husband who gives me all the time and space to write. I love you!

Special thanks to sensitivity reader, Erin M.

Thank you to my Reines for **everything** you do.

Thank you to Brandi Doane McCann for the amazing cover art and extreme patience.

Thank you to Colleen Wagner, editor extraordinaire.

And thank you to my wonderful beta readers.

This book would not be what it is without all of you.

ABOUT THE AUTHOR

Award-winning author, Jordyn Kross, is an unapologetically naughty novelist who spent years honing her writing skills with tech manuals and marginal poetry before finding her passion for writing sexy, boundary-stretching happily-ever-afters.

When she's not writing, she's attempting to garden in the desert Southwest, hiking with her insane pound posse, and admiring that handsome man wandering around her house who continues to stay.

Jordyn enjoys saucy double entendres, pretending to be an extrovert, and is well-known for having no filter. And when she's not in social media jail, she can be found on Facebook, Instagram, and Goodreads, or hiding in a dark cave peering out at Twitter.